TREACHERY IN TUSCANY

Previously published Worldwide Mystery titles by
PHYLLIS GOBBELL

PURSUIT IN PROVENCE

TREACHERY IN TUSCANY

PHYLLIS GOBBELL

W★RLDWIDE

TORONTO • NEW YORK • LONDON
AMSTERDAM • PARIS • SYDNEY • HAMBURG
STOCKHOLM • ATHENS • TOKYO • MILAN
MADRID • WARSAW • BUDAPEST • AUCKLAND

WORLDWIDE™

ISBN-13: 978-1-335-90132-3

Treachery in Tuscany

First published in 2018 by Encircle Publications LLC.
This edition published in 2023.

For questions and comments about the quality of this book, please contact us at CustomerService@Harlequin.com.

TM is a trademark of Harlequin Enterprises ULC.

Harlequin Enterprises ULC
22 Adelaide St. West, 41st Floor
Toronto, Ontario M5H 4E3, Canada
www.ReaderService.com

Printed in U.S.A.

ONE

Sunday morning, my first glimpse of Florence since I was twenty-one. Sunday morning in the spacious *piazza*, quiet, except for the chime of church bells from an ancient bell tower. My jet-lagged brain tried to take in *everything*, all at once. No sign to identify the *Convento di Santa Francesca Firenze*, but the GPS on our rental car had directed us to the imposing fifteenth-century convent. A white Alfa Romeo with a blue stripe and the words *"Polizia Municipale"* along the side pulled away from the curb as we took our luggage from the trunk of our Fiat. A waif-like teenager standing some distance away waited until the police car had departed before she came closer to us.

"*Convento?*" I said.

She said something in Italian, to which I could only reply, "*Non capisco.*"

"*Sì.* It is the convent," she said.

So my Italian left something to be desired.

The girl gave the stark terra cotta façade a measuring gaze, then darted us an uncertain smile, hitched up her rucksack on her thin shoulder, and headed through the arched entrance. At the double wooden doors, she pushed a buzzer, and a loud click announced the door was unlocked. We filed in behind her, pulling our luggage-on-wheels.

"Exactly as I imagined," Alex declared.

I was traveling with Alex, my uncle, as I had done twice before. Travel-writer Alexander Carlyle was in Florence to research his third book, and I was here to keep an eye on him.

Not exactly as *I* had imagined, but it was a *convent*, after all, not a Ritz-Carlton.

We entered a grand space that brought to mind the nave of a cathedral but without any adornments. Gray tile floor, beige plaster walls, table with a faded cloth on it, scarred wooden bench, frayed chair. Alex's travel guides would always direct tourists to unusual places like the convent, in the not-so-touristy district called Oltrarno. Apparently, the nuns, the Franciscan Missionaries of Mary, rented rooms to help pay for their missionary work. Clean, safe lodging. Nothing fancy.

From an anteroom that appeared to be the office came an anxious voice. A statuesque nun in full gray-and-white habit, with a silver cross hanging from her neck, leaned toward a young woman seated at a computer. Her gestures were as animated as her speech, and I was reminded of Catholic school, where I was scolded regularly by the nuns. But the office worker didn't appear threatened. She nodded agreement and contributed a phrase here and there. The undercurrent of worry in the Sister's voice was unmistakable. Several times she said something about the *polizia* before she realized we were waiting, and exited through a side door.

Our new acquaintance was quick to approach the counter, but it was apparent from the exchange—not angry, but rapid-fire Italian—that there was no hurry. Her room was not ready. Nor were our rooms ready. I asked how long it would be. The answer—"Soon"—did not give comfort to this weary traveler.

"If you wish to get food, you may leave your luggage with me. *Piazza Santo Spirito* is not far. Or you can wait in the gardens. In the hall you will find cappuccino, coffee, many choices in the machine." The young woman was trying. And her accent was delightfully musical.

Alex and I agreed we weren't ready to be out and about. I remembered our car. With elaborate gestures, the young woman told me where to park, down a side street, then turn back behind the gardens.

Alex went with me, though I told him I could manage by myself. Sometimes I look after him, and sometimes he looks after me.

A stone wall covered with greenery obscured any view of the gardens, just the tops of a few trees. Several other cars were parked in the tiny gravel lot. A good thing we were in a Fiat, not an SUV. Alex pointed out the building adjacent to the parking area, speculating that it was probably where the nuns resided. Much more recently than the fifteenth century, the smaller structure had been built with materials and architectural elements similar to the building that housed our rooms. My attention was drawn to the windows, bordered with intricate stonework, while Alex talked about the nuns—only twelve left, he had read, while once there had been fifty.

We walked back around the convent and pushed the buzzer. Inside, I peeked in the office and told the young woman we would wait in the gardens. She directed us down a long hall.

Leaving the building through French doors, I had to catch my breath. The gardens were impeccably landscaped, with cobblestones marking a path through the grass, flowering bushes, gently-bending trees, and hedges that formed a maze. Soft breeze. Floral fragrance.

The focal point was a large fountain with water flowing from the mouth of a lamb, its sweet face upturned.

Curled up on her side on one of the stone benches, her head resting on her rucksack, was the girl we had met, her name yet unknown to us. Her dark curly hair was tangled. Low-slung jeans and cropped top revealed a belly button with a ring that matched the ring in one eyebrow. Her blue rucksack was too clean, too new-looking for a runaway who had spent time on the streets—and she did, apparently, have a reservation here. In sleep, her face could have passed for a young child's. A butterfly swarmed around her and settled on her knee, where a hole in her jeans showed her skin.

And that was how I would think of Sophia Costa—Sophie—even when nightmares blurred my memories.

TWO

THE WORD THAT came to mind when I saw my room was *spartan*. Not a monastic cell, but simple and frugal. Twin bed with a plain dark-blue coverlet, heavy old wooden desk and dresser—ebony wood, maybe—and a chair of a much lighter wood, not so old. A small closet, and a sink with a mirror and metal shelf above it. The drain pipe from the base of the sink to the wall was exposed, and a wastebasket had been placed under the trap.

The young office worker, Ivonna—I had asked her name, and it seemed to please her—had shown me to my room, most likely so I wouldn't get lost. It was by no means a straight shot from the first floor—officially the ground floor—more complicated than getting on the little elevator, getting off, going down the hall. This was a structure of intricate mazes that I would enjoy exploring, once I learned the way to and from my room.

Ivonna regarded the wastebasket and made an apologetic face. "A small—*drip, drip*—when the water drains. Luigi will repair it tomorrow. He has not been here for three days, I think. Luigi is our"—she gestured, groping for the word.

"Handyman? Maintenance man?"

She nodded. "I am sorry that we have no one else to repair these things. Luigi has been with the convent for many years. He is very devoted to his work. I do not know that he has ever missed even one day before this."

Noting the emotion in Ivonna's voice, I said, "I hope Luigi is all right."

"He was—he is OK. Today is Sunday, for family. *La nonna* prepares the big meal for all the children, grand-children, aunts, uncles"—she let her voice trail off, gesturing as if to say, *and more.* "Sister Assunta said Luigi will be back tomorrow. He is well now, I think. I am sure he will take care of this—this *leak.*"

"Not a problem," I said, but I couldn't help wondering what the real story was with Luigi.

No air conditioner, but the room was cool. The open window and the transom over the door—an added feature that dated back probably only to the early 1900s—provided good cross-ventilation.

And what a view! The shutters were open on the window that my architect's eye judged to be about twenty-four by thirty-six, something close to that. I wasn't sure standards for window sizes were in place in the fifteenth century. I do historic renovations in Savannah, but this convent—I had to get used to thinking *Convento di Santa Francesca Firenze*—this structure was three hundred years old when Savannah's first buildings went up. I leaned on the wide sill. No screens, but it felt safe. My room was on the second floor, officially, but it was the third story, high above the gardens, looking out on the tops of other multistory terra cotta buildings and a church with a colorful dome. A view worthy of a luxury hotel.

"What's the name of that church?" I asked, pointing to a distant spire.

Ivonna came up behind me to get a closer look and made a pouty face. "I'm sorry I don't know. So many churches in Florence. That one is not"—she gave an apologetic shrug—"not *important*."

She handed me the heavy key ring that looked like a barbell. I had a good weapon—a six-inch length of solid metal! Too bad we had to turn in our keys when we were going outside the convent. Ivonna pointed out the two keys attached—large one for my room, small one for my bathroom across the hall. "The bath is *private*, only yours," she said. "No one will go in except the woman who cleans in the mornings. I will show you."

The private bath was no more than four diagonal steps across the hall. Long, narrow, airy space with a small square window facing the street we'd used to drive around the building. Light-colored tile, shower stall and fixtures that might have been decades old, but not centuries.

Next to my room, directly across the hall from the bath was a large access panel. I would have paid no attention to it, but Ivonna was quick to identify a faint rumbling noise as "nothing in there but *tubi*." With both hands she made a picture in the air, something long and cylindrical.

"Pipes?" I recognized the sound and just hoped that my room, next to what was apparently a mechanical shaft, wouldn't be too noisy.

"Yes!" She laughed, and her plain face changed. She was a pretty girl when she laughed. Slender, about six inches shorter than my five-foot-ten, with shoulder-length brown hair. She wore a modest black dress and flats that would have suited a more matronly woman. I doubted she was more than twenty-five.

"I'm an architect, so I'm curious about the building," I said. "You won't mind if I ask questions, I hope."

"Not at all. Whatever you need, please ask." Turning to go, she reminded me, "Please remember to always lock the bathroom door."

I appreciated the attention to safety, but, as I maneuvered the heavy, noisy, old-fashioned lock, I thought of the visit by the police. And Ivonna did tell me to ask questions, so I asked: "Can you tell me why the police were here?"

"Oh, it is nothing!" she said, but her voice, a little too breathless, didn't match her words. "Nothing to worry you. The *polizia* came about *il furto*, a—burglary—someone robbed a shop near *Borgo San Frediano* last night. We have many artisans in Oltrarno, you know. I think it was a shop where the artisan made jewelry."

The Oltrarno neighborhood, where the convent was located, was "old Florence," Alex had explained, the best place to become immersed in the day-to-day life of the residents, to get a feeling for where they lived and worked. We were south of the Arno River. North of the Arno was the more touristy area.

"So were the police just asking if you'd seen anything suspicious?" I said.

"Yes. That is why they came." Her nod seemed a little too eager. Still, it was reasonable to think the police would warn people in the neighborhood to be alert. It also made sense that the Sisters wouldn't want their guests to worry about their safety. The nun I'd seen in the office may have been complaining that the *polizia*'s presence would cause alarm.

"Please do not worry, *Signora*. The convent is very safe. OK?"

"OK," I said, not completely convinced. "Thank you." Ivonna gave another bright smile and left me to it.

UNPACKING AND PUTTING AWAY was easy in my spartan room. It was still early afternoon. Hard to say whether I was hungry. Exhausted, yes. Florence was six hours ahead of home—home being Savannah, Georgia, for me, and Atlanta for Alex. I'd left Savannah over twenty-four hours ago. I can never sleep on planes. Alex, with the aid of two glasses of red wine, had a restful sleep for three or four hours, the best I could tell.

I texted Alex, who had brought a cell phone on this trip, unlike our other trips, and we agreed to go out and look around. It wouldn't be a bad idea to get a light, late lunch. Ivonna gave us a map of the city and marked the route to *Piazza Santo Spirito*. "Many places to eat," she said.

And she was so right. We found the popular area with no trouble. So many outdoor eateries ringed the *piazza* that we simply chose the first one we came upon. At a table under a colorful umbrella, we shared a pizza—nothing like the pizzas back home. Much lighter. Next time, I reminded myself, I could probably eat the whole thing.

We each had a glass of wine, which measured about two fingers. "This is why the Italians can drink wine all day," Alex said.

Sitting down for lunch with a small glass of wine was relaxing, and also refreshing. I felt I could keep going till night. I knew the best way to handle jet leg was to stay awake the first day and then get a good night's sleep.

A *Polizia Municipale* car crept around the edge of the *piazza*, reminding me of the burglary in the Oltrarno neighborhood. I told Alex what Ivonna had said. He didn't share my curiosity. With an expression just short of scolding, he said, "Jordan, I hope you're not going to start imagining some sort of intrigue, as you have been known to do."

"And for good reason," I reminded him, "but no, I'm not going to imagine anything. Inquiring minds want to know. That's all." I was not surprised that Alex ignored me.

He took out his little notebook. "Let's see what our day looks like tomorrow."

"I take it we have reservations for something."

"The *Duomo*. The museums are closed on Monday but not the *Duomo*." Alex had made a big production of getting advance reservations to the *Duomo*, the *Uffizi*, and the *Accademia*. The ticket lines for these landmarks were supposed to be long, even in September.

We spread out the map that Ivonna had given us and, by measuring how far we'd come from the convent to the *Piazza Santo Spirito*, we judged how far it would be to the *Duomo*. We lingered a while longer, polishing off a two-liter bottle of water that cost nearly as much as the wine. Alex gave me a little map lesson. He had spent several weeks in Florence when he was a young man and, though that was a long time ago, he remembered many of the sights. I had spent a semester in Italy—that also seemed long ago—but our group was based in Venice. Our time in Florence was limited to a few days. Architectural students sketching cathedrals, as I recalled.

Alex wasn't fluent in Italian but the names of the churches and museums rolled easily off his tongue. The *piazzas* dominated by the magnificent churches, *Santa Croce* and *Santa Maria Novella*, the *Piazza della Signoria* with its old Town Hall, and the Medici family's palace, the *Pitti*. We would see all of Florence's attractions, but Alex's travel guides were unique in that they always went beyond the main tourist attractions.

As he folded the map, he said, "And Tuesday, the Moretti Villa. A glimpse of the Tuscan region." His casual reference betrayed the expression in his blue eyes, the memories there, the anticipation of seeing the matriarch of the villa, the woman who once captured his heart, he'd confessed. Angelica Moretti.

THREE

BACK IN THE SUMMER, one sultry evening, Alex and I had met for dinner on the river after one of his board meetings. Alex is on a handful of boards in Savannah, so we see each other every month or so when he drives over from Atlanta. He was already making plans for Italy.

"Your first guide was just released," I said, "and you haven't even done edits for the second one, but you want to travel again in September? So soon?"

"I'm seventy-three, Jordan." He took a final bite of his crème brûlée and put down his spoon. "At this age, a man needs to make use of every minute. Not that there's anything wrong with me, so please don't jump to conclusions, as you're prone to do."

My first trip with Alex, I was skeptical about traveling with my uncle, but I was worried about his health. After Provence and then Ireland, it was more or less assumed that I was going along to whatever destination Alex chose for his travel guide, doing both of us a favor.

We examined our calendars. Alex already had flight information to give me, with options. By mid-September I should be able to get away from work. "Fine," he said, "but you need to let me know—shall we say by the end of next week?" He's such the professor: prepared, methodical, expecting the same from others, which is the part that's sometimes exasperating.

We left the restaurant and walked along the river,

heading toward where my car was parked. We might have walked from my house on Abercorn if the heat hadn't been so oppressive when we'd started out a couple of hours earlier. The evening was cooler now, just a hint of a breeze coming off the river. Music came from some of the restaurants, nice music for walking, not the loud, obnoxious music that would blast from the bars later at night. We settled into an easy stride, and Alex told me about Angelica Moretti.

He and a friend from college days, Victor Morse, had spent a summer bumming around Italy on Eurail Passes in the sixties. Why Italy? True, Alex loved history and art, but Victor's dream of owning a winery in Tuscany was the driving force behind the trip to *Italia*.

"Rome was wonderful," Alex said. "The Vatican, the Coliseum, all the ancient ruins. We took in everything. We were serious about our adventure. It wasn't just about drinking and picking up girls, though we did our share of that. Then we spent some time on the Amalfi Coast. Breathtaking scenery—but I was eager for the museums of Florence, and Victor was ready to visit wineries in Tuscany. So we made our way into the Tuscan hills. We spent a little time in those charming hill towns like Montepulciano and San Gimignano. I've read that they're overrun with tourists these days, but not so when Victor and I visited. I can't even describe how lovely they were—authentic Italy! Finally, we went to Florence for our last six weeks." His smile had turned nostalgic. "We met a young woman who was studying art in Florence. She captured my heart—and Victor's. We were both quite smitten."

Obviously, Alex had not won her affections. I waited

for the rest of the story and was surprised when he said, "Actually, I think she was in love with both of us."

"Couldn't have been a good thing for your friendship," I said.

Alex seemed more amused now than reminiscent. "I suppose things were a bit tense for a while, but when all was said and done, I returned home. Back to Atlanta, as I'd always intended. Victor stayed. And he realized his dream of owning a winery. He changed his name from Morse to Moretti, and began producing the Moretti label. Yes, he married Angelica."

At the time Alex and I were having this conversation, Victor had been ill for a long while. Congestive heart failure, with diabetes and other complicating factors, Alex explained. He had been e-mailing with Angelica. "She tries to be brave—tries to be optimistic. But Victor has been in and out of the hospital several times in the last year. It sounds quite serious."

I knew then that a big part of Alex's hurry to travel to Italy was to see his old friend.

But he carried on with his story, his manner brisk. The Moretti Villa had been taking in tourists for a few years. "Something about tax breaks for what they call *agriturismo*," Alex said. "I'm reading between the lines of Angelica's e-mails, but it seems that as Victor's health has declined, their sons—one of them, at least— convinced the family that they couldn't continue to be profitable on the strength of their winery. I think it was always rather small. So now they produce vegetables, honey, olive oil, jam—all kinds of agricultural items. Tourists come in for wine tastings, horseback riding— oh, it all sounds fascinating. And this *agriturismo* is an angle that would add so much to my travel guide."

He took a long breath. "I had *so* hoped we could stay at the Moretti Villa, but lightning caused a fire earlier this summer that damaged the wing of rooms they rented to tourists. They won't be able to take in tourists for a few months. All of that, and Victor's illness—Angelica and her family have their hands full. She and Victor had twin sons who must be about your age."

"So—where are we staying?" I'd asked.

Alex scratched at the side of his face. "Do you know why I appreciate you so much as a traveling companion, Jordan?" He didn't let me answer. "Because you enjoy adventures as much as I do. You will love this. Angelica suggested the *Convento di Santa Francesca Firenze*. She went to school with one of the Sisters when they were children. Imagine a fifteenth-century structure, and it's right in the heart of old Florence."

"*Convento*?" I repeated. "Sisters? Alex, are we going to stay in a convent?"

"It will be wonderful!" he said.

BY EARLY AUGUST, plans for our trip to Italy were laid out in full. On a Saturday morning, not later than eight o'clock because the mercury would soon rise into the nineties, I was pulling weeds in my backyard. My phone rang, and I saw Alex's number pop up. It was not like him to call so early on a Saturday.

"My old friend is dead," he said.

Alex has many old friends, but somehow, just the way he said it, I knew.

"Victor, in Italy," I said.

"I had hoped I could say goodbye."

He sounded matter of fact, but I sensed he was making a huge effort.

"I'm sorry, Alex," I said—and then, "Should we postpone our trip?"

"Oh no. As a matter of fact, Angelica's email was emphatic. We must carve out enough time for her. That's how she put it. I don't think she was just being kind. A month from now, we can provide a welcome distraction."

I could imagine the benefits of a visit from Alex, who had known Victor—and Angelica—when they were all young. I could see that Victor's widow might find that comforting.

It would not be long now. On Tuesday we were expected at the Moretti Villa.

FOUR

OUR LONG SUNDAY-AFTERNOON excursion through the Oltrarno district ended back at the *Convento di Santa Francesco Firenze* as the sun was sliding behind the building, leaving rosy streaks in the sky. Neither Alex nor I had the inclination to go back out later for a real dinner. We had picked up some tasty-looking figs and fat grapes at a little market along the way. The vending machine at the convent held a variety of drinks and snacks that would save us from starvation.

Which meant we were eager for breakfast, both of us standing at the double doors to the breakfast room before they opened at seven-thirty the next morning.

"Sleep well?" Alex asked.

"Not as well as I would have expected," I said. "Old buildings are noisy. I was surprised to hear so much commotion in the halls. Everything had seemed so peaceful in the afternoon."

"A bevy of French-speaking women checked in late last night," Alex said.

"*Bevy?*"

He shrugged. "The word that comes to mind. Poor Ivonna. She was all alone, trying to get them situated, and they were behaving like irascible children. Maybe their flight had been delayed or something had gone wrong with their tour. I was buying a bottle of water, and they practically *mobbed* me, trying to get to the machine."

"And then I suppose it took a while for all of them to finish in their bathrooms," I said. "Pipes rattling. Locks clanging. Doors slamming in the hall."

"About the private bath, Jordan." Alex made a most earnest face. "I really thought we both had bathrooms *en suite*. That's what I requested. You should have taken my room."

I gave a wave of dismissal, just as an unsmiling woman of indeterminable age opened the doors and admitted us to the breakfast room. Maybe it was bad form to be so eager for breakfast. Or maybe she just expected tourists to ignore her. Her expression softened a bit when I greeted her with *"Buon giorno."*

Hungry as I was, I had to stop and examine the charming space—vaulted ceiling, walls a soft, buttery color, a large window that opened onto the garden. Small tables with white tablecloths, each with two or four straight-backed chairs, except for one long table for eight. At each table were place cards with numbers printed on them.

"That's ours," Alex said, nodding at the table designated with numbers 4 and 17.

"Wonder why we can't choose our own seating arrangements. Seems a little rigid," I said, but I didn't dwell on it. The aroma of coffee beckoned me.

The coffee, provided via machine, was a puzzler. Several options were offered: *Caffe Latte*, *Espresso*, *Caffe Lungo*, and some variations and combinations like *Cappuccino Scuro* and *Latte Macchiato*. I had no clue what might come closest to the good old American coffee I brewed in my kitchen, which is what I craved. The attendant was watching me. I motioned to her. "American coffee?" I said.

"*Americano,*" she said, pushing the *Caffe Lungo* button. I thanked her, and she responded with a kindly nod, if not a real smile.

By the time she'd stepped away, I had my coffee, about two fingers' worth. About the same amount of wine in a glass. I punched the *Caffe Lungo* button again. Others had come into the breakfast room, and a couple of French-speaking women had made a queue behind me. It was probably a good thing I didn't know exactly what they were saying, but I believed I had made another *faux pas*, this time by taking *so much* coffee when others were waiting.

I took my three-quarters-full cup to our table before I went to the food offerings on the sideboard. Alex was just finishing up. He had a roll, jam, and thin slices of cheese and ham. I wondered if he was thinking of Grace O'Toole's scrumptious Irish breakfasts or the lavish breakfasts at our little hotel in Provence. But this was a convent. Frugality was the rule. I chose something that looked like dry oatmeal and poured milk on it. I passed over the only fruit option, which appeared to be canned peaches. A hard roll and a spoonful of jam rounded out my meal.

A minute later, I said, "This is actually quite tasty. I never thought about eating uncooked oatmeal—if that's what this is—but it's filling enough."

"Maybe I'll have some of that," Alex said, as he had devoured his cheese and ham in a few bites. He picked up his empty coffee cup. He must have pushed the coffee button only once.

The room continued to fill. Next to us, a woman close to my height pushed a small man in a wheelchair up to the table. Their number was 11, which meant we were on the same floor. She was heavily made up, more appropriate for a night at the opera than a morning at the convent. The man had a thin mustache and wore black-rimmed spectacles. A blanket covered his legs, the toes of his shoes peeking out. She spoke to him in Italian and left him alone at the table.

I saw that their key—the key ring that looked like a barbell—had apparently slipped from the man's lap to his footrest. I picked it up from between his shoes—his feet jerked a little—and laid it on their table. "*Grazie*," he said in a whispery voice, but his frown made me wonder if I'd done something wrong.

"You're welcome," I said. I made a mental note, for what it was worth: Peculiar couple.

And then I noticed the girl we'd met yesterday. She was giving the room a once-over. I waved to her, and she came to my table.

"What are these numbers?" she asked, pointing to the place cards.

"Our room numbers," I said. "What's yours?"

"Twelve." Also down the hall from mine. She looked around and spotted her number at the long table. "So am I supposed to sit with the old women because I am traveling alone?"

"Why don't you sit with us?" I raised my finger, signaling for her to wait. Trying to be as inconspicuous as possible, I crossed the room and removed the chair and the place card with number 12 from the long table. My smile and cheery "*Buon giorno*" seemed to satisfy the three elderly women who were seated at the table. I pretended not to notice the attendant's scowl as she watched me relocate the chair.

"You are kind," the girl said with a little laugh. We

introduced ourselves, and I finally learned her name—
Sophia Costa. She said we could call her Sophie.

She brought back some of everything from the sideboard. Nothing wrong with her appetite. Like Alex and
me, she had gone out Sunday afternoon and had something to eat but hadn't eaten since, she told us. "I went
to sleep so early," she said, between bites. "I did not
sleep the night before because I was in the train station
in Rome, and there is no sleep there."

I had learned with my own children—five of them,
all grown up now—that you had to show a willingness
to listen without showing *too much* interest in what
they're telling you. Especially true of teenagers. Once
she'd started talking to us, no prompting was necessary.
Though Alex didn't comment, if Sophie had checked
his expression more closely, she would have noticed the
wrinkle between his brows that appeared when she'd
said she spent the night in the train station, and how
that wrinkle grew more pronounced as she continued.

"My friend goes to *università*. She wanted me to
meet her friends, so we went with them to hear music,
and when it was close to the time of the last train to *Firenze*, she took me in her car to the *stazione*. But a terrible accident had shut down the streets." Sophie bit into
a hard roll and chewed vigorously for another minute.
"We sat in traffic for a long time—an hour, I think! I
believed I could still make the last train. I hurried to
purchase my ticket, but I had not imagined how confusing it would be in the *stazione*." She hunched her shoulders. "I missed the train by a few minutes. You know
the trains in Italy are always on schedule, never late."

She had planned on the night train, she explained,
thinking she could sleep between Rome and Florence

and check into the convent early on Sunday. "To save money," she said.

"Wouldn't your friend have come back to the station for you?" Alex asked. "You could have stayed the night with her."

Sophie made an incredulous face. "I could not ask her to do that! She had met my train in the afternoon and had brought me back that night. No, I told myself I would wait for the early train to Florence, and that is what I did. A few hours, not so long." She turned up her palms. "But I did not sleep. I did not know that it would be such a long time before I could get my room."

Her phone rang, and she pulled it from a small purse hanging from her shoulder. I couldn't understand the exchange—in Italian, of course—but I heard her annoyed "*Mamma*!" several times, and I recognized her tone—that universal tone teenagers use with parents.

She finished the conversation, darted a sheepish look between Alex and me, and said, "*Mamma* worries so much."

"A daughter your age, alone in Florence—I can see why your mother might be concerned," I said.

"I am eighteen," Sophie said with a bold little twitch of the shoulders, "and the convent is safe." Then her lips curled. "*Mamma* does not know I am in Florence. Or *Papa*."

I had to clamp my teeth to make myself remain quiet as she went on. "They think I am in Rome with my friend at *università*. Still they worry. And why is that, when they say I myself should go to *università*? *Papa* more than *Mamma*. He calls me *il mio piccolo gattino*. Little kitten." She was trying hard to look annoyed, but the warmth in her voice betrayed her.

So tempting to say there was probably a good reason for her parents to worry, given that Sophie was lying to them, but that would likely end our conversation.

She scooted her chair back. "I am still hungry," she said, and she headed for the sideboard again.

Alex gave me a stern look. "Not your problem, Jordan."

"I know," I said. "I know."

THE DOOR WAS OPEN when I returned to my room. My unease lasted only a minute, though. A wiry little man with a shock of gray hair and a jet-black mustache was working under my sink.

"*Buon giorno*," he said—and something else that may have been *I'm fixing the leak*.

"*Buon giorno*," I said—and added, "*Grazie*," for good measure.

He was tightening a coupling nut. He'd probably replaced a gasket, a job I could've accomplished with a proper wrench. Sitting on my bed, I waited for another minute while he finished. We smiled and nodded our goodbyes. I saw a bandage on one side of his head.

I had met Luigi.

FIVE

The *Duomo*, according to our calculations, was about a mile and a half from the convent. "After such a *hearty* breakfast," Alex had said, with heavy irony, "the exercise will do us good."

Crossing the Arno for the first time, we entered the bustling "tourist zone." The narrow streets were jammed with traffic, and if there were rules of the road, I couldn't figure out what they were. I'd had a taste of driving in Florence on our way in from the airport, but we hadn't come through this congested part of the city. Motorscooters zipped along at an alarming speed, using the sidewalks to pass cars if it served them to do so. Kiosks were plentiful in the *piazzas*, advertising tours and selling souvenirs. But in the midst of it all, architectural gems, some that weren't even "important," as Ivonna might have said, kept inviting me to stop and gaze.

In the *Piazza della Repubblica*, children's squeals rose from a colorful carousel. We stopped at an open-air market for *cappuccinos*. Alex took a photo of me under the "new" arch, dating back only to the nineteenth century, and then he hurried us on. But as we were leaving, he pulled a brochure from the inside pocket of his jacket and slowed down to look at it.

"I thought so. *Vivere la Toscana!* is located in the *Piazza della Repubblica*. Has to be somewhere close by."

"And what is *Vivere la Toscana!*?" I said.

"Translated *Experience Tuscany!*" Alex stopped and showed me the brochure with its photo of the arch. "It's the tour company Angelica told me to contact. Her granddaughter is a chef with them. She does their cooking classes. The company has an arrangement with the Moretti Villa. They take groups out to the villa for that authentic Tuscan experience."

"Cooking class. Sounds like something we ought to do," I said.

"Not *we*, my dear. But *you* might enjoy it."

Alex tucked the brochure back inside his jacket. "Maybe we can look up *Vivere la Toscana!* when we come back through the *piazza* this afternoon. We need to get on to our tour."

We had plenty of time before our ten-thirty tour. Alex, however, liked to be not just on time but early. *Very* early.

Before we'd finished our *cappuccinos*, we were looking up at the magnificent dome that defined the Renaissance, the crown of the grand cathedral, *Il Duomo di Firenze*.

"THE CHURCH IS free to enter, so the line is always long," Alex said.

The *Cattedrale di Santa Maria del Fiore*—translated: the Cathedral of *Saint Mary of the Flower*—is the main church of Florence and, if not the main attraction for tourists, *one* of the top must-see sites. Knots of tour groups dotted the vast pedestrian space, the *Piazza Duomo,* and a long line that began at the steps of the church extended all along the front of the huge building.

"Our tickets allow us to skip the line, and also to climb to the dome and the bell tower—if we want to— and our tour guide will take us through the Baptistery as well as the interior of the Cathedral. We could have made our own reservations, but we get so much more with the tour. I think it's a good value," Alex declared, checking our tickets against the signs that tour guides held high. He pointed to a bright yellow sign. "There— that's our tour."

We joined the group that grew to about fifteen before the tour began. Earphones were provided, not a bad idea for a large group when some are necessarily in the back. The volume, however, was not the problem. Our English-speaking tour guide was *barely* English-speaking, her heavy accent more suggestive of Eastern Europe than Italy, I thought. I was sorry for Alex, who exchanged a frown with me several times, so I knew he was not understanding some of what she said, either. Tours are *his* thing. I am more the self-guided type.

Much of what the tour guide told us—what I *think* she told us—I knew, and no doubt Alex knew, as well. The *Duomo*, as the Gothic Cathedral is ordinarily called, was begun in 1296, but left unfinished. It was not until the 1400s that a goldsmith named Brunelleschi, who had no formal architectural training, created the dome that completed the structure. I remembered my visit to Florence as an architectural student and how our professor had marveled at the spirit of the Florentines. "Imagine building something as grand as the *Duomo* and leaving a hole in the roof, hoping that someday the technology would be available to finish it," he'd said. "What optimism!" I remembered also that public opinion had not always favored the Neo-Gothic façade of the church, which dates only from 1870. Some ridiculed the "busy-ness" of the green, pink, and white Tuscan marble panels, the mosaics, and the pointed arches, but

I was in the camp with those who think the decorative façade is stunning. I could have lingered much longer than the tour guide allowed before she announced, "Now—our time—we go in!"

The huge nave, with its paintings and busts and stained glass windows—forty-four windows in all—could have held my attention for another hour. Most impressive of all, at the front of the church, were the bright frescoes covering the interior of the dome. Gazing up until my neck hurt, I was still not ready when our guide moved us along. The Baptistery was next on our tour. Another inspiring mosaic ceiling—and copies of Ghiberti's famous doors. The originals were housed in the *Duomo* museum, and much to Alex's dismay, the museum was closed, undergoing a major renovation.

After a few minutes at the *Campanile*, Giotto's Bell Tower, our tour guide bid us *arrivederci*. At that point, Alex and I had to make a decision. Nearly five hundred steps led to the dome of the *Duomo*. The view of Florence was supposed to be glorious. But even with our advance reservations, we would have to wait in a long, slow-moving line to make the climb. Several in our group had heard it would take two hours. An alternative was to climb the 414 steps of the Bell Tower. Shorter line, moving faster.

I was not sure Alex should attempt either. I had been on hand for one of his attacks of angina, which had occurred the night after a strenuous walk uphill to see a windmill.

"It would be a shame to miss the view," he said.

"Yes," I said, "but I'm not very patient."

"That is true."

"And I'm even more ill-tempered when my stomach is growling. Are you hungry?"

We agreed to have lunch and come back. Our tickets were good for the rest of the day.

"You'll be more patient after you've had a nice lunch," Alex said.

All around the *Piazza Duomo* were outdoor cafés. We chose one with *Trattoria* as part of its lengthy name, as *trattorias* are most often family-owned, offering home-style cooking. One small table on the sidewalk was empty, calling our names, so to speak. I chose zucchini and smoked mozzarella risotto and Alex ordered a ravioli dish. We thought both might be heavy for lunch fare, but somehow we managed to clean our plates. We enjoyed coffee that tasted somewhat *Americano*—another half-cup or less, and no one offered refills. People-watching was delightful. At two-forty-five, we started back.

Plenty of time to climb to the top of either the *Duomo* or the *Campanile*, even if there was a long wait, but both of us conveniently failed to mention it. Surely there were other glorious views of Florence. Alex pulled out his brochure and said, "*Vivere la Toscana!* must be nearby." We asked at a couple of shops. The tour company was not actually *on* the *piazza*, but around the corner, up a creaky set of stairs, with just a small sign visible from the sidewalk. But once we were upstairs, we found a lively place of business. The tour that was assembling had a large group of Americans, from the distinctive sound of their voices.

A young man in a green *Vivere la Toscana!* tee shirt met us with a pleasant smile. "Are you here for the walking tour?" he asked.

"Not today," Alex said. And he began to explain that

he was a friend of Angelica Moretti, and we were going to the Moretti Villa on Tuesday and perhaps would book tours later, but today we just came by, hoping we could meet Angelica's granddaughter. "I don't know her name," Alex said, "but she's a chef with your company, I believe."

The young man's smile widened. "I know her well. Marisa's my wife. I'm Jake Endicott." We introduced ourselves. He glanced around. "Marisa's here somewhere."

"I see her." Alex's gaze settled on a petite young woman across the room. Jake's expression was something between amusement and puzzlement. Marisa was just one of two young, attractive females in green tee shirts, but Alex had apparently picked the right one.

"She's the image of her grandmother when Angelica was nineteen," Alex explained, still staring, as if transfixed.

Jake showed us where to wait—two bright green molded-plastic chairs beside a rack of brochures advertising tours and other offerings. Marisa was getting the walking tour organized. Jake spoke to her, and after the other young woman left with the group, Marisa came to meet us.

"I am Marisa," she said, with a lovely accent and a lovely smile.

Alex was absolutely beaming. He said he was an old friend of her grandmother's. "And your grandfather, too. Victor and I were traveling together when we met Angelica." Marisa said her *nonna* had told her about him. I took that to mean that Angelica had told her Alex would be visiting Florence and the Moretti Villa, but Alex may have thought she meant something else. He seemed not to know exactly what to say—a rare occurrence.

He gave a little chuckle. "It was a wonderful time in our lives."

I chimed in. "Did your grandmother tell you that Alex is writing a travel guide?"

"Oh, yes. That is very exciting. She said you might need information about tours in Tuscany, and we have much information, as you can see." She indicated the rack of brochures.

I picked up a brochure about cooking classes that just happened to have a photo of Marisa in an apron and chef's hat on the front. "I'm thinking about this one."

She gave another bright smile. "We will have the class at the estate on Friday."

Jake finished with a customer and came over to join us. I asked how long they had been married. Just ten months, they both said at once, looking a little starry-eyed at each other. Alex asked where Jake was from, and he said the Chicago area. He'd come to Florence two summers ago, met Marisa, who was studying to be a chef, and just never went back.

"Like your grandfather," Alex said to Marisa.

A shaggy-haired man in one of the green tee-shirts entered the office and immediately began to shout at Jake. "I have to go," Jake said. "The Vespa tour group is about to come in."

"The motorscooters. I will help him," Marisa said. She added in a whisper, "I'm sorry."

Alex and I both made expressions of dismissal. No problem. We would see her later. "Maybe the cooking class," I said.

As Marisa headed toward the door, the man spoke

to her—not in the same bark that he'd used with Jake, but in a mocking voice. She gave us a quick glance and went behind the counter, to the computer, instead of outside to help Jake. The disagreeable man greeted us effusively. "If you are interested in any of our amazing experiences, I can help you. I am Cristiano, the owner of this company." He smelled like a three-martini lunch. Maybe in Florence it would be a bottle-of-wine lunch.

Alex straightened his lapels and said in his most disgruntled tone, "No thank you. We have changed our minds." And we walked out.

MY PHONE STARTED RINGING as we went down the unstable steps outside the office. I fumbled in my big purse that held everything from a water bottle to my travel information to one of those rain jackets that folds up into a small package. Alex was grumbling. "A nasty man, that Cristiano fellow. I would have *nothing* to do with his tour company if it weren't for Marisa."

The phone had gone quiet when I found it. I smiled when I saw the caller's name.

"Something you need to attend to?" said Alex, frowning. He is not quite on board with cell phone etiquette, and I knew he was irritated by the intrusion. "Someone from home?"

"Not from Savannah. From Paris."

"Ah, Paul Broussard."

Paul Broussard, the charming patron of the arts I'd met in Provence. We had flown to Paris in his private plane, but a murder had interrupted our plans. We'd spent an afternoon in Dublin—too short. Things had always been exasperating between us.

"And when will Monsieur Broussard be arriving in Florence?"

"That's probably what he was calling to tell me," I said.

I listened to Paul's voice mail the moment I was alone, even before I reached my room. Wednesday. He was flying into Florence in just two days. On this trip—unlike the others—we would have the luxury of *time*. The thought made me faintly giddy.

SIX

In the convent's sunny breakfast room Tuesday morning, I suggested to Alex that we should not arrive too early at the Moretti Villa. The drive would take approximately ninety minutes. Angelica had mentioned lunch. Lunch was never before one o'clock in Italy—often later.

I was able to delay our departure until nine-thirty.

Alex was pacing in the front room, the entrance hall, when I came downstairs. He glanced at his watch but couldn't reasonably scold me because I was still five minutes early. I laid my heavy key ring on the counter in the office and greeted Ivonna, who seemed to work extraordinary hours. Only once had I seen another other young woman in her place. Ivonna's smile was always cheery, and she always looked up a moment from the computer screen, as she did now, with a greeting beyond the simple "*Buon giorno.*"

"Please be very careful driving in Tuscany," she said. "The roads have many curves." She made an "S" in the air that started at the bottom and went up, a drawing of winding roads.

As we headed around the building to get our car, Alex said, "While I was waiting for you, I learned the names of the couple who sit at the next table in the breakfast room. Carlo and Varinia Santoro. I was telling Ivonna about the Moretti Villa, and they came up and began to make a huge fuss. The woman. Not the man in the wheelchair."

"A fuss about what?"

"It seems the cleaning woman was unlocking their door when they returned from breakfast, and they've requested that no one go into their room except when they are present. Ivonna said the woman left *in a bad temper.*"

"Wonder what they have in their room that's such a secret," I said.

"Ivonna said almost the same thing. She said it was silly to think anyone would want to prowl in their room." Alex chuckled. "I had to supply the word *prowl.*"

"Maybe the man has special equipment or clothing, special—I don't know—I suppose it's just a privacy thing," I said. I would not be more specific, but Alex nodded that he got it.

"I heard something else while I was waiting." He cut his eyes at me to emphasize that he'd had to wait. "Two women from England, I expect, were talking about the caretaker for the convent who was mugged last week, outside the convent wall at the trash bin. I think I saw him yesterday. A little man with a big bandage above his ear."

"Luigi. He fixed a leak under my sink yesterday," I said.

Alex raised his eyebrows. "I'm surprised you didn't mention the mugging. But I'm glad you didn't make too much of it. I considered whether I ought to tell you or keep quiet about it."

"I didn't know he was mugged. Ivonna said he'd been out for a few days, but not why."

Not far from the car was the garbage bin. I said, "It

is a little worrisome, that someone was mugged just outside the convent walls. And there was that robbery, not far from here."

"Inside the convent, we are safe," Alex said. "What are you doing?"

I was digging around in my purse. "I hope I didn't leave the car keys in my room."

Alex frowned, and I knew he was calculating the minutes we'd lose if I had to go back.

"Found 'em," I said, dangling the keys.

Alex glanced at his watch. I didn't think I'd ever seen him so antsy.

IVONNA WAS RIGHT about driving in the Tuscan hills on the narrow, spiraling roads. There wasn't as much traffic as in the city, but cars zipped around us as if we were sitting still, and oncoming cars flew past us in a blur. Sometimes they barely missed each other. The views of the countryside were spectacular, tempting me to take my eyes off the road—not a good idea. As the GPS directed us, we found ourselves on a tiny lane, snaking upward, with a steep drop to the valley below. We had left the traffic, which was a good thing because two cars couldn't easily meet. When we did meet, both of us had to slow to a crawl. At last, at a proper hour, eleven o'clock, we approached our destination—the Moretti Villa, sitting high on a hill.

Eventually, I pulled into a gravel parking area with three other cars. Standing at the knee-high stone fence, I would have been content to keep looking out over the valley, but I heard a woman's voice: "Alex! Oh, Alex!" she called, her arms outstretched.

Alex opened his arms wide and they met in a long,

affectionate embrace, murmuring about how good it
was to see each other, how long it had been. As I came
closer I noticed the resemblance that Alex had seen
when he'd first met Marisa. Angelica was petite like
her granddaughter, a bit heavier in the way that has
more to do with age than actual weight. The eyes, as
blue as the Tuscan sky, were the same as Marisa's. Her
hair was so black that at first I thought she must have
colored it, but from the random sprinkling of gray, I
decided it had to be natural. She wore it swept up in a
twist that seemed a little old-fashioned—but elegant.
She was dressed in a loose turquoise blouse with bead
work on the neckline, white pants, and white sandals.
A beautiful, stylish woman.

At last Alex remembered me—yes, I think he had
forgotten.

"Angelica, this is my niece, Jordan Mayfair. Jordan,
please meet my dear, dear friend, Angelica Moretti,"
he said, quite formally.

Angelica broke away from Alex, grasped my hands,
and did the European cheek to cheek thing.

"*Benvenuto in casa mia.* Welcome to my home, Jordan! This is a beautiful moment for me!" she said. "I
could hardly wait for today to come!"

"We've been looking forward to it, too—very much,"
I said, darting a smile Alex's way. "Angelica, your villa
is lovely."

"Please, come with me. Let us go to the *loggia.*"
She walked between Alex and me, holding both of our
hands, until we reached the heavy, ornately carved door,
at which point she led the way through spacious rooms
to the back of the house. "Marisa telephoned me and
said you had been to *Vivere la Toscana!*" she said. "I

am so glad you met my dear Marisa. She is very smart! She can tell you everything you should know to put in your book, Alex."

We came out on a terrace—the *loggia*—beside a pool. The pool itself was not large but the landscaping was exquisite. It overlooked the same valley we'd seen when we parked. "That is Raffaele's wife, Bianca," said Angelica, indicating the woman who was swimming. I thought I caught a note of disapproval in her voice. Perhaps she'd expected the daughter-in-law to get out of the pool and greet us, but Bianca seemed to be in her own world, gliding through the water, her backstroke slow and rhythmic.

"Please," Angelica said, indicating a wrought iron table for eight, sheltered by a huge striped umbrella. A wine goblet with a trace of red wine in the bottom sat on the table.

I couldn't resist walking over to the edge of the *loggia*, to get the full panoramic view. The valley was a patchwork of vineyards and golden fields, fencerows defined by tall, slender cypress trees. Not far away a couple of other villas dotted the landscape, and across the valley a village, distinguished by terra cotta roofs, was nestled in the dark green hills. All under the cloudless blue sky. It was the kind of vista that always appeared in advertisements of Tuscany.

I returned to the table where Alex was sitting, his expression one of perfect contentment.

Angelica had removed the nearly-empty wine glass and had gone inside, but a minute later she returned with a plate of cheese, bread, Italian meats, and olives. "This is my *other* daughter-in-law, Ambra. Roberto's wife," she said, indicating the woman who followed her with a pitcher of lemonade and three goblets. There was as much approval in Angelica's voice as there had been disapproval when she'd spoken of the swimmer, Bianca.

Ambra was a few inches taller than Angelica, medium height, with dark curly hair, cut short. With her comfortable manner and relaxed smile, she was easy to like, immediately.

"Is Marisa your daughter?" I asked her.

"Yes, mine and Rob's." Ambra's face glowed with pride. She began to pour our lemonade.

"Aren't you going to join us?" Angelica asked her.

"I cannot. I am making ricotta cheesecake. Do you know this dessert?" she asked Alex and me. We both said we'd had cheesecake but probably not the *Italian* recipe.

"You will like it, I think," said Ambra.

"We have a bike tour arriving for lunch," Angelica said. "Ambra works so hard and not just in the kitchen."

"There is work for everyone on the estate," Ambra said.

"Yes, there is work enough for everyone who will do it," Angelica said, with a cut of her eyes at the swimmer.

Ambra went back to the kitchen. Eventually, Bianca got out of the pool, wrapped a towel around her sculpted body, and came to the table. She was pleasant enough when her mother-in-law introduced us, but after the obligatory greeting, she excused herself. "Don't expect me for lunch, Angelica," she said, over her shoulder. "I have a board meeting, the museum in Siena."

"I apologize for my daughter-in-law," Angelica said, when Bianca was out of earshot. "Sometimes I am so angry with her I could scream! And sometimes I am sad for her. I think she would not be so *cold* if things were different with Raff." Angelica explained that for years

Raffaele had done all the marketing for the Moretti wines, and he traveled much of the time, meeting with wholesalers and suppliers, attending sales conferences. "I am afraid they have grown apart. And there was never a child. That would have made a difference, I am sure. Marisa has brought so much joy to Rob and Ambra—to all of us."

Suddenly she raised her hands as if surrendering, and her voice became musical once again. "Enough of that! Let's talk of happy things. Alex, tell me about your books!"

That was the line that always made Alex smile.

SEVEN

IT WOULD BE a while before the late lunch that was customary in Italy, so Angelica asked if we wanted to see around the estate. We did, of course. She looked at our shoes—we had both chosen comfortable footwear—and declared, "Perfect!" Looking at her own dressy sandals she said, "I can't go in these, so give me a moment." She left us to finish our lemonade, the best I'd ever tasted. As we waited, Raffaele came out and introduced himself.

"You're one of the twins," Alex said.

"I am the smart and good-looking one," Raffaele said, with a laugh.

I didn't know about smart, but he was good-looking, all right. Thick silver hair that he wore stylishly long. Blue eyes like his mother's, accented by the blue in his shirt. Tall and slender but muscular enough, he wore tan chinos and loafers without socks. Preppy. Friendly, too. He sat with us, lit a cigarette, and asked how we were enjoying the sights of Florence.

"Have you met Sister Assunta, *Mamma's* friend?" he asked.

We said we hadn't met any of the nuns, but we hoped we would.

Angelica returned in the midst of our exchange and added, "My friend from childhood, Assunta, has managed the convent for some time. Mother Superior resides in the nunnery but I have heard she is ill, perhaps near death." Changing course, she laid her hand on her son's shoulder and said, "I hope you are planning to stay the rest of the week, Raffaele. You must remember that the photographer will be here Saturday."

"Oh, *Mamma*! Why do we have to do that?" he complained.

"Because the website designer said it would be a good thing to do!"

Angelica turned to us and explained that someone was working on the Moretti website. The present site had only a few photos. "The designer wants to show pictures of what we do and who we are—the Moretti family! He insists that it is necessary to have these photographs!"

"I understand photographs of the vineyards, everything about the *agriturismo*"—Raff's brows pulled together as he said the word in a deep, dramatic tone that indicated a measure of distaste—"but no one wants to see *us*. Who cares about how the Morettis look?"

"Let us talk about this later, Raffaele," Angelica said. "Now I promised Alex and Jordan a tour of the estate. You are welcome to come with us."

He exhaled a long stream of smoke. "*Grazie*, but no. I have seen it all many times."

THE MANNER IN WHICH the villa was tucked into the hills was deceptive. This was a much larger enterprise than I had imagined when we'd arrived at the gravel parking lot, with that glorious view of the valley. None of the farm buildings had been visible from the front of the villa or the side where the *loggia* and pool were situated.

Angelica led us out to the back through the large kitchen with its delicious aromas, where Ambra and another woman worked. "Watch your step," she said. Construction was in progress, the new wing to replace the one fire had destroyed. A highly antimated Angelica gave a play-by-play of how lightning had caused the fire, and only by the mercy of God had the two families of tourists been spared and the fire contained before spreading to the rest of the villa.

Near the kitchen was a low building used by the *Vivere la Toscana!* cooking classes. Beyond it was the winery and tasting room, a massive old building with rows of barrels and gigantic vats, shelves of bottled wine, and a group of chairs positioned around a table—apparently for the wine tastings. The aroma was faintly intoxicating, the lingering bouquet of years of wine-making. Angelica called to the man at the other end of the building who held a cell phone to his ear. "Roberto!" Her son, Raff's twin, waved and pointed to the phone.

"Important call, I think," she said. "We'll see him at lunch."

"So this is where the magic happens," Alex said.

"Yes—and no. Victor would have said the magic is in the grapes, the vineyards. He tended the plants with such love." Angelica's smile was reminiscent as we left the winery and began walking on a stony path, through thick shrubs—some rose bushes, I noted. "Victor could tell you which vines produced well last year and which did not. It was rather amazing—how he knew each plant like a parent knows a child."

"How many acres do you have?" I asked.

"The estate? I think twelve hectares. We plant two hectares in grapes now. It was more when Victor was well, when he could oversee the vineyards. Now we have the olive groves."

Alex clarified that a hectare was about two-and-a-half acres. Five acres in vineyards still seemed like a lot to me.

Our tour took us past small outbuildings, an equipment shed, stone walls—high and low. Angelica pointed to a large building, somewhat distant, that housed the olive oil processing. "Milling and bottling," she said, without enthusiam. She didn't offer to show us inside. Olive oil, I gathered, meant little to her—just another product to sell. None of the emotional attachment that she felt to the wine.

We came to a large vegetable garden with beautifully tended rows, and a stand of fruit trees. A short, stout woman met us with a basket of apples. Angelica took three apples from the basket and gave one to Alex, one to me. "Please, taste," she said. "It is a good season for the apples. We grow strawberries and peaches, too, and we sell our jams and preserves."

I bit into the crisp, sweet apple and made a groan of approval, chewing. Angelica paused as we came out on a flat grassy strip. In the distance were a barn and corral with four horses. "We offer horseback riding to our tourists. Rob and Ambra ride when there is time, but there is little time, as you might imagine. Do you see, on the hill behind the barn—those are our goats. We sell goats' milk and cheese."

"When did you become an *agriturismo*?" Alex asked.

"Ah—it is what families like ours must do in these times. These *economic* times," she clarified. "Victor had the gift of the grape. That is what we always said about him."

Alex nodded, with a fond smile.

"When Victor had his first problems with his heart—

ten years ago—he would not hear of changes. He believed Roberto could take his place. Raff has always tended to the business, the accounting, marketing—that was his contribution and a very important one. Roberto had his father's love for making wine. They walked in the vineyards together in the mornings. I have seen both men in their long aprons, with their hands in the pulp as the grape mixture in the bins moved along the convyer belt."

It was a beautiful thing to imagine—to *remember*, in Angelica's case. A moment passed while she blinked. Then she explained that as Victor's health problems became greater, Roberto had finally said, "I have your love of the grape, *Papà*, but not your gift."

"The *agriturismo* was Rob's idea," I interjected.

"It was his idea and his work that made it happen," Angelica said. "Raff did not agree. He was very much against it. But Victor himself realized that our profits from the Moretti wines were not what they once were. The small wineries like ours could not compete with the large companies and foreign markets. He saw the wisdom in the *agriturismo*. The tourist industy was booming!" She laughed. "Victor said yes, we should 'jump on the bandwagon.' It was a leap. We knew nothing but making wine. But we jumped on the bandwagon."

"He said something like that fifty years ago," Alex said, "and I'd say he was right."

"Fifty years ago, the investment in a winery was a good thing," Angelica said. "But times change, and the *agriturismo* is now a good thing. It is a great benefit for taxes. Our agricultural products do very well, and it has been most profitable to take in tourists—until the fire. We hope it will again be profitable. The new wing is"—she took a deep breath and exhaled slowly, noisily—"very expensive!"

I wondered about insurance but didn't think I should pry. Even if insurance had paid off well, as it should have for a fire caused by lightning, I knew from my years in the building industry that new construction always costs more than is expected.

We finished our apples and tossed the cores, walking up the gentle slope toward the vineyards. Separated by a lane that a vehicle could drive on was the olive grove, but the vineyards took precedence, plants laid out in perfect rows that began at the base of the hillside, extending to the top. Angelica led the way at a brisk pace, seeming not to notice that Alex was lagging a bit behind. She took us between the rows of vines, taller than our heads. Stopping at last—and I was glad both for Alex and for myself—she broke off a small cluster of grapes from a larger one and pulled off grapes for Alex and me.

"Taste," she said. We tasted and approved. "Soon they will be ripe, ready to harvest in a few weeks, but already they are not bitter. Even the skin is sweet. Already they have the personality of the wine they will become."

I smiled at her use of "personality." I might have said "character," but her expression gave a deeper level to the description. Alex smiled, too, probably for the same reason.

"We have good soil here—just the right sandy component. It makes an elegant wine," she said. "Do you know that Victor could taste the difference in these"— she touched another cluster—"and the grapes grown higher on the hill? I cannot. But I can taste the difference in a Moretti wine and any other." She pushed back a strand of dark hair that had come loose in the soft breeze.

I thought I could read the thoughts behind Alex's wistful smile. He must have been thinking that Angelica and Victor had been perfect for each other, that fifty years ago, things had turned out for the best.

EIGHT

A DOZEN OR SO bikes were parked next to the low building that Angelica had said the cooking classes used. "That's one of the tours," she said, when we were making our way back to the villa. "They're having lunch now. A traditional Tuscan lunch comes with their bike tour. I am sure *you* are ready to eat, yes?"

It was two o'clock. Yes, the *hearty* breakfast offered at the convent had worn off as had Angelica's tasty refreshments. Our lunch was served on the *loggia*. As we took our places at the wrought iron table, Jake Endicott came by to say hello. He had led the bicycle tour from Florence.

"All the way from Florence?" I asked, thinking of our ninety-minute drive over hilly terrain.

Jake laughed. "That would be quite a bit to expect of most tourists. No, we stop along the way to pick up the bikes. We ride about twenty-five kilometers."

"That would be plenty for me," I said.

"It's enough of a challenge so they feel like they're getting their money's worth," Jake said. "They go home with their photos and have something to show their friends, and if they say twenty-five kilometers, that sounds pretty impressive."

Before he left us, he reminded me of the cooking class on Friday. "Marisa wanted me to tell you she hopes you'll sign up."

I was thinking of Paul Broussard. He'd be in Florence Wednesday—but on Friday he might very well have appointments with movers and shakers of the art world. That was what he did, what he'd do on this trip, though we had an understanding: We'd spend lots of time together.

"You *must* do the class!" Angelica interjected before I could answer. "Alex and I can visit while you cook!"

"Sounds delightful," Alex said. "You can tell me more about the *agriturismo*."

"Sure—you can meet the group out here. No problem," Jake said.

I took a deep breath. "What can I say?"

Angelica clapped her hands and then declared, in the voice of a true matriarch, "So it is settled!"

THE TRADITIONAL TUSCAN LUNCH was lovely. *Bruschetta* and goat cheese made on the estate for starters, and homemade pasta with cherry tomato sauce for the main course. Plenty of wine.

We were well into the meal when Roberto joined us. He was shorter than Raff, his hair cropped close, still dark, like Angelica's. I wondered if Victor had been prematurely silver-haired, like Raff. There was a resemblance between the twins in their strong facial features, but Rob was more solidly built, his hands thick. In his jeans and shirt with rolled-up sleeves, he looked more like a working man than his brother.

Profuse with apologies to his mother and to Alex and me, he said, "A matter of business that could not wait." He glared at Raff.

"I told you I would take care of it," Raff said. He caught Angelica's eye. She sat at one end of the table—

the *head* of the table, it would seem—and drew her shoulders up as if she were about to speak. But Raff reached for her hand. "It is nothing, *Mamma*. The insurance payment is slow, but there is no problem. I will call. I said I would call today, and the day is not over."

Roberto raised his palms in a halting gesture. "It is fine. I myself spoke with the agent and the contractor."

"*Mio Dio!* What was the rush that you could not let me do my job? Why do you not trust me, my brother?"

"Should I trust you, my brother?"

"Please!" Angelica's voice was stern. "We have guests! I am sorry, Alex and Jordan. My sons were not brought up to be so rude!"

"Please forgive me," Roberto said to Alex and me. "It is true. I was impolite."

Raff raised his glass. "To our friends. You honor us with your company." I couldn't tell from his tone whether he was entirely sincere or putting up a façade, but glasses clinked, and it was all over. His charm, I gathered, often allowed him to forego an apology.

THE GIRL WHO SERVED the ricotta cheesecake couldn't have been more than fourteen, but she was well-trained. Angelica told about the family that worked on the estate: Fernando and his sons, his wife, daughters, and his mother. "Family means everything to us," Angelica said. "Fernando's family has been devoted to the Moretti family since Rob and Raff were just boys—his father before him."

The wine flowed freely, and I was sorry I had to limit myself because I'd be driving us back, shortly. Our lunch was, I surmised, a typical Italian meal, with everyone talking over everyone else. The conversation came to an abrupt halt when Raffaele's cell phone rang.

"Please, Raffaele! We do not take telephone calls at the table," Angelica said.

Raff, who was sitting next to me, was checking the number. "Ah, perhaps my brother has not resolved everything with the insurance company, after all. This is the insurance agent calling me."

"Let him leave a message!" Angelica said.

Raff silenced the phone and returned it to the clip on his belt.

When lunch finally ended after at least two hours, Angelica invited Alex and me into her spacious living room, and the teenage girl she called Pia brought coffee.

"Please forgive my sons for their bad manners today," she said. "It has been hard since Victor's death."

"Sounded like the kind of bantering I remember, growing up," Alex said. "Jordan's father and I couldn't be in the same room for ten minutes without fussing. That's what it was, just fussing. Nothing serious."

Angelica nodded, but I could tell she thought there was something more with her sons.

Rob and Ambra joined us briefly. Both had coffee, and we talked about the Morettis' relationship with *Vivere la Toscana!*

"Marisa is the connection, of course," Rob said. "She met Cristiano when she went to the cooking academy. He is a chef, himself, but with limited talents, I think. He was not happy with offering cooking classes only. To his credit, the tour company he created has done very well."

I could see, from Alex's expression, that he wanted to say how much he disliked what he knew of Cristiano, but he remained silent.

"I like Jake," I said. "He and Marisa make a lovely couple."

"They do, don't they?" Angelica said, proud grand-mother.

"Cristiano is a horrible man," Ambra put in. "He is a drunk and he uses women in the most terrible ways."

Alex had his opportunity. "I don't like him, either—though I've only spent five minutes with him."

Rob touched his wife's arm. "Marisa and Jake can take care of themselves."

"I hope they can," Ambra said. "I am a mother. I worry." And she began a tirade against Cristiano. Apparently Jake was already working at *Vivere la Toscana!* when Cristiano brought Marisa into the company to do cooking classes. He didn't count on the immediate attraction between Jake and Marisa. He threatened to fire Jake, but Marisa told him she would leave, too, and so they both continued to work for Cristiano, but he had never given Marisa the responsibility he had promised.

Angelica motioned to the girl who stood in the doorway. "More coffee, please, Pia." To Alex and me, she said, "You did not expect all of these—problems! Our family's problems."

"All families have problems," I said.

We left the estate at about five o'clock. That would put us in Florence, past all the narrow, crooked roads, when it was just getting dark. As we went to our car, we saw Raffaele and waved to him. He was standing beside his car, using his phone. But the phone he had used at lunch was still clipped to his belt. Why did he need two phones? When I posed the question to Alex, he told me I was being nosy. But I couldn't help it. I remembered the glint in Roberto's eyes when he'd asked, "Should I trust you, my brother?" and I wondered.

NINE

AFTER THE MARVELOUS late lunch at the Moretti Villa, I was content to munch on an apple and call it dinner. Angelica had sent a bag of apples and a bottle of wine with each of us. I went out in the evening for a short walk to the bridge—one of several bridges that crosses the Arno—joining an amazing number of people, for a Tuesday night. All ages, from babies in strollers to the elderly, they were out and about. Student-types, couples, children, and dogs. Evening turned into night. I was not afraid to be on the medieval streets of Oltrarno, just cautious, but as my path to the convent took me past artisans' shops that were now dark, I knew it would be prudent to head back. Stretching out on my narrow bed, I realized how tired I was. Sleep came within minutes.

Voices woke me sometime in the night. I had left my window open for the fresh air. Strange that there were no screens. Alex said he was keeping his window closed at night because he'd seen a mosquito. Though my window overlooked the garden, a haven for insects, I'd had no such problem. Maybe being on the second floor—the third story—made the difference.

Several uniformed officers with flashlights searched the perimeter of the garden. I watched for a minute, listening to their voices, wishing I spoke Italian. Then I went into the hall, to the bathroom and back. I heard no sounds at all from my floor or from anywhere inside the building. Back at my window, I kept watching for another ten minutes or so, until the police left. This time it took a while to settle down enough to sleep.

ON MY WAY down to breakfast, I decided I'd ask Ivonna what she knew about the night visitors—if she was working. She wasn't. Another young woman was in the office. I'd seen her before but didn't know her name. I didn't feel comfortable asking her what was going on in the garden at three a.m. The corridor that led to the breakfast room took me past the double doors with an elegant little sign that said "*Cappella.*" The tall, stately nun I'd seen talking to Ivonna on Sunday came out of the chapel. She gave a nod and a half-smile. I took advantage of the opportunity.

"*Buon giorno,*" I said. "*Mi scusi.*"

"Yes?" she said. "You speak English?" So far, my few lines of Italian hadn't led anyone to believe it was my native language.

"I'm sorry to bother you, Sister, but could you tell me what happened in the garden, why the police came last night?" I asked.

She visibly stiffened. "I am sorry if they disturbed your sleep," she said, tucking her hands in her sleeves.

"That isn't important," I said. "I just want to know what the police were doing out there in the middle of the night."

She took a few steps away from me, and I wondered if maybe she'd simply chosen to ignore my inquiry, but she went to a nearby bench and sat down. "Please," she said, indicating with a nod that I should sit beside her. Her hands were still hidden in her sleeves.

"The police were here Sunday, when my uncle and

I arrived," I said. "I know there was a burglary Saturday night. So—did something else happen last night?"

She studied me for a moment. "Are you and your uncle perhaps friends of Angelica Moretti?"

"Yes! I'm Jordan Mayfair. You must be—Sister"—I searched for the name.

"Assunta." She smiled a genuine smile for the first time, and the stern lines of her face softened. Having made the connection with her friend, who was Alex's friend, Sister Assunta was less reticent, telling me about the police. Yes, there had been another robbery in the Oltrarno neighborhood last night, another artisan's shop, another maker of jewelry.

"This time—a very sad thing." Sister Assunta's countenance turned sorrowful. "A man did small jobs for the artisan and slept in the shop because he had no place to go. The burglar had not expected anyone to be there. The man was killed during the burglary."

A chill traveled down my spine. This had happened nearby. I thought about the shops I had passed, after dark. And I knew now why Ivonna hadn't given me straight answers.

"But what were the police looking for, in the garden?" I asked.

Sister Assunta took her hands from her sleeves and began using them to gesture. "Last night, a drunken man, lying in the street, told the *polizia* that someone came onto our grounds and disappeared, and so they began a search in the middle of the night."

"How was the culprit—the burglar—supposed to have made it over the wall?" I said, remembering that the wall surrounding the property had to be twelve feet high.

"And the gate built into the wall would have been

locked. So you see why I think there is a mistake." She said it with an air of finality and stood up. To continue on the topic at that point seemed disrespectful. I stood, as well.

She gave another half-smile. "Angelica was my best friend when we were children, taught by the Sisters of Mother Mary of the Passion. Oh, how I wanted to be like her! To have such joy! I was too shy. But I found my joy in our Lord, in my calling." She didn't wait for me to respond, and what could I have said?

In the breakfast room, I saw that our table was set for one, which meant that both Alex and Sophie, who had been seated with us since that first morning, had already finished. Checking the time, I assured myself that I wasn't late. Alex and I had reservations at the *Accademia* at ten-thirty. Two hours—plenty of time. I visited the coffee machine and sideboard for my usual morning meal. Funny how I'd come to find the food offerings quite enough and, in fact, appealing. This morning there was actually a big bowl of assorted fresh fruit, cut up, a welcome change from canned peaches. Settling at my assigned place, I noticed that the wife of the man in the wheelchair—Varinia? Was that what Alex had said her name was?—was alone at the next table. She was as dressed up as always, wearing a silky caftan, her hair and make-up looking as if she'd come straight from the beauty salon.

I decided to strike up a conversation with her—if she spoke English. She did. Though she wasn't chatty, her manner was pleasant. I started by commenting on the fruit and then the perfect weather and then the sights of Florence. I was surprised that she said she and her hus-band had been on a hop-on, hop-off bus tour of the city.

"We did not hop on, hop off, of course," she said. "My husband—you have seen him—in his chair, he cannot do many things that others do, but the bus ride was enjoyable. More than two hours seeing all around Florence. The busses have"—she gestured, trying to find the word—"*lifts*. The trains, also."

"The museums are accessible—I would assume," I said, thinking of the requirements for handicapped accessibility in the States. I couldn't say for sure what the requirements were in Europe, and I thought Varinia might not understand *accessible*, but she gave an eager nod.

"The elevators make it possible for Carlo. But so many people"—she made a face and shrugged—"it is not easy with the chair when it is so busy. Have you been to the *Uffizi*?"

"Not yet," I said.

"After we went through the left wing, the medieval art, the tour was too much for Carlo—too much for both of us. But for you—yes, you should go."

I wanted to say I admired her—and her husband—for getting out and about, given the difficulties with the wheelchair, but I didn't want to sound patronizing.

She picked up the napkin and silverware at Carlo's place. "Carlo is not feeling well this morning," she said. "I need to take him something to eat."

"I hope it's nothing serious," I said.

She gave a wave of dismissal. "It happens sometimes."

I thought she might elaborate, but she didn't. "How long has he been in the wheelchair?" I asked, even as I was thinking that Alex would surely be saying, "*Nosy, nosy.*"

Varinia did not seem to take offense. "A few years. Six years, yes, since the automobile accident, near Naples. He was fortunate to live. He will never walk, poor Carlo."

Questions bubbled up in my brain, beyond normal curiosity. I had seen his feet move. But that didn't mean he could walk. Or did it? Nosy as I was, I would not pursue the topic of her husband's injury. I asked, "Is Naples your home?" I asked.

"Yes."

Now, maybe I really *was* being too inquisitive. But I asked one more question. "Did you hear the commotion last night—the middle of the night? The police, in the garden?"

"Our room overlooks the street, on the side, not the garden. I heard nothing," she said. "Now I must prepare a plate for Carlo," and she left the table, heading for the sideboard.

I wondered why she didn't ask what the commotion was all about? Didn't she wonder why the police were there? Maybe she just wasn't as naturally curious as I was.

I finished the last bites of fruit and drained my glass of the red-orange juice I'd learned was the product of Sicilian blood oranges. There was still time for two fingers of *cappuccino*.

WHEN WE MET in the front room at nine-thirty, Alex was studying the map, checking the distance from the convent to the *Accademia*. He was afraid we'd miss our ten-thirty tour. We could do it, walking at a brisk pace, I thought, but Alex might exert himself too much. I asked the young woman in the office to call a taxi for us, and it arrived within minutes.

"It's a good thing we didn't walk," Alex said, when the taxi left us at *Via Ricasoli*.

It was five minutes past ten. To Alex, that meant we were right on time.

While we were waiting for all the tours to assemble, watching for a guide with a bright yellow sign, my phone rang—jingled, actually. I retrieved it from my bag and saw the caller's name. "I'll be right over there," I told Alex, pointing to a storefront, a leather shop, that didn't seem crowded. "Hello—Paul?" I said. Alex pursed his lips, amused.

It always thrilled me to hear Paul's voice, to hear him say my name. Technology being what it was, we could have made phone calls—had Facetime chats—every day, could have texted every hour, but that kind of constancy was not a feature of our baffling relationship.

"I took the liberty of making reservations for dinner. I hope you are agreeable," he said.

"I'm agreeable," I said.

"It's a little *ristorante* that overlooks the Arno. I wanted to be sure we had no trouble getting in." I couldn't help smiling. I'd probably been smiling the whole time, but I was wondering when Paul Broussard had ever had trouble getting into a restaurant.

"Sounds lovely," I said.

He said he was staying at the Westin. "I enjoy the small, *local* hotels when I travel, but the manager of the Westin is an old friend of mine. He would not forgive me if I came to Florence and stayed in another hotel." I could imagine that twitch of his shoulders. *C'est la vie.* "The rooftop bar has a spectacular view," he said. "I might suggest a drink there before dinner."

"Perfect," I said.

Ever the gentleman, he offered to pick me up at the convent, but since he was staying at the Westin, it only made sense that I should take a taxi and meet him there. I had to insist. Eventually he agreed that it was the most reasonable plan. He'd meet me in the lobby. Then he said, "Jordan, I did not know this until yesterday, when Bella arrived unexpectedly in Paris, that she will be flying to Florence with me. You remember that I told you about Isabella?"

Certainly I remembered. We'd had a long conversation in Dublin about the daughter he hadn't known existed until less than a year ago.

"She has her own plans, of course," Paul said. "She will be going to Cortona this weekend, where a friend of hers is renting a villa. I think there was a movie, set in Cortona."

"*Under the Tuscan Sun,*" I said.

"Probably. I think it was a story that made young unmarried women believe Cortona was the place to find romance." Paul gave a little laugh. He had such a warm, rich laugh.

"Will I get to meet her?" I said.

"Of course. Tomorrow is her birthday, a perfect time for you to meet her and her to meet you—and Alex, too—at a little dinner party. What do you think? Yes?"

"Yes. I'll ask Alex, but he's usually up for dinner parties."

"And then Bella will leave for Cortona. Her plans should have no bearing on ours, Jordan," he added, as if he might have read my mind.

Alex was motioning to me. I said, "Our tour is about to begin, Paul."

"Until tonight, then," he said. "Seven?"

"I'll see you at seven." Already I had started counting the minutes.

TEN

THE TOUR GUIDE, unlike the one we'd had for the *Duomo*, spoke perfect English. I couldn't help being distracted, but as we made our way through the entrance and checked our belongings through security, I tried to convince myself that Paul would be true to his promise, that Isabella would not intrude on our time together. In Dublin, when Paul had told me he'd recently learned he had a daughter in her thirties, I couldn't help being skeptical, even though Paul had established, to his satisfaction, that she *was* his legitimate daughter. What was it that nagged so at me? After celebrating her birthday with her father—and why shouldn't she?—Isabella had her own plans. Meeting her might be just the thing to dispel the doubts I had about her, qualms that had no logical basis, misgivings that were likely petty, much as I hated to admit that to myself. And it occurred to me for the first time that Isabella might have felt the same way about me. We simply needed to get to know each other.

I suspected Paul knew what he was doing. He usually did.

OUR GUIDE LED US through the lobby, made a turn, and stopped, letting us all catch up, giving us a moment to take in the statue at the far end of the long hall, Michelangelo's masterpiece, *David*.

The young guide—pretty, but needing attention to the dark roots of her blonde hair—pointed out the *Prisoners*, unfinished figures that seemed to be struggling to emerge from the stone, as we made our way along the hall. "See the bending of elbow and knee, the movement, the restless energy," she said. She tried to engage us with stories of Michelangelo as we waited for our turn at the statue we had all come to see. She told how at eighteen Michelangelo opened a corpse, and with the aid of a candle, studied the human body in order to accurately represent human proportions. He often worked night and day, in a kind of manic state. It was said that he slept with his boots on. Michelangelo, who lived in the palace of Lorenzo the Magnificent, of the powerful Medici family, carved *David* from a block of marble that other sculptors had rejected. "Many said there were 'no good artists' after Michelangelo," our guide told us.

The various tour groups were well-behaved, moving on when their time was up, and then it was our turn at the seventeen-foot-tall statue. "The woman who dusts *David* has the best job," the young guide said. A titter of laughter went up. I took photos from all sides. Alex was standing quite a distance back, his arms folded, just staring upward, into the mesmerizing eyes.

"Jordan!" someone said.

It was Sophie Costa, sitting on the floor, legs crossed, her back against the wall. Pen in hand, she had apparently been sketching in a small sketch book.

"Do you think the shepherd boy has already slain the giant?" she asked.

I moved closer until I was looking down at her. She raised the sketch book—more the size of a journal—to her chest, as if she wanted to hide what she was doing, but I'd already seen that her drawing of the statue showed a great deal of talent.

"The guides say that is what Michelangelo intended, but I think—look at his eyes. I think this is the moment of his decision," Sophie said. "Not *after* he killed the giant, but *before*."

"You know your Bible story, don't you?" I said.

Alex had joined us. He said, "You've brought up a longstanding debate. I think I agree with you, Sophie. The way I see it, David is sizing up the giant. He's ready with his slingshot. He knows, by the power of God, he can take down Goliath."

"Wouldn't he be brandishing the head of Goliath if he'd already killed him?" I said.

"That's how Caravaggio painted it." Alex regarded Sophie and clarified, "Baroque artist who painted *David with the Head of Goliath*."

"I like *this* David," Sophie said. "He has such gentleness in his face. He does not want to kill the giant, but he must do it. That is how I see it." She stood up, picked up her rucksack, and draped the strap over her shoulder. "I will go with you," she said.

"Aren't you with a tour group?" I aked.

"I was, but I stayed when they went on. I have listened to many of the guides as I sat here," she said, looking proud of herself.

Our guide caught my eye and motioned for us to join our group. As I was considering whether Sophie might be able to just tag along, she strode up to our guide, and they spoke. Probably in Italian, but with the strident voices of other tour guides and the general noise of the crowd, I couldn't have heard what they were saying, anyway. After a moment she returned to us. "I told her I was lost from my group and she said I could stay with this one but she couldn't give me earphones. I don't care about that."

All the tours handed out earphones and collected them at the end. I wondered if our guide had believed Sophie or assumed she hadn't paid to be part of a tour. I was considering that possibility myself. I asked, "Where are *your* earphones?"

"I gave them back to my tour guide," Sophie said. "I told her I was not feeling well, and that was why I couldn't stay with the group. Better than saying I was bored, I thought."

Alex and I exchanged a look. Sophie was certainly not bound to the truth.

"Let's not get left behind," Alex said. He checked his brochure. "I think our next stop is the *Rape of the Sabine Women*."

Sophie finished the tour with us. I enjoyed watching her, seeing her expression when something resonated with her. She touched the ring in her eyebrow when she seemed to be thinking hard. Alex clearly relished in dispensing his own knowledge of art and history. When we left the gallery, Alex suggested lunch at the *Ristorante Accademia*, right around the corner. He was, of course, better acquainted with the guide materials than I was.

"My treat," he said. Sophie accepted the invitation with a simple nod.

I tried pasta with black truffles that proved to be an excellent choice. Alex had a tortellini dish with spicy sausage, and Sophie ordered a pizza. Alex and I each had a glass of wine. I expected that Sophie might order a glass as well. This was Italy, and she was eighteen.

But she ordered tangerine Italian soda. Maybe she was *not* eighteen. That wouldn't have surprised me.

Whenever I'd had a meal with Sophie, her appetite was always impressive. I had a feeling she might not be eating much except breakfast at the convent—an economic consideration. She bit into a cheesy slice with a fierceness that suggested she wouldn't have any trouble devouring the medium-size pizza.

She told us, mostly with her mouth full, that she was from Casa Vitoni. "A village at the toe of the boot of Italy," she said. "Near the Amalfi Coast. You know the Amalfi Coast?"

"Yes indeed. I was there many years ago," Alex said, "and I imagine it is still one of the most beautiful places in the world."

"I think so," Sophie said, "but I have not been to all the beautiful places in the world, not even a few." She laughed at her little joke.

With urging from me, Sophie talked about her parents. Her father was a sales agent for a company that produced olive oil, based in Sicily. Her mother kept accounts for some of the businesses in Casa Vittoni—a pharmacy, a man who owned fishing boats, a few others.

"Do you have brothers or sisters?" I asked.

"No, I wish, but it is just me," she said, reaching for another slice of pizza.

"Will you be going to college?" I asked. Alex gave me a sidelong glance, as if to say, *Too many questions*.

"Not now but—later—I don't know. *Mamma* would be too lonely when *Papa* goes to Sicily." Sophie filled her mouth, chewed, and swallowed. Then she changed the subject. Looking from me to Alex and back, she asked, "Do you have children?"

"Not I," said Alex.

I told her about my five—Holly, Claire, and Julie, the twenty-somethings, and my twins, Michael and Catherine, who were nineteen, second-year college students. Sophie's reaction was typical, when I say *five*. Wide eyes, an intake of breath. "And your husband?"

"He's been dead a long time," I said. Sophie had turned the tables, quite deftly, actually.

The waiter appeared then, took Sophie's order for pistachio gelato, and when he was gone, conversation turned to touristy subjects. Sophie had gone on a hop-on, hop-off tour of Florence and had spent an afternoon at the library. "I used a computer there," she said, as if she knew we might be wondering what a teenager was doing in the library when she was on holiday. "On Friday, I will go on a Vespa tour, out into the Tuscan hills. We will have lunch at a villa."

Alex said what I was thinking. "Would that be the Moretti Villa?"

"That is the name."

"We'll be there on Friday, too," I said. "I'm taking a cooking class. Alex is a friend of Angelica Moretti."

"I met Angelica fifty years ago," Alex said, with a reflective smile. "The same trip that took me to the Amalfi Coast. Angelica married the man who was traveling with me. Victor. He established the Moretti vineyards, and now, I understand, it is an *agriturismo*. Victor died a few months ago."

I could tell from her distracted gaze that Sophie was only half-listening. Alex may have realized that he was going on a bit. He touched the stem of his glass and swirled the wine.

"You must have been doing business with *Vivere la Toscana!*" I said.

"Doing business?" Sophie frowned.

"I meant you must have gone to *Vivere la Toscana!* to sign up for the Vespa tour. It's the tour company that has an arrangement with the Moretti Villa. Marisa Moretti, the chef who does the cooking classes, is Angelica's granddaughter." I paused, thinking now *I* was going on a bit.

"Marisa, yes. She has been kind. I went to their office near the *Piazza della Repubblica*, where I met Marisa, but first I found *Vivere la Toscana!* online." Sophie looked up. The waiter was back, delivering a large dish of gelato that made me wish I'd ordered one, also, but there were gelato shops everywhere if I was in the mood later. Then my plans for the evening with Paul flashed through my mind. I had to keep myself from smiling.

Sophie did not dig into the gelato as I would have expected. She took a small bite from the tip of her spoon, so different from the manner in which she usually attacked her food. Her pensive manner seemed a prelude to the question she asked after a moment: "Do you know any of the Moretti family with the name Bianca?"

"Why, yes, that's Raffaele's wife." Alex spoke and then his expression changed as he apparently began to wonder what I wondered: Why was she asking?

"Raffaele is Angelica's son. Marisa's uncle," I said.

"I think *Papa* knows Bianca Moretti," Sophie said. "I have seen her name on his phone—the phone that is for his business. It is supposed to be for his business. I am not supposed to use it, but I have seen the name, Bianca, many times. Many calls have come from Bianca Moretti." She was holding the bottle of soda with both hands, her grip tight around it.

I wasn't sure what to say. Alex remained silent, too, probably at a loss, as I was. After a long awkward moment, I said, "Maybe he does business with the Moretti family. They seem to all be part of the *agriturismo*. Did you ask your father?"

"I could not ask because—the phone, it is for his business." Sophie searched our faces and then gave a little laugh, pushing back the dish that was still half full. "I will meet you outside," she said. She didn't wait for us to reply before she headed to the door.

"Now that was odd," Alex said, after a moment of stunned silence.

The waiter left the check, and Alex counted out Euros. Through the window, I could see Sophie. She was smoking a cigarette, pacing back and forth.

ELEVEN

SOPHIE WALKED WITH US for a short distance, but near the *Duomo*, as Alex and I headed toward the *Piazza Santa Maria Novella*, the direction that would take us eventually to the convent, Sophie went another way. She said she had not been to *Ponte Vecchio* yet, and she wanted to see the famous bridge, lined with shops that sold silver and gold. "I will not buy the silver or gold, but I can look," she said. Since lunch, Sophie didn't seem as spontaneous as before. I was sure she had said more to us than she had intended to say. Now she was more guarded.

Alex and I avoided the main street by the *Duomo*, with its heavy pedestrian traffic, but kept walking toward the grand *Church of Santa Maria Novella*. I said, "I suppose we know now what Sophie is doing in Florence."

"*You* may know, but I'm not sure I do," Alex said.

"It seems obvious to me, Alex. She has come to Florence to meet—should I say *confront*?—Bianca Moretti," I said. We stopped to wait for a light.

"Confront? Do you think she'll cause a scene at the villa on Friday? And how, I wonder, would her father have met Bianca? I suppose in the course of his travels—and we don't know much about Bianca. She may take trips on her own, without Raff."

"Ah, Alex, you're becoming as curious as I am," I said.

"I sincerely doubt it," he said, as the light at the crosswalk turned green.

Farther on the main thoroughfare, *Via Dei Fossi*, I remembered to tell Alex about my conversation with Paul.
Dinner tonight—just me, and that was fine with Alex,
as I knew it would be. A dinner party tomorrow night
that would include Alex and Paul's daughter, Isabella.

"She's here? In Florence? With Paul?" Alex gave a
dubious look.

"Apparently she's going to visit a friend in Cortona
this weekend, but tomorrow is her birthday. That's the
purpose of the dinner party," I said.

"Should we take gifts?" Alex asked.

I hadn't thought of that. I groaned, not that I minded
buying a gift, but choosing for a stranger was hard. "I'm
sure we should. How about if I get something from
both of us?"

"Excellent idea," Alex said.

After Dublin, I had told Alex about the revelation
that Paul had a daughter. It wasn't as if there was anything *wrong* with Isabella's sudden appearance in Paul's
life. Her mother had divulged, just before she died,
that Isabella's father was Paul Broussard. They'd had
a whirlwind marriage in New York thirty-something
years ago, and when it had ended, she was pregnant,
but she didn't tell Paul. He had returned to Paris and
never knew about Isabella.

There was the logical question: Was Paul absolutely
certain? Yes, DNA testing had confirmed that Isabella
was, indeed, Paul's daughter. His thorough investigation had caused a huge problem. When Paul had first
insisted on the test, Isabella attempted suicide. Since
that time, Paul had rented an apartment for her in Paris,
besides her New York residence. I'd confessed to Alex
that although Paul had a great fortune to spend as he

wished, I hated to see Isabella taking advantage, if that was what she was doing.

Alex had reminded me that it was Paul's decision, whether wise or foolish.

"So—we'll get to meet Isabella," I said now. I told Alex that Paul apparently had been surprised when she'd arrived in Paris. Obviously they communicated on a regular basis, and she knew he was flying to Florence, but she hadn't *asked* if she could hitch a ride so she could visit a friend. She had *assumed*. Wouldn't you expect a thirty-four-year-old daughter to *ask*?

"She sounds a little like Sophie—who is eighteen. So she says," Alex said. We laughed. We had crossed a bridge and now were in the Oltrarno district, not far from the convent.

"Why don't you go on, and I'll look around for a birthday gift for Isabella?" I said. Alex was easily persuaded. I could see the fatigue in his drooping shoulders. I'd tried not to walk too fast, but it had been a long way from the *Accademia*.

I began to window-shop. I was thinking of a piece of jewelry for Isabella—not expensive, of course. A bracelet, necklace, or earrings. I expected that she had pierced ears, but what if she didn't? So earrings were out.

On a side street that I took because it was on my way to the convent, I passed a shop that was dark, with a notice on the door that looked official. Strange, in the midst of all the other lively activities. Next door was a cheery ceramics shop. I went inside, looked around, and struck up a conversation with a woman who was rearranging some of the items on the shelves. Yes, she said, the shop I asked about was the one that someone broke into Tuesday night. A terrible thing, she said, that the man who slept there was attacked and died before he reached hospital.

A robust man came out from the back, scowling, and spoke sharply to her. I didn't have to know Italian to understand. He didn't want her talking to me. Her husband, I imagined, both of them near my age. She turned to me and said in an apologetic tone, "Is there anything else?"

The man continued to watch me but said nothing. I bought a colorful ceramic bowl for myself, thanked the woman, and left the shop.

Still looking for a birthday gift, I paused at a few shops that sold jewelry, but the merchandise in the windows was too pricey for my purposes. In one of the high-end shops, Varinia from the convent was bending over a display case. Carlo, leaning forward in his wheelchair, was also examining the jewelry. Apparently he'd made a swift recovery.

Maybe tomorrow, I thought. Tomorrow I can shop for a birthday gift. The afternoon was getting away from me. And then in the window of an unpretentious little shop, I saw a simple silver bracelet with delicate filigree, similar to one my husband once gave me from Tiffany's. I still wore it often but hadn't brought any jewelry of value with me. Losing my luggage on the trip to Provence had made an impact. I went inside the shop, found that the bracelet was not inexpensive but was affordable, appropriate as a gift from both Alex and me. I bought it, had it wrapped, and hurried to the convent. In just three hours, I would be seeing Paul.

BUT THAT DIDN'T HAPPEN.

I had left my phone in my room while I showered in the bathroom across the hall. The text from Paul—Call me, please, Jordan—told me something had gone awry. I could practically hear the regret in the written words. Isabella, I thought. Something Isabella had done or not done had spoiled our plans for the evening.

As it turned out, I was wrong about Isabella but not wrong about our plans for the evening. Paul was still in Paris. His plane had a mechanical problem and was being repaired as we spoke. A minor thing, he assured me. I'm sure he saw no reason to get technical about the problem. The mechanic was confident that everything would be in working order, everything checked out, absolutely, and the flight could take place tonight.

"But I am sorry to tell you"—that regretful tone—"that even if we could take off within the next two hours, it will be late when we land at Peretola, and as you know the airport is some distance from Florence, so by the time I arrive at the hotel, I think it will be—*too* late."

"I get it," I said.

"Jordan, I am disappointed, too," he said.

Realizing how impertinent I must have sounded, I amended my tone. "It's not your fault. I know that. Yes, I'm disappointed, but I'll look forward to the dinner party tomorrow night. By the way, Alex is delighted to accept your invitation."

"I am delighted to hear it. But must you and I wait until then? We have tomorrow." He quickly added, "I understand that you may have plans—but perhaps you would find a small window of time for coffee, a glass of wine in one of the *piazzas*, a walk along the Arno?"

"Alex and I have reservations for the *Uffizi*," I said, as certain as Paul surely was that I would find a *small window of time* for him, but not making it too easy.

"The *Uffizi*. Ah, a most wonderful gallery. If you would enjoy—shall we say *a V.I.P. tour*—I am sure I could arrange it with the director. He is a friend."

Of course he was.

"It would give me great pleasure to take you and Alex through the gallery."

I would have felt silly now, saying that Alex and I already had tickets for a tour. No tour could match what Paul Broussard could show and tell us about the famous gallery. We made our plans for late morning. Paul said again how sorry he was that this thing had happened, and I said, "So am I." We were silent for a moment, and I wondered if he was thinking what I was thinking, that something *always* seemed to get in the way, as if destiny did not want us together.

Paul wouldn't hear of meeting at the gallery. He insisted on coming to meet us at the convent. "Until tomorrow, then," he said, and I echoed his words, trying to be excited, knowing that it wouldn't be long, knowing that it would be wonderful. But I couldn't shake my disappointment.

Alex was expecting me to be with Paul tonight, and I would leave him to whatever plans he had. I would tell him at breakfast what lay in store for us tomorrow.

I spent most of the evening in my room, reading about the *Uffizi*, hoping I would be at least conversant with Paul as he led us through the gallery that holds the greatest collection of Italian paintings in the world. After night had settled, I went to the vending machine. Luigi passed by, carrying a tool box. We exchanged nods and smiles. Luigi, like Ivonna, worked long hours. I took my sparkling water to the garden for a while. The air was sweet. I sat on a stone bench close to the fountain.

The water flowing from the mouth of the lamb into the base of the fountain made a soft mist that was refreshing as it reached my arms. I looked up at what was Alex's room and saw that the light was on, but after a few minutes, the room suddenly went dark. An early night for my travel-weary uncle wasn't a bad thing. I smiled as I imagined Alex's delight upon hearing who our guide at the *Uffizi* would be tomorrow.

I made it an early night, myself. After texting with my children—only Michael and Catherine taking the time to text back, but then they were college students who were most likely *always* on their phones—I put on my jammies. The night air had turned cool. As I shut my windows, I saw Sophie in the garden, lighting a cigarette. Ivonna joined her and lit up, as well. Maybe Sophie had found a friend. I had the feeling she really needed one.

TWELVE

PAUL ARRIVED IN a hired car, not a taxi. Seeing him for the first time in months, I was struck by the thought that was exciting and comforting, all at once: He was always as I imagined he would be. His salt-and-pepper hair, always a little long on his collar, never seemed to get more silver in it. His usual attire was a crisp shirt, blindingly white against his dark jacket, and that was how I always thought of him. His strong jawline. His blue eyes that always seemed to be looking straight through me. He never changed.

I would not have expected anything more than a welcoming greeting from Paul—for both Alex and me—but once we were in the car, with me between Alex and Paul, I loved it that he took my hand and kissed it, and whispered, "I am so glad to see you."

Then he was all about business.

Every visitor to the *Uffizi* should have a Paul Broussard clone as a guide.

Not only did Paul move us smoothly through each checkpoint and take us into "Private" areas to see works that were not on display, but his boundless knowledge of the paintings, the artists, and the periods made for a seamless tour. Beginning in the room full of Medieval Madonna-and-child paintings—represented on heavenly thrones with floating angels—Paul explained how the art was evolving from flat, crude, ethereal representations to more realistic images. I'd studied art history, but Paul made it all come alive.

So many masterpieces were housed in the *Uffizi*. More than a few times, I had to catch my breath as we viewed familiar works. Paul paused a long time at Botticelli's *Allegory of Spring*. "The Renaissance was blossoming, and, as you can see, the two-dimensional, medieval religious paintings have given way to the art that glorifies the beauty and grace of the human body," he noted. Botticelli prints and reproductions in books were nothing like the original painting, the curves of the bodies visible through gauzy nightclothes.

On to the works of Leonardo da Vinci, and Paul was ready with one of the many stories that seemed to come as easily as I could tell anecdotes about my children. "Legend has it," he said, "that when Leonardo was just a boy, he painted an angel for his teacher, who then gave up painting forever, knowing his own talent would never match his student's."

And then the classical sculpture room, which gave Paul further opportunity to be "professorial." He explained why sculpture was so important as artists of the Renaissance studied the human body, and I was pleased that Alex seemed so engaged, since he usually liked being the professor. We spent a long time viewing works of the High Renaissance. "If you compare *Venus* with Titian's nudes," Paul said, "obviously we see the difference in the way the Renaissance played out in Florence—the pure innocence—and in Venice—the hedonism, the pagan spirit. I do love the rich color that Titian used for the hair of his subjects. The same color as yours, Jordan." Alex cleared his throat and pretended to be interested in another painting.

The final leg of our tour allowed us to view Raphael, Rembrandt, and Caravaggio. Alex said, "I thought Caravaggio's *David with the Head of Goliath* was here." Paul said no, the painting was housed at the Galleria Borghese in Rome. I thought of Sophie, our conversation about David and Goliath, and wondered if she had used the ticket to the *Uffizi* I'd given her at breakfast. She'd thanked me and said she would go. But with Sophie, you never knew.

After our marvelous three-hour tour, we had lunch at a *trattoria* that was tucked away so far from the main street that it would seem hard to find. But it was packed, and when my codfish with pappardelle pasta was served, I understood why patrons managed to locate it.

We shared a bottle of wine, laughed, and recalled some of our adventures in Provence. Conversation was easy, until Alex said, "I was surprised Isabella didn't join us at the *Uffizi*." I felt a scowl come on, and I was immediately ashamed. Why did the thought of Paul's daughter always bring such negativity to my mood? Was I jealous? The very idea was disgusting.

"I invited her, but she said, as we checked into the hotel last night, that she might go out later and she would most likely sleep in this morning." He turned up his palms and said, with an indulgent smile, "You know how the young people are."

I touched my forehead but couldn't make the furrows go away. So he *had* invited Isabella. What could I say? I'd brought my uncle along. But when I thought of *young people*, carefree, high-spirited, flitty young people, I thought of college students or twenty-somethings. Isabella was thirty-four. I was an architect and mother of five when I was thirty-four.

Paul called for the hired car, and we returned to the convent. Alex and Paul said their goodbyes, shook hands, and Alex went to the double wooden doors to push the buzzer. Paul and I stood beside the car, the first time we had been alone. For a long moment, we were silent.

I wondered what he was thinking, but then it didn't matter. He touched my face, tilted my chin and kissed me. It was a brief, sweet kiss, a promise. He walked to the double doors with me. I pushed the buzzer. "I am very glad that we are here, together," he said, and then he was gone, leaving me a little dazzled, as so often was the case with Paul Broussard.

Isabella Broussard was late.

Broussard, yes. She had legally changed her name when it was settled that Paul was her father. He told us this—Alex and me—as we waited for her at the restaurant. Paul had come to the convent in the hired car, but Isabella was not with him. She had returned late to the Westin that afternoon, after a shopping excursion, he explained. "Perhaps I should not have mentioned the fashion center of Florence," he said, laughing. "But I think Bella would have found it anyway."

He selected a wine from an extensive wine list and ordered a plate of cheeses and meats, fruit, olives, and bread—enough for a meal, as was usually the case with the *antipasti*. Checking his phone, he said with confidence that I didn't quite buy, "I am sure it will not be long."

We spent another pleasant half hour, seated at the outdoor table, overlooking the Arno, with its soft river breezes, before Paul checked his phone yet again, and said, "*Pardon, s'il vous plait.* I should try to reach Bella, to see if there has been a problem."

I didn't think he actually believed there was a problem. Isabella, in my mind, was like a lot of people who don't respect other people's schedules. The purpose of this occasion was her birthday, and she had not made the effort to be even *close* to on time. But I was trying hard not to be judgmental. I kept making assumptions about Isabella, and I really didn't know her at all.

Paul left the table and walked to the edge of the terrace, punching on his phone. I wondered if it was an act of courtesy—as restaurants frown on patrons using cell phones at the table—or if he had words for his daughter that he didn't want us to hear. I was betting on courtesy, knowing Paul. When Isabella appeared, before his call ever went through, he met her with a smile and a quick embrace that seemed to say all was forgiven.

She must have inherited her mother's looks because she had none of Paul's strong, striking facial features, but she was tall, as he was. A leggy blonde in a short black dress that emphasized her curves and cleavage, Isabella was not just beautiful; she was movie-star beautiful. Straight hair, with stunning highlights. Wide green eyes with long dark lashes. Full, glossy lips. Red lustrous nails, not too long or too short. The thought struck me that her reason for being late could've been that she'd spent a long session with a make-up artist and hairdresser.

Paul did the introductions and we all did the requisite nice-to-meet you greetings. I expected a *Sorry I'm so late*, but there was none of that. Bella looked around. "What a quaint place you picked for my birthday! Thank you, Paul," she said, leaning a bit toward him, bobbing her head a little, a gesture that made me think of a doll. Quaint? I wouldn't have chosen that word. I might have said elegant. It was not trendy. Maybe that was what she meant.

She and I sat across from each other, as did the men. "Happy birthday, Isabella," I said.

"It's Bella. This is thirty-five, and I don't intend to have any more birthdays. So I'm going to enjoy this one!" she said.

Paul had poured her wine, finishing the bottle, and he made a motion to the waiter to bring another. Bella raised her glass. "To good times!"

"To you, Bella, on this happy day," Paul added. I wondered if he'd had another toast in mind, but Bella had taken the wind out of his sails.

We clinked glasses and sipped the excellent wine.

I couldn't help staring at Bella, trying to get a read on her. Something wouldn't quite come into focus. She didn't ask anything that indicated she wanted to know about Alex and me, but she wasn't eager to answer my questions, either. When I mentioned Cortona, giving her the opportunity to elaborate on her plans, she simply said, "It seemed like something fun to do."

Paul did an admirable job directing the conversation, but Bella showed no interest in the travel guide Alex was writing. She showed no interest in me. "You may remember that I told you Jordan discovered how the art was being removed from the Museum de Chateau in Provence," Paul said. She responded with a nod that seemed to say, *I vaguely remember.* The waiter's appearance from time to time gave us a reprieve from the awkwardness. The menu was in Italian, of course, and although Alex and I had managed with most menus, picking out recognizable names or ingredients, this time ordering was a big production. Paul, fluent in Italian as he was, read the menu, followed by the waiter's elaborate descriptions of each dish we considered.

Alex took out his pen and little notebook and began to write, copying from the menu.

"What are you doing?" Bella asked, with amusement that edged toward sarcasm.

Alex explained that he kept notes about restaurants and dishes that he might mention in his book. "I have a feeling I'll be making a recommendation," he said.

Bella pursed her lips and nodded, as if she thought Alex was a most *eccentric* character.

The arrival of the first course—the pasta course, as I'd come to think of it—was a welcome diversion. Each of us had a different pasta. Mine was a scrumptious linguini with peppers, eggplant, tomatoes, and mozzarella. As Alex finished the last of his gnocci with spinach, he said, "I should not have ordered a second course." Generally, he did not, nor did I—or if we ordered a main course, we skipped the first. But Paul had insisted, and I reminded myself that my mother's order to clean my plate did not have to apply tonight. The servings were not huge—usually the case in fine restaurants—and the sea bass I had ordered, apparently a dish for which the restaurant was well known, was something I should not miss.

Bella seemed more interested in the drinks than in her food. By the end of the first course, she had finished her second glass of wine and had ordered a martini. It was a while before the main course arrived. I tried once again to engage Bella in conversation. "Paul says you have an apartment in Paris now, so you spend part of your time there," I ventured.

"Paul is so generous," she said, with another of those odd little gestures, leaning toward him. I didn't want to think the word *flirty* applied. I wasn't going to go there. But I saw no discomfort in Paul's expression, no recognition that Bella's behavior didn't align with the way young women typically behaved toward their fathers— and that bothered me. For the first time, Bella became talkative, telling about her flat that overlooked the Seine, and how much fun she'd had picking out the furnishings and art. "Paul and I didn't always agree about the art, but we compromised. I'm more contemporary. More— *out there* in my tastes!" She gave an elaborate shrug. "That's just how I am."

"You're fortunate to have Paul advising you," Alex said.

He gave a modest smile. "Some Parisian artists are doing interesting things with *found art*," he said. "It is not a new movement, but some young artists have taken a new twist on it. We worked with an extremely talented young man who used birdcages for one of his pieces and candy wrappers for another. And his best—don't you think, Bella?—is the one with parts of computers and other electronic devices. It's quite stark. Quite imaginative."

I tried to be interested. I really tried. But I was getting a headache. I excused myself and visited the ladies' room, taking my time. When I returned, a stranger had joined our table. A chair had been added between Bella and Alex. Paul stood, pulled back my chair, and said, "Jordan, please meet Eli Schubert, a friend I have not seen for some years—and here we are, incredibly, both in Florence. He is a fine journalist. Eli, this lovely woman is Jordan Mayfair."

"My pleasure, Jordan," Eli Schubert said, and I knew from his three words that he was an American. He stood, reaching across the table to shake my hand. Round-faced, with round, wire-rimmed spectacles, he had an engaging smile and a firm grip as he pumped my hand twice. He looked me in the eye. I had the feeling that he was scrutinizing me and that I had passed the first-impression test. I was glad he had happened along. Our evening might take a different direction.

THIRTEEN

AND IT DID take a fascinating turn, as Eli and Paul rehashed old times.

"We met in Paris," Paul said. "Eli was doing a story for the *New York Times*."

"It was Lyon, at an INTERPOL conference, where we met, but we may have done some carousing in Paris," Eli corrected, with an easy laugh. He recalled for our benefit that he'd gone to Lyon to cover a meeting INTERPOL had convened to deal with stolen art and antiquities from Iraqi museums. Paul was present at the meeting as a member of the International Council of Museums, and he had provided Eli with a useful source, a specialist in illegal export of art.

Paul directed a wry smile my way, and I knew he was remembering that once I'd thought he was involved in art theft. Hard to believe now, that there was ever a time I had not trusted him. I smiled back and felt a surge of warmth, having our private moment.

"I wound up following INTERPOL's incident team to Iraq for two months. Turned out to be a helluva story," Eli said.

"And since then, have you continued to chase stories around the globe?" Alex asked.

The waiter set down a tall glass in front of Eli. It looked like a soft drink, Coke or Pepsi.

"Yeah, for a while I did." Eli rubbed his hand through

thinning hair. "I spent over a year on a series about human trafficking. Talk about chasing stories. I was in Romania, Singapore, West Africa—every story led to another that was more gruesome." He picked up the glass and took a long drink. "I hit a rough patch, professionally and personally. Took some time off."

"You're back at it now?" Paul asked. "Or are you here on holiday?"

"Oh, I'm back at it."

"Can you say what you're working on?" I asked.

"Sure. It's no secret."

I was captivated as he told about an investigation by INTERPOL into a ring of jewel thieves working in Italy. "Petty criminals, all connected to the Camorra," Eli said.

"Camorra," Paul echoed, and he explained to the rest of us that the organization was a mafia-type crime syndicate, one that had operated in Italy for many years.

"These thieves work all over Italy. They move the jewels through the ports of Naples, to Sardinia, and then on to Nice," Eli said.

A shadow crossed Paul's face. "I wonder if you have come across the name of Antonio DeMarco. He is a collector in Nice. A ruthless, immoral man, the kind who would be connected with the Camorra."

Another memory—Paul telling me that his brother had gone to prison because of Antonio DeMarco.

"Not a name I recognize, but I'll bet INTERPOL has him on their radar," Eli said.

"Tell me about these petty criminals," I said.

He described how the jewel thieves worked, pulling off small capers, moving through several towns or cities until it seemed the authorities were closing in on their trail, and then they simply disappeared. When he'd finished, I mentioned the robberies in the Oltrarno district.

"The Italian police are not very forthcoming, so I don't know what they have, so far," Eli said, "but, yeah, I've been following those."

Bella's voice suddenly rang out. "Can we *please* stop talking about crime?"

Paul looked as confounded as I'd ever seen him. Eli stood up and said, "Hey, I apologize for crashing your party. I couldn't resist saying hello to my old friend. Forgive me."

"Eli, please, there is nothing to forgive." Paul stood, as well. "Don't go, please."

Eli pulled some bills from his wallet, and in spite of Paul's protests, he tossed a few beside his glass.

Paul walked around the table. The men shook hands, embraced in a loose, *manly* sort of way, Eli a good six inches shorter than Paul. He pressed a business card into Paul's hand. "That's my number. Call me," he said, and Paul agreed that he would.

Eli bid us all good evening. When he had gone, Bella said, "A nice enough man, but honestly, I did not want to spend my birthday listening to his tales of criminals."

"It is your birthday, of course," Paul said, with a smile that was forced, if I was any judge. He motioned to the waiter. "It is time for the cake and champagne."

BELLA SEEMED TO genuinely appreciate the simple silver bracelet from Alex and me. But our gift paled miserably in comparison to the gift from Paul, which happened to be another bracelet. Rich blue sapphires in an exquisite setting, the bracelet had to cost ten times what ours had cost—or more than that! What did I know of precious gems? Bella slipped it on her small wrist and held it out admiring it, saying it was just *too much* before giving Paul an enthusiastic hug.

"I have missed every one of your birthdays until this one," Paul said in what struck me as a somber tone—or maybe it was just sentimental. "It is not too much."

Bella held out her glass for more champagne. I had stopped counting how many drinks she'd had. So far, she'd shown no effects of the wine, martini, and champagne, but with this glass, her speech turned a little woozy. "I think I'll wait until Friday—no *tomorrow* is Friday. Isn't it? I mean *Saturday*. I think I'll wait until Saturday to go to Cortona. I'm having too much fun in Florence." She raised her glass to her lips, no longer *sipping* the champagne.

Paul motioned to the waiter. I didn't know if the word he mouthed was French or Italian, but I was sure he'd called for the check, to bring this night to an end.

"Can we go to some of the museums tomorrow, Paul? That famous one—the one with *David*? You invited me today, but you don't mind going back, do you?" She tried to say *Uffizi* a couple of times but gave up, laughing after she couldn't get it right.

"Today we were at the *Uffizi*," Alex chimed in, with heavy emphasis on the word *Uffizi*. He was in his professorial mode now, the mode in which he had little patience for nonsense. "Michelangelo's *David* is at the *Accademia*. Two distinctly different galleries."

"I'm afraid I have an appointment tomorrow," Paul said. He directed his apology to me. "Jordan, I did not get a chance to tell you that I have two business meetings scheduled during my time here, and one had to be tomorrow because the gallery owner is going on holiday."

"I'll go with you to the gallery," Bella said. "It'll be fun."

"No, it is not appropriate. This is a business appointment," Paul said.

I was very glad I could say, "I have plans to do a cooking class in Tuscany."

"A cooking class? How delightful," Bella said. "Where is it?"

"In Tuscany," I said.

"At a villa that belongs to a friend of mine," Alex said. I gave him a warning glance, fearing that Bella would ask to come along. "It's arranged through a tour company," he added.

"Do they have other tours?" Bella asked.

Alex said yes, certainly they did, and when she asked directly, he had to give up the name: *Vivere la Toscana!* I sighed. How I hoped she didn't wind up in the cooking class!

Bella gave a dismissive gesture. "I might just go on to Cortona," she said. She admired her bracelet again, holding it against the light, making the sapphires shine.

"I'll call for the car now," Paul said, rising from his chair. He went inside, where I imagined he would settle the check, as well.

"I think Paul is a little miffed. Do you think so? All I did was ask to go along—he knows how I love galleries. Was that what made him mad?" Bella asked.

"Oh, I don't know," I said. "He didn't seem mad to me."

She scooted back her chair. "I'm going on to the hotel. It's not far. I can walk."

Alex and I both protested. She should not leave. Paul

would be right back, and the car would be here soon. But Bella grabbed up her purse and the gift boxes.

Alex stood up, reaching out in a pleading gesture. "Please, Bella. It isn't safe to walk by yourself." I thought of the expensive bracelet on her wrist. How foolish!

She looked around for a way to leave. All that separated the terrace with its now half-empty tables from the sidewalk were large planters with lush greenery. Bella squeezed through a space between two planters. By now I was on my feet, too, calling to her, but she was running down the street. Paul came back just in time to see her before she disappeared into the night.

"She wanted to walk back to the hotel," Alex said. "We tried to stop her."

"*Mon Dieu!* What was she thinking?" Paul turned to us, his face drawn. "I am so sorry, but I think I should go after her. Everything is taken care of, and the car— you will recognize the driver who brought you here. He is on his way."

"We'll be fine," I said.

He hesitated, and then with composure that was typically Paul, he said, "I am so sorry, Jordan. I will call you."

"Go," I said.

He did.

I WONDERED HOW Paul had imagined the night would end. I wondered, as I lay awake in my small, firm bed, in the absolute silence, the absolute stillness of my spartan surroundings. Maybe he would've had the driver drop Bella at the Westin and Alex at the convent and he and I would've gone on to a little café for late-night music and quiet talk. And then, a walk along the Arno, with the lights shimmering on the water. Would we have wound up at his hotel? As I pondered the possibilities, the fantasies, my phone made the noise indicating that I had received a text, and Paul's words brought me back to reality.

Bella returned safely to the hotel. Apparently she took a taxi. She answered her phone at last, saying she is in her room. I am sorry this is how the evening ended, Jordan, more than I can say. I wanted to let you know so you will not worry. Sleep well, and we will talk soon.

So he was thinking the same thing I was—how the night might have ended. But he was giving me too much credit if he thought I was *too* worried about Bella. She might have been a temptation for muggers, with her pricey bracelet, but I couldn't muster up more than a smidgen of concern as I pulled the thin coverlet up to my neck and—eventually—drifted into a sound, dreamless sleep.

FOURTEEN

BREAKFAST WAS IN full swing when I arrived. Alex was already at our table, but from the looks of the food before him, I gathered he'd just sat down. I had to stand in line for the coffee machine, but it was well worth it. I desperately needed the caffeine. When I returned to the table with my usual breakfast fare, I told Alex about the text from Paul sometime after midnight.

"Whatever was Bella thinking, running off like that?" Alex said—the same question Paul had voiced.

Maybe it took a woman to guess what she was thinking. "Trying to get attention," I said.

"That makes no sense. She's an attractive woman. She should have no difficulty getting attention," Alex said.

I surmised it was Paul's attention—his unconditional approval—that she craved, but I didn't say it. I changed the subject. "Have you seen Sophie?"

He had not. Sophie didn't show up while we were at breakfast. I knew she was planning to go on the Vespa tour, so I assumed we'd see her at the villa. I wondered what she would say to Bianca Moretti. I hadn't had a chance to talk with Sophie since the revelation that her father had Bianca on speed dial. These young women with their daddy-issues! Sophie was a teenager. Some of her actions might be forgiven. But Bella was no child. Her behavior was ridiculous.

Alex and I finished breakfast, met in the lobby a few minutes later, and headed to the Moretti villa. Since it was my second time to navigate the hairpin curves as we spiraled into the Tuscan hills, I was more prepared for the challenge, but those wild Italian drivers kept me from paying too much attention to the breathtaking views of the valleys far below the twisting road.

Once again, Angelica Moretti met us with an effusive greeting, declaring that she had been counting the hours since we were there Tuesday. We sat on the *loggia*, drinking that amazing lemonade from the Moretti lemons and sharing a plate of *bruschetta* topped with capers and black olives, until Ambra came to tell me the *Vivere la Toscana!* van with the cooking class had arrived. Alex and Angelica were already reminiscing when I left them.

"Jordan! I am so glad you are here," called Marisa, the first to get out. She stopped to help a plump, short-legged woman climb down. I could see the van was crowded.

"Looks like a large class," I said.

"A full house, as they say."

A full house for their cooking class was a good thing, wasn't it? Somehow, though, I sensed that Marisa wasn't delighted. As I was wondering why, Bella stepped down from the van.

"Good morning, Jordan!" she said, more chipper than I would have imagined she'd be this morning. No indication of a hangover. Incredible! "I decided to take your suggestion."

I clenched my jaws to keep from saying I had *not* suggested that she join the cooking class, but Marisa may have guessed, from the surprised look on my face.

"It is a good thing you were meeting us here," Marisa

said to me. "I am not sure where we would have put one more person in the van."

Cristiano, his hair slicked back into a ponytail, came out of the driver's seat. "We could not refuse the beautiful woman who joined us this morning."

Marisa darted him a look that made him laugh a lecherous laugh. I read her look as *Only because she's beautiful.*

Ambra showed the group to the *toilette* for handwashing, in the old building that housed the winery and tasting room, while Marisa and Cristiano unloaded the van. The women and the two young men in the group talked about the market. Ambra told me, "I am sorry you missed the *mercato*. Most of the ingredients for the class come from here, the *fattoria*—the farm—but Marisa says it is important to visit the *mercato* for the experience, so they buy some items there."

"I'm sorry I missed that, too," I said, but I thought of Marisa's comment about the full van, and I was glad I wasn't sitting on someone's lap, or someone sitting on mine.

A few minutes later, Ambra directed us to the low building where our cooking class would take place. She told me, with a smile, "We will take good care of your uncle."

"I'm sure Angelica is doing just that," I said.

THE BUILDING IN WHICH the kitchen for the cooking class was located may not have been centuries old, as the winery must have been, but it was old, built of stone, with an uneven tiled floor. Upgrades that obviously had been necessary for the cooking class were the new appliances—commercial quality refrigerator, ovens, and stovetop—and the marble-topped U-shaped work counter around which we gathered, elbow to elbow. While Marisa washed vegetables in a deep sink, Cristiano poured wine for everyone and Ambra brought a *piatto di biscotti*, a plate of the crispy pastry, flavored with almonds, dusted with sugar.

A young woman from Australia named Iris positioned herself on the high stool beside me. We struck up a conversation and I was fascinated by the fact that she had served in the military in Iraq. She was on leave. "My fiancé and I met in Florence for a short holiday before I have to return," she was saying, when Bella edged in between us. Like a puppy, underfoot.

"Now we begin our work!" Cristiano made a show of dropping two whole carrots, two sticks of celery, and two large red onions into a pot, saying, "For the *brodo vegetale*, the vegetable broth that we will use to boil the *ravioli* you will prepare. Together we will prepare *ravioli* with sauce, and you will prepare strawberry *tiramisu*." A round of light applause followed. "Now you must prepare the vegetables for our sauce," he said. Marisa distributed tomatoes, zucchini, carrots, and scallions, and gave each of us a chef's knife. Cristiano then gave brief directions on the safe use of the knife.

"Not a lot of room to work," Bella, who was standing, said in a stage whisper. "My kitchen is probably this large, just for one person!"

Iris, the Aussie, did not disguise her irritation at Bella. I wondered what Bella might have said or done on the trip from Florence. "Not so bad for eight, but tight for nine," Iris said.

Bella's neck stiffened, her eyes rounded, as if to say, "How rude!" By the conspiratorial look she darted my way, it seemed she had no clue that *she* had done anything unseemly.

Clearly, Cristiano was the head chef and Marisa was his sous chef. I don't know for a fact that the sous chef is *supposed* to do all the work while the head chef pontificates, but in this case, that's how it was. Cristiano pranced about the room, leaning over shoulders, at times reaching in to hold a pretty young woman's hand and guide her in the proper manner of dicing. To the plump woman Marisa had helped off the bus, he said, in a most officious tone, "Do not think you are *beheading* the carrots! *Dice! Dice!*" Marisa didn't join the chorus of laughter; I suspected Cristiano had made the same remark in so many classes that it had grown stale.

To me, he said, "Perfect, *si*," meaning he did not care to lean into *this* woman who was well over thirty-something, and that was just dandy with me. I had diced plenty of vegetables in my day, so I didn't need his instruction. It came as no surprise that as he reached Bella, she suddenly let out a yelp. She had cut her finger—a little knick on her pointer. Not much blood, but she had Cristiano's attention. He made a huge deal of it, taking her to a corner cabinet where a first aid kit was stashed, playing doctor. He gushed over her sapphire bracelet, much too extravagant to be worn in a cooking class, I thought. Finishing with the bandage, Cristiano pulled a stool from what must have been Marisa's station, poured another glass of wine for Bella, and said, "Doctor's orders! Let someone else finish your task," and he pointed to me.

Iris, who was young and pretty enough, gave him no chance to get close. She stepped back from the counter, held the knife for him to take, and said, "Show me."

He didn't take it. He made a wave of dismissal and said something in Italian that must have meant, "You're doing fine. Carry on."

Marisa collected our vegetables in a large pot and set them aside. "Now we will make strawberry *tiramisu*," Cristiano said, and he actually snapped his finger at Marisa. She doled out the ingredients: eggs, sugar, Mascarpone cheese, Ladyfinger biscuits, milk, and strawberries. A thin sheen of perspiration had popped out on her forehead as she rushed around while Cristiano sashayed about the room. Only when he decided he wanted a cigarette did he give Marisa a chance to take charge. She was patient and helpful as we separated the eggs, combined the sugar and egg yolks, and beat the whites with a whisk. Incredibly, some of the younger women had no idea how to separate eggs or use a whisk to fluff egg whites into peaks. I was glad I had taught my daughters that much—probably not my son, I confess. The young men in our class knew what they were doing. One of them said they were both training in a culinary program.

Bella pushed her bowl of eggs toward me, her bracelet catching the light. "Can you do mine, Jordan?" she asked. "My finger is too sore."

It took longer than one might imagine for the group to finish folding the cheese into the yolk mixture, adding the fluffy whites, and spreading a layer into individual serving dishes. Marisa directed us to dip the Ladyfinger biscuits into the milk and arrange them on top, along with the sliced strawberries. She was demonstrating the final touches when Cristiano returned.

Immediately he took over. "Now," he said, reaching for a Ladyfinger.

Marisa whispered to him, and he went to the sink and washed his hands. *"Now,"* he said again, and he turned to glower at Marisa. *"You* cook the meat for our sauce."

When we'd finished decorating the creamy mixture, Cristiano apparently saw that Marisa should tend to the meat she was browning in a large pan, so he actually made the effort himself to open the refrigerator door. One by one, we put our individual *tiramisu* serving dishes on a shelf to chill. He made a brusque comment to Marisa, and she answered.

"It seems our sous chef needs more time with the meat," Cristiano said, "so we will take a break before we begin to prepare the *ravioli*. More wine?"

FIFTEEN

THE KITCHEN HAD become stuffy. I was glad to get some fresh air. I thought I might check on Alex, but why did I need to do that? I didn't. Sounds from the construction site drew my attention. Two workmen were using a forklift to unload pallets of terra cotta roof tiles from a small truck. I saw Rob Moretti and called to him. He waved and called back, "Come! I will show you."

"Do you have time?" I asked.

"For the *architetto*, of course!"

"I'd love to look around," I said. The ground was uneven, and I had to pick my way through rubble. Rob cautioned me to be careful. I laughed and said, "It's not my first construction site."

From behind me came a voice that I was beginning to know all too well. "Jordan! Wait! Wait for me!"

I had not paid much attention to Bella's three-inch heels until now, but as she made her way toward us, stumbling on the rough ground, I couldn't help saying, "Bella, you'll ruin your shoes." That, I thought, would be more likely to dissuade her than to say she might hurt herself.

"I'll be careful," she said, and her steps became more dainty.

The workmen had stopped their work to watch this striking woman in her high heels, tight Capri pants, cleavage-revealing top, not to mention the sapphire bracelet, as she navigated through the debris. Rob appeared to be momentarily mesmerized, but he quickly regained his senses. "You are most welcome, *signorina*, but are you sure? The site may not be safe for you. It is not a clean place for a woman."

I took no offense that he wasn't worried about the cleanliness where *I* was concerned.

"You are so kind," she said, and I swear she batted her eyelashes. "I'll be fine. I'm Bella."

"I am Roberto," Rob said. Bella extended her hand. I noticed she held her bandaged finger, on her left hand, at an odd angle, and sure enough, Rob asked about it. She described her injury as not *too* deep or *too* painful, her words at odds with the *brave* face she put on.

I felt an obligation to add to the introductions. "Roberto Moretti lives here. This is his family's villa. And Bella is visiting Florence with her father, who is a friend of mine."

"A very *good* friend, it seems," Bella said, with a contrived smile.

I turned to Rob. "We'll have to get back to the cooking class in a few minutes."

"*Si.* Come with me," he said, and we went inside the structure, Rob leading the way, Bella blundering along behind me.

I was a little surprised that the project wasn't farther along, but I knew that construction delays can be caused by any number of factors. From the conversation at the Morettis' table on Tuesday, I knew there had been some issues with the insurance, too. The framing was up. It was easy to see the layout of the rooms. A plumbing crew was doing the rough-ins. Rob took a minute to speak to one of the plumbers in a bathroom, maybe something about the location of the fixtures. The plumber took a measurement and pointed to the plans. Their Italian was rapid, but it didn't sound angry. Just working out one of the many glitches construction requires.

As Rob showed us around, I could see he was both knowledgeable about the new wing and proud. I wondered where Raff was, the brother who showed little interest in the project.

"Would you like to see the views of the valley from the balconies?" Rob asked. An extension ladder was propped up, giving access to the second floor.

Bella, who'd been looking bored while Rob and the plumber spoke, said, "Oh, let's do!"

I wouldn't have minded using the ladder to go up; my hikers were good for climbing. But Rob suggested we use the staircase at the end of the hall, and it made sense, for Bella's sake. He led us through the hallway, which was strewn with tools and power cords, bunches of pipes and rods. We came to a tight spot. Bella was so close on my heels that I thought she would run into me. I was about to turn, to tell her to give me a little room, but I didn't get a chance before the noises came—the clanging of pipes rolling and a shriek from Bella. She was on the floor, wailing. All of this in an instant. In another moment I was kneeling beside her, asking, "Are you all right? What happened?" and Rob was standing over us, murmuring something in Italian that, if he were in the States, would be, *"Please, God, don't let her sue."*

Abruptly, she stopped crying and sat up, refusing the hand I offered her. Her face seemed about to crumple as she said in a pitiful voice, "Why, Jordan? Why did you push me?"

I was momentarily speechless, but I caught my breath. "I didn't."

"You *did*. Why?"

I looked at Rob for support, though he'd been leading the way so he wouldn't have known what happened behind him. His expression revealed only a mix of worry and bafflement.

A nylon strap had been loose around a bundle of threaded rods, and I figured she must have tripped, but I wasn't going to point it out, and throw Rob under the bus. Bella just *might* sue.

"You stumbled. It was an accident," I said.

"Are you able to stand, *Signorina*," Rob reached out with both hands, and she let him help. He sighed, clearly relieved that nothing seemed to be broken. "Ah, it is not so bad."

"It's my ankle. I hope it's not a bad sprain," she said, working her ankle back and forth.

"Doesn't look like it's swelling," I observed.

The glare she gave me could have cut a diamond. I tried to sound genuinely sweet as I said, "I'll help you get back to the kitchen."

"I don't need *your* kind of help, Jordan. I can't imagine why you pushed me."

"But I *didn't*. Bella, I'm sorry this happened, but you're mistaken. I didn't push you."

She whirled around. A handsome young workman cleared a path for her, and she left.

"Maybe I'll get another chance to look around," I told Rob, "but I'd better go back now."

I still couldn't detect whether Rob believed me, but the words of Hamlet's mother rang in my mind: The lady doth protest too much. Bella knew I hadn't pushed her. I would be truthful with Paul, but I would remember it was counterproductive to protest too much.

NEITHER OF US spoke on our trek back to the class. Bella hiked out several paces in front of me, looking like she might fall again as she teetered on her high heels, putting on a good show of limping. She was not injured. I was sure of it. The more I thought about it, the more bizarre it seemed. Was it possible she had *deliberately* taken a fall in order to accuse me? What an outrageous idea! I told myself.

Outside the door to the cooking class, some in our group were smoking, some on their phones. I wondered if Paul might have called while my phone was silenced to plan for tonight. He had come to Florence so we could spend time together. I felt a stitch in my chest at the thought of another dinner with Bella. Considering what had just happened, I doubted she'd want that any more than I would. My big tote bag was in the car, but I'd brought a small purse with a shoulder strap to keep my phone and car keys with me. As Bella turned toward the winery, where the *toilette* was located, I headed toward the vegetable garden and a low stone wall, and drew out my phone.

Yes, Paul had called, but he hadn't left a message. I hesitated, not sure what I might say about Bella. Then I took a deep breath and returned the call.

"One moment, please, Jordan," Paul said, and he spoke to someone for a full minute before coming back on the line. "Now we can talk. I have been consulting with a gallery owner but we are finished until we meet for lunch."

"I forgot about your meeting," I said.

"It is not important. Tell me, how is the cooking class?"

"I've learned how to make *tiramisu*. We're taking a break." I just had to say it. "Paul, did you know Bella was planning to be here?"

"I did not know until this morning. She was already at the tour company, ready to leave for the market, when she sent the text."

I couldn't detect either approval or disapproval in his voice, and that annoyed me. Why couldn't he give me some indication that Bella was *not* pulling the wool over his eyes? But this was not the time to go any further with Bella. I said, "I should get back to the cooking class."

"We must make plans for tonight, yes? Will you call later?" And before I could answer, he said, "Ah, I almost forgot! Do you know about the festival in Florence tomorrow night?" I didn't, and Paul enlightened me. The *Festa della Rificolona*, the Festival of Paper Lanterns, would begin at *Santa Croce* at dark Saturday night and pass through the piazza in front of the *Convento di Santa Francesca Firenze*. "I have never experienced the festival, myself, but I am told there will be many people marching with banners, playing music, carrying colorful paper lanterns high on poles. My friend at the Westin told me about it, and he has reserved a table for us at the café across the piazza from the convent—before it's too late to reserve. I hope you don't mind that I made these arrangements."

"I don't mind. I'm delighted, Paul. Why wouldn't I be?"

"I never want you to think I am"—he seemed to search for the word and came up with "presumptuous."

How could I be annoyed at this man? "Bella will go to

Cortona tomorrow," he added, "but I am sure Alex will want to join us for a spectacular view of the festival."

For a fleeting moment, I felt a prickle of shame that I couldn't find it in myself to be as generous toward Bella as Paul was toward Alex. But I got over it.

We said goodbye with promises to talk in the afternoon. The prospect of such a delightful festival took my focus off Bella's fall as I made a quick trip to the *toilette* for handwashing before we would likely knead pastry.

SIXTEEN

MAKING HOMEMADE PASTA had to be the highlight of the day. In all my years of cooking for my family—lots of lasagna, spaghetti, and fettucini—I'd never made the pasta from scratch. Flour, eggs, olive oil, and salt—all on the marble surface. Make a well in the flour, crack the eggs into it, and add olive oil and salt. Whisk the eggs with a fork while continuously blending in flour. Then came the time when we had to get our hands into it.

Bella screwed up her face. She might've asked me to do the kneading for her, but she hadn't spoken to me since we'd returned from the construction site. Nor had I spoken to her. Iris and I had chatted, looking around Bella. Cristiano came by, saw what Bella was doing—*not* doing very well—and called for Marisa. Poor Marisa! No sooner did she knead the dough, pat it out, and show Bella how to use a rolling pin to roll out the pastry than Cristiano was ordering her to distribute ricotta, parmesan, and eggs for the stuffing. Several in the class were having trouble getting the pasta thin enough and sealing it properly around the stuffing to make one huge ravioli. I wound up helping Bella with hers because Marisa was so busy assisting others and Cristiano was not getting his hands dirty. For a moment I thought she might be reconsidering her accusations after her fall in the construction area. We were civil, talking about the pasta.

Sounds from outside, the growling of motorscooters, caused us all to look up. The Vespa tour had arrived. I thought of Sophie and wondered if I'd get a chance to talk with her, but was immediately drawn back to Cristiano's instruction.

"You may wash the flour off your hands here," he said, pointing to the deep sink. It was more than just flour. It was flour that had mixed with eggs and olive oil and then dried—much like a thin glaze of concrete. Cristiano continued, as we began to move around the kitchen, "Observe! Marisa will combine the vegetables you have prepared and the meat she has sautéed to make a rich sauce for the pasta. The sauce will thicken, and the ravioli will take only ten minutes to boil in the *brodo vegetale*. Lunch will be ready in less than one hour."

I checked my watch. It seemed it should be much later than two-fifteen. The cooking class would have been so much more enjoyable if Bella had not decided to join it.

And I didn't know the half of it yet.

As Bella washed her hands, Cristiano, of course, took notice. "Where is your beautiful bracelet?" He joked, "I hope you have not lost it!"

Bella gasped. "My bracelet!" She pressed her hand to her mouth, letting a little cry escape.

"*Signorina*!" Cristiano exclaimed. "*Dio mio*!"

Dio mio, indeed. What would Paul say if she'd lost that fabulous bracelet? He wouldn't care about the cost, but how had she been so careless with his precious gift?

By now, a hush had fallen over the room. Everyone was gathering around.

Bella's hand slid to her chest, as if she were trying to still her racing heart. "I might have left it in the restroom," she murmured, "at the sink when I washed my hands."

"Ah, yes! That must be what happened!" Cristiano put his hand over his heart, much as Bella had done. Relief! And then to Marisa, "Go to the *toilette* and bring the bracelet!"

I spoke without thinking through what was happening here. "I went to the *toilette* just after you were there, Bella, and I'm sure your bracelet wasn't at the sink."

"It *must* be!" Cristiano said. And then in a flurry he ordered everyone to look around the room, on the floor, on the work surface which was still cluttered with bowls and utensils.

Marisa returned, shaking her head, and Bella began to weep.

Someone suggested searching everyone's purses. The plump woman was offended by the idea that anyone in our group could have taken the bracelet. Voices rose, and the word *police* caused Cristiano to shout, "No *polizia*! We will not call police! We will find the bracelet!"

I was convinced Bella had just misplaced it. "Are you sure you had the bracelet after you fell, on the construction site?" I said.

"I didn't *fall*. I was *pushed*!" Her crying had turned swiftly to yelling. "And I *told* you—I took the bracelet off at the sink, so no I didn't lose it at the construction site."

Iris chimed in, "Check your purse. Maybe you dropped it in your purse and forgot."

"I *didn't*!" Bella had been at the deep sink, but now she marched to her place at the work station—no indication of a sore ankle—and bent down for her purse. It was about the size of mine. She dumped the contents on

the counter—phone, wallet, lipstick, a few other mis-
cellaneous items, nothing of much interest. She hiked
her chin and said to Iris, "There. Why don't you check
yours?"

Iris did just that, and others followed. The two young
men emptied their pockets. Even the woman who'd been
offended by the idea at first, said, "Let's just get it over
with." No one had counted on spending the cooking
class like this, and no one was enjoying it.

I picked up my purse and turned it upside down. The
sapphire bracelet fell out.

ALL THE SURPRISED GASPS sounded like air leaking from a
room full of balloons. No one was more surprised than
I. "Bella, I have no idea how this happened," I said.

And then I saw through her expression and I knew
exactly how the bracelet had wound up in my purse.
She overdid the shock just a bit. A *pop-eyed* look, the
"O" of her mouth big enough for an orange, her hands
clasped at her throat. Too dramatic, like something she'd
seen in an old movie. I was not fooled, but from the
murmuring that started up in the room, I gathered that
the others *were*.

"*Why*, Jordan? You pushed me and then you took my
bracelet. I don't understand." Bella's pleading voice was
much more convincing that the earlier high-pitched accusations. She snatched the bracelet from the counter
and, in a manner that could only be described as *lov-
ingly*, she slipped it on her wrist. As if rehearsing to
show her daddy how she treasured his gift.

Cristiano tried to intervene, beseeching me, "I am
certain there is some explanation. *Signora*, did you per-

haps find the bracelet at the sink in the *toilette* and you
meant to give it to the *Signorina*, but you forgot?"

"No, that didn't happen. I haven't touched the bracelet," I said.

"Then how do you explain yourself?" Bella said.
"You were in the bathroom after I was. It's *your* purse.
I just can't think why you would do it. My father would
buy you a beautiful bracelet, too, if you asked him." Her
voice kept edging toward a whine.

One of the women chimed in, "If it were mine, I
would call the police and try to get to the bottom of it."
The voice of an American. I didn't look at her. My gaze
was locked with Bella's.

"No *polizia*!" Cristiano exclaimed, and then, in a
more controlled tone, "It is all a big misunderstanding,
an unfortunate thing to happen, but the bracelet is back
with the *signorina*, yes? It will be explained, I am sure,
but we must now finish our work! Please!"

Low voices and shuffling noises followed. No one
made eye contact with me except Iris, and she seemed
more perplexed than sympathetic. Surely Marisa believed me, but she was at the stove, stirring the sauce,
so I couldn't see her face.

Someone called to Bella, asking to see her bracelet,
and her mood suddenly improved.

All at once she had young women gathering around
her, their voices soothing. Flash of *déjà vu*. Junior high
girls.

I couldn't deny that it stung me to think Bella had
managed this ploy. I grabbed my purse and the items
that had spilled after the bracelet had fallen out. Cooking class was over for me.

I LET MYSELF into the villa through the back door, expecting to hear Alex and Angelica talking, but all was quiet. Even in the kitchen, where I expected to see Ambra or the girl, Pia. I assumed they were in the winery, serving lunch to the Vespa tour. Just as well. I needed a few minutes to collect my thoughts. I helped myself to a glass of water and took it out to the *loggia*.

Paul was expecting me to call him, but I supposed he'd still be at lunch. Three o'clock was sometimes just the middle of the Italian lunch, and a business lunch might extend even longer. If I were honest with myself, I didn't know what I'd say to Paul about Bella, and how could I talk to him at all if I didn't tell him what had happened today? Truthfully, at this moment, I just wanted to talk to Alex.

A sound came from the kitchen through the bank of open windows, and Pia appeared at the door. She may have wondered why I was there, but the well-trained girl simply smiled and asked, "May I get something for you, *Signora*?"

"*Grazie*," I said, "but no. Have you seen Signora Moretti and my uncle?"

"I saw them before they went out to walk. I think they are in the vineyards or looking at the horses," she said. I thanked her, and she went on her way, back to the winery, I presumed.

A few more minutes had passed when Marisa showed up with a tray. To my delight, she'd brought a plate of pasta—my *ravioli* with sauce—and the *tiramisu* I had made. I was surprised Cristiano had let her get away, but she said the others were eating now.

"I know you did not take the woman's bracelet," she said.

"No, I didn't. Please, sit with me," I said.

"I cannot stay," she said. "I wanted to tell you that I *know* someone put the bracelet in your purse. You would not do such a thing."

"Thank you, Marisa," I said. "I'm not sure Cristiano believed me, but it means a lot to me that you do."

"Cristiano"—she gave a shrug—"he simply wants it to be over, without *polizia*. He was in trouble a long time ago. Drugs, I think. He was very young when it happened."

That made sense now, though I had assumed he just didn't want the negative publicity for *Vivere la Toscana!* that would come with police involvement.

Marisa said, with some hesitation, "I do not know this to be true, but I think the woman herself may have put the bracelet in your purse."

"I think that's exactly what happened," I said.

Marisa's eyes widened. "Why did she do such a thing?"

"She doesn't like it that her father is fond of me. I'll just leave it at that," I said.

"Ah, yes." Marisa nodded. "Do not worry, Jordan. Nothing will come of this."

She wouldn't have known that what really mattered— *who* mattered—was Paul and what *he* thought of Bella's version. How it would play out with him, I couldn't predict.

SEVENTEEN

IN SPITE OF EVERYTHING, I hadn't lost my appetite. Cristiano had mentioned that he would give all of us the recipes we'd used today. I could contact Marisa for those. I had no plans to see Cristiano or anyone else in the cooking class again.

Well on the way to cleaning my plate, I again heard sounds from inside. More noises later, after I had finished the exquisite *tiramisu*. Food has a way of cheering me, and my mood had improved after the lunch that was absolutely perfect. Maybe it would have been a bit more perfect with a splash of the wine Cristiano poured so freely, but water would do. I went to the kitchen to refill my glass.

Bianca was filling a glass of wine for herself, emptying the bottle. I didn't get the sense that she'd been assisting with lunch in the winery. She was too "put together"—sundress, low-heeled sandals, flawless make-up, and hair that must have been just now blown dry. A floral scent enveloped her. It was likely she was fresh from a shower after swimming.

"It is too bad I took it all," she said, holding up the bottle, pretending to inspect it. "I will open another if you like."

Holding my glass under the faucet, I said, "It's probably better that I have water."

"Water is never better if you can have wine." She laughed. I realized she was a little tipsy.

And then, her gaze shifted, and I saw that Sophie was standing just outside the kitchen, in the dining room. Bianca walked toward her and asked something in Italian—*Who are you? What are you doing?* would be my guess. I was continually amazed that the Italians seemed to know when to use their language and when to use English, even before the other speaker said a word.

"Sophie?" I said, but she didn't acknowledge me. She began to spew Italian at Bianca.

Bianca set her wine glass on the counter with such force, I was surprised it didn't break. The heels of her sandals made urgent clicks on the tile and then the hardwood as she went toward Sophie and followed her into the living room, each talking over the other. At first, I didn't move. This was the scenario I had imagined—Sophie confronting Bianca about her father. Not my business. But I stayed. Something about the exchange was too disturbing. I set down my glass, went to the doorway between the kitchen and the dining room, where I had a view into the living room. I caught a glimpse of Sophie pointing; then she moved out of my line of vision. The voices grew louder, angrier, and when I heard a crash, I couldn't stand by any longer.

Another crash as Sophie hurled a framed photograph into the wall. Bianca was screaming.

"Sophie! Sophie, stop it!" I shouted, and, for whatever reason, my words seemed to jolt her. She blinked as if she were waking from a trance, and then she turned and ran out the front door. Almost in the same moment, Bianca brushed past me, sobbing.

Two photos—the glass broken on both. The frames

had hit the wall, the corners making deep gouges. I picked up the damaged photographs and laid them on a side table. One of them was a wedding picture of Raff and Bianca. One appeared to be the whole Moretti family, and it must have been taken not long before Victor died because the frail-looking man was sitting, with the family gathered around. Sophie had taken those from an arrangement of more than a dozen family photos on a marble-topped bureau. I had thought Sophie might do *something*, but certainly not anything like this.

As I studied the photographs, Alex and Angelica came in the front door. They must have met Sophie flying from the house. Both asked what had happened, what this was all about, and then, with a little moan, Angelica spied the damaged photos and rushed to examine them.

I made a helpless gesture. "I'm not sure. Something between Sophie and Bianca."

And then I noticed how pale Alex was. He took his handkerchief from his pocket. His forehead was slick with perspiration. Before I could even ask, he said, "I've already swallowed one of my tablets. I'll be all right, but I need to lie down."

Angelica, flustered as she was by the photos, shifted her attention. "Alex became too tired. It is my fault. I myself walk all over the *fattoria* so it is easy for me, but I should know that my visitors are not accustomed to such exercise."

I doubt that made Alex feel any better.

He shook his head. "Please. As I told you, these attacks of angina just happen. I don't always know the reason. The nitroglycerine tablet will do its job shortly."

"We must let you rest." Angelica took his arm and

began to lead him away. "Jordan, will you get your uncle a glass of water? He will be in a bedroom on that hall. You will see." She indicated with a nod. Her hands held tightly onto his arm.

When I had Alex's water, I went back through the living room, taking a minute to look out the window. I didn't really expect to see Sophie. She was supposed to be with her Vespa group in the winery. But there she was, sitting on the low rock wall, with the Vespas parked all around her. And sitting beside her, Cristiano.

ANGELICA PROVIDED A colorful afghan for Alex, who was lying on top of the covers. She and I both sat with him for a few minutes, until he said, "Ladies, I can't rest very well under your eagle eyes. Please, go about your business, and I promise I'll be fine."

Angelica glanced at me, her expression questioning, and I nodded. Outside the bedroom, I said, "He's sounding more like Alex now."

"I was so worried when his breathing became difficult, and his face turned very white," she said. "I wanted him to sit, to wait, to let me get help, but he was determined to go on."

"That's Alex—bull-headed."

We heard the growl of the motorscooters, and I went to the window to see if I could spot Sophie leaving with the Vespa tour. I thought I picked her out, but from the back, several of the riders wearing helmets looked alike, male and female. Moments later, I could still hear the faint noise of the motorscooters, down the mountain, when the van from *Vivere la Toscana!* took the cooking class—with Bella—away. Angelica joined Ambra and Pia, who had returned to the kitchen with trays and carts from lunch in the winery. I went to the *loggia* again—such a peaceful setting—with a coffee that Angelica had pressed upon me. A soft breeze had come up, making gentle ripples on the water in the pool. Surely there would be no more drama today. Alex would be fine, after resting a bit. I had settled down, myself, a little, when Paul called.

"Are you all right, Jordan?" he said, with a note of urgency in his voice, and I knew Bella had already called him, giving him her version of the missing bracelet. How tempted I was to rush ahead with my side of the story, but prudence won out, and I remained silent.

"Bella and I have talked. She is very upset about what happened, and I can imagine you must be distressed, as well."

"To be honest, Paul, I'm more angry than anything," I said. "I've never been accused of stealing before."

A beat of silence followed, and then Paul said, "Bella should not have worn the bracelet to a cooking class. Someone took the bracelet, of course, and when Bella announced it was gone, that person dropped it into your purse. Bella said yes, that had to be what happened, and she is so sorry about—how all the others reacted when the bracelet was found."

All the others? My jaws were so tightly clenched that they began to ache. A moment passed. I was supposed to reply, of course, but I couldn't come up with the right words.

"Jordan, are you there?"

"I'm here."

"I have assured Bella that you are completely trustworthy, that I do not doubt you for one moment," he said. I was reminded of the time in Provence when I'd had to come to a place of trust in Paul, and it wasn't easy. It had to mean something that he had no doubts about me.

"What should matter to Bella is that she has her bracelet back," I said. "And what matters to me is knowing you trust me."

"With all my heart, Jordan," he said.

This was not the time to mention Bella's accusation that I made her fall, as we'd toured the new wing of the villa. Maybe she hadn't told Paul about that, when she'd realized it was not so easy to deceive him about me. Perhaps I would just have to accept Paul's faith in Bella, as long as she was unable to shake his trust in me.

"And now—can we make plans for tonight?" he said. "Just the two of us?"

"It's a lovely thought," I said, and I meant it. What I didn't say was that I couldn't imagine Bella would let it be just the two of us. "I can't be sure what time Alex and I will return to Florence. He's had another attack of angina, and he may need to rest here for a while longer."

Paul was concerned and understanding, as I knew he would be. He asked me to call him later, and that was how we left it. It could be worse, I told myself.

WE DIDN'T LEAVE the Moretti Villa until six o'clock. We might not have left then, but Alex insisted that we should get past the most treacherous roads before it was absolutely dark. Thinking of me, my dear uncle. Though he made a joke of it: "Given how Jordan drives, we'll be much better off not taking those switchbacks in the dark."

He and Angelica seemed to have a hard time saying goodbye, with one long embrace and then another and promises not to lose touch again. Angelica wiped away tears, and as Alex turned to go, she reached for him again. "Could you come back? You will be in Florence for a few more days. Could we have another afternoon, perhaps?"

Alex and I exchanged a look, and finally I said we might. We couldn't promise. "I would love more time," he said, and they embraced yet again.

He was quiet in the car. I asked a couple of times if he was all right, and he assured me that he was fine. But he wasn't *fine*.

I had waited all this time to tell him about Bella, and as he listened, nodding, making disapproving faces now and then, I felt a weight lifted. Though Marisa believed me and Paul believed me, Alex was the only one I'd been able to tell *everything*, including how Bella had managed to make Paul think she was just an innocent victim. So deceptive, so manipulative.

"Is she still going to Cortona tomorrow?" Alex asked. "Wasn't that her plan?"

I managed to smile for the first time all afternoon. "*Mon Dieu*, as Paul would say, I certainly hope so."

And then I told Alex what Sophie had done, throwing photographs into the wall, and how she and Bianca had screamed at each other. By now, I was feeling removed enough from the incident so that it seemed like something I'd read or seen in a movie. Regardless of the warm feelings I had for Sophie, her problems were not mine, and she had not sought my advice.

Alex shook his head, "What a day this has been."

"Too much drama," I said.

A shadow crossed his face, a strange expression that made me ask, "Is there something else, Alex?"

He didn't answer for a moment, and then he nodded and murmured, "Yes."

EIGHTEEN

"How do I begin?" he said. His lips curled into a weak smile. "Actually, that is what Angelica said. 'How do I begin, Alex?' and then she said, 'I was pregnant, with our child.'"

I almost ran off the road. Alex, who rarely swears, roared, "Damnation!"

"Sorry. We're OK," I said.

"I can wait to tell you this if you aren't able to drive and listen at the same time."

"I'm sorry. Please. I'm listening—and watching the road, I promise."

And so he told me.

"I didn't know, when I returned to Atlanta, and Victor stayed in Florence. Angelica didn't know, either, until after I had left Italy. She would have written to me about the pregnancy, but she lost the baby. It was early—too early to know if it was a boy or girl."

I glanced from the road just an instant and saw Alex's expression of sadness and regret.

"Hearing this today must have been—terrible," I said.

"I haven't processed my feelings yet," he said, in a most professorial way.

"Did Victor know?"

"He did. He was a comfort after her miscarriage, she said." Alex cleared his throat, and I wondered if emotion was about to overcome him, but I didn't look at

him. He went on. "I understand now why Victor may
have stopped writing. We didn't have all the technology then, you know. Friends wrote letters. His were
brief and finally they stopped altogether after the twins
were born. I always believed he felt some guilt that he'd
won the girl and now they had a family—his dreams
had come true. But now I'm seeing his guilty feelings
through a different lens. He knew what he had might
have been mine—could have been, but for a quirk of
Nature. Because if Angelica had told me she was having our baby, I would have returned to Italy. If she had
given birth to our child, both our lives would have been
very different."

"I'm sorry, Alex." It sounded so lame, but I didn't
know what else to say.

Alex took a long breath, exhaling noisily. "No one is
to blame. Angelica has had a good life, and so have I."

I had the feeling he said it to convince himself, but
I agreed. He'd had a wonderful life, I told him. He had
many accomplishments to his credit. But I knew even
as I said it that it wouldn't make him feel any better.

By now night had fallen, and a big orange moon—
three-quarters full—was rising. I brought up the Festival of Paper Lanterns, Saturday night. It was the first
chance I'd had to tell Alex that Paul had reserved a table
for the three of us at the café across from the convent.

"You and Paul have had no time to yourselves," he
said. "I'm sure I could watch the parade from the convent."

"Your window doesn't overlook the *piazza*."

"Nevertheless," he said, "Paul was probably just
being kind when he included me."

I told him he was being ridiculous. "Paul and I have time," I said, though the truth was, time was getting away.

ON THE OUTSKIRTS of Florence, we stopped at one of the few gas stations we'd seen. I bought sparkling water and little packaged cakes from their vending machines. It was nearly eight o'clock. I texted Paul: Just now coming into Florence. I will call later but do not want to leave the convent tonight because of Alex.

An hour later, after I'd seen Alex to his room, amid protests that he didn't need a nursemaid, I received a text from Paul: Please come to the entrance of the convent for a delivery.

I took the stairs with a lightness that made me think of being sixteen again. And there was Paul Broussard, standing in the glow of the convent's security lights, attired in his signature white shirt and black pants and black jacket, holding two flat boxes that, from the aroma, contained pizza. A cloth bag swung from his arm, with the neck of a wine bottle visible. The sight of him brought a wide grin and a rush of pleasure that I'd been needing all day.

"You don't look like any delivery boy I've ever seen," I said.

"It is my first time, I assure you," he said. He looked uncomfortable, his stance, the way his elbows jutted out. "My driver said this particular *pizzeria* is very good," he said. Ah, yes. I couldn't imagine Paul going into a *pizzeria* and ordering at the counter.

"Come in," I said. I had been standing in the doorway so I didn't have to buzz us in.

"I thought perhaps we would have to sit in the *piazza*," he said, with a wry smile. "I wasn't sure the

Sisters would allow me inside." He held out the boxes, and I took them.

"I think we'll be fine in the garden," I said.

He nodded approval and followed me through the common room and on through the ground floor of the convent. Through French doors, we entered the garden, and Paul said, "I did not imagine this!" It was true that tonight the spacious garden courtyard, bathed in moonlight, seemed it might belong to a palace, rather than a tired, fifteenth-century convent. A few lights from rooms on the two floors above *piano terra*—the second and third floors but officially the first and second—offered some illumination near the building, but Paul and I followed the cobblestones farther out, past the fountain with water pouring from the lamb's mouth, to a stone bench in the midst of some flowering bushes. Nice to have some privacy at last.

"There is enough pizza for Alex, too," Paul said, with an inflection that seemed to say he hadn't really believed Alex would join us. This time he *was* just being polite, I thought.

I pointed, identifying the dark window between two windows that were light. "That's Alex's room. Looks like he's already called it a night. He's had an exhausting day."

Paul produced the bottle of wine, a corkscrew, and two wine glasses wrapped in cloth napkins. He'd thought of everything. And then we dug into our meal—a hearty sausage pizza and another festooned with colorful vegetables. I should say *I* dug into the vegetarian pizza, leaving the other for my second course. No matter what happened, what emotions churned inside me, or how much I'd consumed at the last meal, my appetite never seemed to fail me. Paul was more fastidious, eating the sausage pizza. The *pizzeria* had been generous with paper napkins.

"And your day—was it exhausting?" he asked, after a few bites.

Was that his way of leading to conversation about Bella? I wondered. I didn't want to talk about her, not tonight, but I said, "Yes. Exhausting."

"I am not sure why Bella wanted to go to the cooking class," he said.

I took my time with the mouthful of pizza. He waited. I swallowed and took a long drink of wine. He was still waiting for my reply. Paul was better at this game than I was. I decided I would be perfectly honest, not protest too much, but I would lay out the truth. I said, "Before Bella accused me of stealing her bracelet, we were in the new wing of the villa, the part under construction. Bella shouldn't have been on a construction site with high heels. She stumbled and fell, and she blamed me for that. I can't tell you exactly what her intentions were, Paul—what they *are*—but I know she doesn't like me. And I don't think she likes it that you *do*."

Now it was Paul who hesitated, taking a long time with a large bite of pizza. "Bella is difficult," he said, finally. "You know she attempted suicide. I worry that she might do it again."

"I can see that would weigh heavily on you." I was sincere. The worry in his voice was touching.

He wiped his hands on a napkin, and shifted his position, signaling that he was finished eating. "Bella has two half-sisters," he began. "This summer I invited both of them to Paris when I knew Bella would be in New York. I wanted to know more about Bella, her family, her background. Only one sister accepted the invitation. The younger one, Jessica. She was somewhat sympathetic to Bella because she said their father was obviously preferential to her and Manette. They were his biological children, of course, but none of the girls knew that as they were growing up. On the other hand, Amanda, mother to all of them, pampered Bella, 'spoiled her rotten,' according to Jessica. So for all of their lives, there was a rift, Bella on one side and her half-sisters on the other."

I closed the pizza boxes and stacked them. Paul poured more wine for us. He gazed past the fountain, beyond the garden walls. And then, after a minute, he seemed to snap out of his reverie. "After Bella learned that I was her true father, it seems she—*gloated*—that is the word Jessica used." I could see he was embarrassed to think of what Bella might have said about his fortune, his prominence. "So I think the rift is beyond repair."

I thought of my daughters, the four of them, how there was rarely a day during their growing-up years that the sparks hadn't flown, but always, they could count on each other in a crisis. And now that they were young adults, they were beyond all that pettiness. I couldn't help feeling a stab of sorrow for Bella that she'd wound up without sisters who had her back, even knowing that her own obnoxious behavior was mostly to blame.

"I take it seriously, being Bella's father," Paul went on, "but I am new to this role. I know she is difficult, but I don't know what to do about it—and perhaps I can do nothing, which is very hard for a man like myself to accept." He took a long breath and reached for my hand. "I am sorry to say all of this to you tonight, Jordan. Can we make plans for tomorrow?"

Sitting close together, we talked for a long time about churches and chapels and museums, and about Savannah, my family, my work. The night breeze grew cooler. We finished off the wine. Most of the lights in the rooms went out, and the moonlight seemed to grow brighter. A few people came and went, to smoke, talk on their phones, or just sit, as we were doing. Ivonna came out to smoke, and we gave her the remaining pizza, which she accepted with profuse gratitude. "I get very hungry at this time of the night!" she said. She snuffed out her cigarette and hurried inside.

Before we left the garden, Paul drew me into the shadows and took me in his arms. Our long kisses seemed to say something we hadn't said before. Even now, we didn't put words to it. Without any words at all, we walked through the French doors, back through the convent, to the front door. Another brief kiss that wouldn't have alarmed the Sisters, and we said goodnight.

This was how I had imagined it might be, our time in Florence.

NINETEEN

SLEEP WAS A long time coming, but when I finally settled down, I may not have moved for seven whole hours. I woke around eight o'clock, refreshed, thinking about the plans Paul and I had for the day. I hurried to shower and hurried to the breakfast room before the doors closed at nine.

Alex and I didn't always have breakfast together. Usually he was earlier, present promptly at seven-thirty when the doors opened. Today I couldn't help feeling relieved that the cup and saucer and silverware at his place had been removed. He'd apparently come and gone, which meant he was up and about—without adverse effects from his angina attack, I hoped.

And I was glad to see Sophie at our table, sketching in her sketchbook. I had worried about her, hard as I'd tried not to. I filled a bowl of the uncooked oatmeal I'd grown to like and chose a double serving of *Caffe Lungo* at the coffee machine. Sitting diagonally from Sophie, I was close enough to see how pale and puffy-eyed she looked. She laid down her pencil and sipped from a glass of the Sicilian blood orange juice.

"Nice work," I said, indicating the drawing she'd made of the breakfast room, with its vaulted ceiling and French doors. A skillful two-point perspective.

She closed her sketch book and toyed with the ring in her eyebrow.

"Have you already eaten?" I asked.

"No. I drank too much last night." She made a face and put her hand on her stomach.

"You might try bread. Maybe a roll with some jam," I suggested.

"I cannot," she said, looking at the red-orange juice. "I am not sure about this, but I thought I should have something."

I stirred brown sugar into my oatmeal and began to eat. Sophie sipped her juice. She looked quite miserable. Maybe this was her first hangover. I had a feeling that getting drunk might have something to do with the incident at the Moretti Villa yesterday. And what was that all about? I wasn't sure my earlier theory was all there was to it. My motherly instincts kicked in, and I asked. "Do you want to tell me what happened with Bianca Moretti?"

She shrugged, a pretense that it was nothing. "I lost my temper. No, I don't want to talk about it. Cristiano was right. He said that parents always disappoint their children, and if you don't believe it, you never really grow up."

"Cristiano from the tour company?" I couldn't hide my astonishment. I'd seen them sitting together on the stone wall at the Moretti Villa but had no idea they knew each other well enough for her to confide in him. Cristiano had to be forty.

"I am not a child," she said, as if she had read my mind. "Cristiano asked me to go out, and I went. I should not have drunk so much, but it was not his fault."

At that moment Carlo and Varinia Santoro appeared at the door of the breakfast room. They were the last ones. The attendant closed and locked the door. Sophie saw them and leaned toward me. "Please don't ask me about what happened at the Moretti Villa. But there is something else. Something I saw when I was going to my bathroom. I was sick," she said, making a gesture of *throwing up*. She directed her gaze at the couple, Varinia pushing the wheelchair toward their table. Sophie whispered, "I can't say it now."

Varinia, hair and make-up perfect as always, situated the wheelchair at the table next to ours. She said, "*Buon giorno*," and I returned the greeting. Sophie took a long drink of her juice. Carlo remained aloof, which was not unusual. Varinia, generally not much friendlier than her husband, turned to Sophie and asked, "Are you feeling better this morning?"

Sophie nodded.

Varinia waited a moment longer, as if she expected something else from Sophie, and then, with an expression that was absolutely vinegary, she said, "It is not good to get so drunk. You seemed very confused! I was worried." Hiking her chin, she headed for the food table.

Carlo darted a glance our way. I had no reason to believe his hearing was impaired, so I didn't ask Sophie to finish what she'd started to tell me. For a minute, we didn't say anything. Sophie looked down at her hands in her lap, and then she said, "I am going home tomorrow, to Casa Vittoni."

"Oh—tomorrow." I picked up my cup and held it a moment, considering. She'd been in Florence a week, but her plan to go home seemed as if it had come about suddenly. "Would you like to meet my friend, Paul Broussard, before you go? I know you're interested in art, and he's quite an expert. I think he'd like to see your sketches."

She shook her head vehemently. "I am sorry. I need to go home to my *Mamma*," she said, scooting her chair back.

Sweet, I thought. Sometimes, a girl just needs her mother.

"Will I see you later?" she said.

"Of course," I said.

She left in a hurry. I saw her again after I had finished breakfast. I was in the hall, going to my room. Sophie was entering the chapel with Sister Assunta.

I TEXTED ALEX to tell him I was spending the day with Paul, but I'd have my phone if he wanted to reach me. He texted back, saying he needed time to work on his book, so he would stay close to home. I was relieved that he wouldn't be out by himself. The rest would do him good.

It was a splendid day for sightseeing—blue skies, abundant sunshine, and a gentle breeze. Paul and I walked all over Florence, starting not far from the convent at the *Brancacci Chapel*, with its impressive frescoes. Still in the Oltrarno district, we toured the *Pitti Palace*, the elaborate palace of the Medici family. It was well past mid-day before we'd seen all the rooms, the galleries, and the gardens. We crossed the Arno and made our way to the *Piazza della Repubblica*, where we stopped at a small *trattoria*. Sitting at an outdoor table across from the carousel, we had a long, leisurely lunch. I didn't mention *Vivere la Toscana!* which was just around the corner. I didn't want Paul to make the connection between the tour company and the cooking class at the Moretti Villa that Bella had ruined for me. Conversation about historic sites was easy and lively, but noticeably, we both avoided mentioning Bella.

Waiting for the check, Paul glanced at his watch. "How the hours have flown by," he said. "We have just enough time to visit *Santa Croce* or *Santa Maria Novella*—one or the other. It is about the same distance to either church but they are in opposite directions from here."

"You choose," I said.

"*Santa Croce* is older," he began. "You will see the tombs of Michelangelo and many other famous Florentines in the floor and the wall. As for *Santa Maria Novella*, the marble façade is remarkable. It is a marvelous blend of the Romanesque, Gothic, and Renaissance. Both churches are architectural masterpieces you will appreciate, each with its own character."

I was smiling, thinking Paul sounded a bit like Wikipedia, but I found it charming. A few more descriptive details of each church, and he decided on *Santa Croce*. "*Piazza Santa Croce* is where they will be setting up for the *Festa della Rificolona* that will begin at dark," he said.

As Paul had promised, the church was an architectural delight. We toured the interior while we still could. Paul presumed it would close to tourists earlier than usual because of the gathering crowds in the *piazza*. On another day, I might have wanted to spend more time viewing the spacious nave, the tombs, and the frescoes, but today an hour was enough. During that time, activity in the *piazza* had intensified. As the staging area for the festival, the square was humming with commotion. People kept arriving with poles bearing colorful paper lanterns. Marching bands were beginning to assemble. I took a few photos of the church's marble façade, but it was hard to focus on architecture with all the hustle and bustle around us. Paul suggested that we get a table and have something to drink. For once, the seas didn't part for Monsieur Broussard. We had to wait. By the time we were seated, the square was so packed with people that I couldn't imagine how it might be this evening.

I ordered a *caffe latte*. Paul was having a tangerine Italian soda, which made me think of Sophie, the day we'd had lunch after touring the *Accademia*, and she had said, "I think *Papa* knows Bianca Moretti." Sophie had seemed guarded with me, ever since. But today at breakfast she was about to tell me something before Varinia and Carlo Santos arrived. Had Varinia's comment simply embarrassed Sophie? I hadn't been able to read her reaction before she left the room in a hurry.

"What is it that they say—a penny for your thoughts?" Paul said.

I apologized for my momentary lapse. "I haven't told you about Sophie, have I?" I said, "The girl who's staying at the convent. I wanted her to meet you. She's a talented young artist."

"Tell me," Paul said, and I could see in his expressive eyes that he suspected there was much more I needed to say. I told him everything I knew.

"I wish I knew what's troubling her—I think it's more than her father's affair," I said.

Paul put his hand on mine. "You have a tender heart, Jordan."

"Alex tells me it's none of my business."

"Perhaps not, but the girl would do well to seek your advice. And, of course, I would be happy to meet her if she is wise enough to let you make the introduction."

I gave Paul's hand a squeeze and took mine away, picking up my cup. "She'll go home tomorrow and I'll never see her again, so I shouldn't involve myself."

Still, Sophie had asked, "Will I see you later?" I'd been out with Paul all afternoon, unavailable if she'd wanted to talk. I couldn't help the nagging feeling that I'd let her down. I promised myself I'd see her before she left tomorrow.

We finished our drinks and took a taxi. On the way to the convent, I finally asked about Bella. It seemed too odd not to mention her at all. "Did she go to Cortona?"

"Yes. She rented a car and drove herself this morning. I thought she should take the train. That seemed a more sensible choice to me, but"—he gave a little shrug—"what do you do?" That was all he said about Bella. He asked about Alex, and I told him I thought Alex was working on his book, perhaps getting some much-needed rest at the convent.

"I might need a short nap myself before we meet at the café," I said. "It has been a lovely—*lovely*—day, Paul." Yet I couldn't help noting that we had been excruciatingly polite with each other.

"Lovely, indeed," he said, perhaps thinking the same thing, and he kissed my cheek as the taxi pulled up in front of *Convento di Santa Francesca Firenze*.

TWENTY

THE CAFÉ WAS directly across the *piazza* from the convent, so Alex and I met Paul there. Though we were early, he had arrived earlier. No surprise. Our table would have had an unobstructed view of the *piazza*, through which the parade would pass, except for the crowd that had gathered. The square was roped off, and police in shirt-sleeves, wearing white caps, made sure the crowd stayed behind the ropes.

Paul had already selected the wine. No sooner had we taken our seats than the server brought the bottle. Paul ordered a platter of cheeses, olives, roasted red peppers, and the likes—the traditional *antipasti*. Not an upscale *ristorante*, the café was, nevertheless, prepared for their patrons to spend the whole evening there, it seemed from the leisurely pace. Probably the management knew no one would leave during the festival, but I hadn't felt rushed in any eatery in Florence, no matter how small or inexpensive. Not like many American restaurants that expect you to order immediately and relinquish the table within an hour.

"We had a most delightful day," Paul said, spearing an olive from the plate. "I hope you did, as well, Alex. Jordan said you were working on your book."

"I did, this morning." Alex gave me a sheepish look. "But when I took a break in the garden and realized what a glorious day it was, I just couldn't go back to my room. I decided to take a hop-on, hop-off bus tour."

I wished he'd let me know where he was, but I knew better than to say it. Apparently he had hopped off several times because he said he had barely made it back to the convent in time to jot down a few notes about the sites he'd seen.

He must have read my mind because he said, "Nothing about the tour was strenuous. I knew tonight we'd just be walking across the square."

I gave him a scolding look and he added, "I feel marvelous!"

"And so do I," Paul said.

"And so do I," I said.

We ordered our first course, continued working on the generous platter of *antipasti*, and the server poured more wine. Dark had settled. "We should hear the music soon," Paul said. "*Santa Croce* is not too far from here." He explained that the festival, dating back to the seventeenth century, was a celebration of the Virgin Mary's birthday. It was a tradition for farmers and peasants from the country to make the pilgrimage to Florence each year. Because they had to leave home before dawn, they came with candles and lanterns on long poles. They also brought their goods to the city to sell—vegetables, cheeses, and homemade items. "The market and the festival have continued to this day," Paul said, as we heard the first faint drumbeats. In another five minutes, the parade entered the *piazza*.

Everyone at the outdoor tables stood up. Musicians led the parade, and drummers continued to show up, keeping the beat. The *piazza* was soon filled with marchers moving through, all ages. Men carried children on their shoulders. Standing, we had a good view, in spite of the crowd that had gathered between us and the square. We had an excellent view of the colorful paper-mâché lanterns, swaying at the tops of high poles. Onlookers clapped and cheered. So did we, as did all the other patrons of the café.

Directly across the square from us was the convent. Why my gaze was drawn to the upper-level convent window, *il secondo plano*, which was the third floor, I will never know. Movement in the window caught my eye, and something fell to the ground.

Screams and cries rose above the sounds of the parade. Pandemonium broke out in front of the convent and rippled through the crowd like rushing waters.

I must have screamed, too. I was vaguely aware of Paul and Alex calling my name. A woman—apparently an American—at the next table was crying out, "Did you see? Somebody fell out of that window! Over there!"

She was pointing at what I had seen.

My throat closed up. I could scarcely breathe. I didn't know if I could speak at all, but I knew I couldn't say what I was thinking: *Sophie's window*.

TWENTY-ONE

"THE CONVENT." My words sounded squeezed-out.

Both Paul and Alex looked across the *piazza* to the convent. Alex continued to frown, as if still trying to understand, but Paul said, "*Mon Dieu!* Is that what you saw, Jordan? You saw someone fall from a window in the convent?"

I nodded. I still could not say *Sophie's window.*

Comprehension washed across Alex's face then, and concern, as he stared at the façade of the convent, whispering, "Oh no." Alex's distance vision, even with glasses, was not perfect, but I was sure he could see that on the second floor, in a couple of windows, people were leaning out, looking down. On the third floor, no windows were shuttered, but only one was open. I couldn't be sure that Alex knew whose window it was. That wasn't something I'd ever pointed out to him, and I didn't say it now: *Sophie's window.*

"We need to go to the convent," I said, my words still raspy.

"We can try," Paul said.

The next moments were frantic. Shrill whistles sounded, as police tried to maintain order. The ropes did not hold back people who headed across the *piazza* to see what had happened—and the square was already packed so there was much jostling for every inch of space. Indistinct strains of music began to die away as the musicians moved farther from the square. Drumbeats sounded from the other direction until police closed off the *piazza*, halting the parade. People were permitted to leave the square, it appeared, just not enter it, but not many were leaving. The screaming had stopped, but the noise level had risen to a roar, and then came the sound of sirens.

It seemed we might not get through at all, but eventually we did, with Paul in the lead, taking us not directly across the square, which was chaotic, but around the edge of the commotion. How long, in minutes, I couldn't say. By the time we reached the other side, where police had already put up ropes to push the crowd back from the front of the convent, several squad cars had arrived. Officials in jackets with the word "*Carabinieri*" on the back blocked our view, but when they shifted to make room for an official entourage to come forward from a black SUV, I caught a glimpse of what I knew was a body, though it was covered. And then the gap closed, and I saw that Paul was speaking to a policeman, one who may have been on site all evening, judging from his short sleeves and white cap, just like the ones we'd seen from our café. Crowd control.

After a moment, Paul was back beside Alex and me, saying, "I told the *gendarme* that you were staying in the convent, but he simply said no one would be allowed inside for some time. Of course, that wasn't what I wanted to know."

"He didn't say how this happened?" Alex asked. And *who*, I thought, but I didn't say it, and neither did Alex.

"He would not give out that information. He does not know me," Paul said. In Paris, it would be different, his gesture, an upturned palm, seemed to say.

I rubbed the gooseflesh of my arms. It was not a cool night, not temperature-wise. Low sixties, I would guess. But I was shivering. Paul said, "Are you all right, Jordan? Please, let me give you my jacket."

"I have a sweater," I said, and I dug in my tote bag. Paul helped me with it, and then he put his arm around my shoulders and drew me close to him. His warmth was comforting, but I couldn't stop shivering.

"It is a terrible thing," he said, and I realized Paul didn't know what I feared—probably Alex didn't, either. But as long as I didn't say *Sophie*, maybe it wouldn't be true.

"Perhaps we should go back to the restaurant and wait. Have a coffee or brandy," Paul said.

I shook my head. "Let's stay—for a while. Please. Maybe we can find out—more." I wanted to know, and I didn't.

A woman from the black SUV had joined the other officials, and it was clear she had authority. Her dark hair was short, worn in a kind of bouffant, a little old-fashioned, but along with her tailored suit, the hairdo seemed right. She bent down, and I lost sight of her as she apparently looked at the body. The next time I saw her, she was at the heavy door of the convent, pushing the buzzer. And then she went inside, accompanied by half a dozen men.

And then I saw Cristiano, from *Vivere la Toscana!*

He was moving through the crowd, going away from the convent. I touched Alex's arm and made a motion toward Cristiano. "Wonder what he's doing here," I said.

"I can't imagine," Alex said.

We kept waiting. Time dragged on. After a while, Paul said, "Ah! There's Eli. There is a man who will have information if anyone does. Excuse me." A minute later, he returned with Eli Schubert. And Paul was right. Eli had information.

"I KNOW A lieutenant in the *carabinieri*," Eli explained. "He called me. I wasn't far from here, at a little *trattoria* on the river."

"And he allowed you to enter the *piazza*," Paul said. It was not a question, but he arched his eyebrows, an expression that seemed to ask *Why? When no one else was allowed to enter?*

Eli responded with a shrug. "I've been known to pass information on to him."

All around us people carried on noisy, highly emotional conversations in Italian. It was not likely anyone was listening to us, but we arranged ourselves in a small circle, the four of us, making it easier to hear each other.

"Why is the *carabinieri* involved?" Alex asked. "Isn't the *carabinieri* a branch of the Italian military?"

"True, but they're charged with domestic law enforcement, too. It depends on the nature of the crime, how serious it is," Eli said. "It's not unusual for the locals—the municipal police—and the *carabinieri* to both rush to a crime scene, both trying to take charge. They've been known to fight—I mean push and shove and yell—over who can claim the crime. But sometimes it's clear, one way or the other. I think the *carabinieri* will be backing off this one. It may not be a crime at all."

"Why do you say that?" I asked.

"This is a convent, for one thing. It's probably an accident. Someone leaned too far out the window." Eli ran his hand through his thinning hair. "I'm not saying it *can't* be foul play—I know better, never say *never*—but that's not the first thing that comes to mind."

"Do you know who it is? The one who fell?" Paul asked.

Eli shook his head. "Nope. Do you know whose window that is?" This, he directed at me.

Sophie's window.

But I didn't have to say it.

Our attention turned to a white van, and Eli said, "Medical examiner." The policemen shifted back to let the van pull into the closely-guarded area next to the building, moving the ropes back, pushing spectators back. Momentarily, the heavy door of the convent opened. The officious woman we'd seen go in now exited. Tall, shapely. Behind her came one of the officers wearing the windbreaker-jacket of the *Carabinieri*.

"That's Chief Inspector Eleanora de Rosa," Eli said. "She's *Polizia Municipale*."

"And the *Carabinieri*?" Paul asked.

"I don't know him. But you can see, she's taking charge," Eli said.

Chief Inspector Eleanora de Rosa was doing the talking, all the gesturing, and then all the officials disappeared behind the medical examiner's van. A few minutes more, and a gurney was lifted into the back of the van. A body bag.

The words spilled out in a hoarse whisper. "Please don't let it be Sophie."

Alex squeezed my arm. His silence said it all. He had feared all along that the window was Sophie's.

Paul took a deep breath. "Ah, I understand," he said. "*Mon Dieu!* The young artist you mentioned to me. Jordan—I pray there is some mistake."

I looked at Eli, who had remained respectfully silent. "That's Sophie's window. Sophie Costa is her name."

The white van began to roll forward. For many in the crowd, the spectacle was over. There was a general movement away from the convent.

"I'll head to the *questura*, the police station. See what I can find out," Eli said.

It felt late, the way nights feel when the party is dying down and the energy is waning, but it was not quite eleven. We returned to the café where our evening had begun. Apparently the bills Paul had pressed into our waiter's hand when we had rushed from our table, our first course not yet served, had been a satisfactory amount—an impressive amount. We were welcomed with enthusiasm by the man who was ostensibly the owner, and the waiter could not do enough for us.

Paul ordered *caffe corretto* all around—coffee with brandy—and the waiter brought a plate of *biscotti*. Alex and Paul kept the conversation going, mostly about the *Festa della Rifocolona*. Paul said the parade would end in a party at the *Piazza Santissima Annunziata*. That *piazza* had been part of Alex's hop-on, hop-off tour today, and he added something he'd learned from the tour guide about the tradition of children shooting spit wads at the paper lanterns. I appreciated that they were trying to distract me, but it didn't work. I sipped my drink and began to feel warm at last, warm from the inside out. The convent was in plain sight now, not many revelers left in the square, and close to midnight, we saw the heavy front door open to admit people who had been waiting outside.

So we called it a night.

We did not linger at the door of the convent. Paul

promised to call in the morning. "I expect I will hear from Eli. He is very good at getting information."

Alex pushed the buzzer. Paul raised my hand to his lips. The heavy door opened.

Ivonna was at her appointed place when we went to get our keys. Her gaze met mine, and her face began to crumple like a child's. She stood up and reached across the counter. I took her icy hands in mine, and she began to weep, murmuring something in Italian. I could make out just one word: "Sophie."

TWENTY-TWO

AFTER AN EXHAUSTING NIGHT without sleep, I finally gave up at about six a.m. Crossing the hall to my bathroom for a shower that I hoped would refresh me, I glanced a few doors down to room twelve. A policeman had been guarding the door when I'd come to my room at about midnight, a sliver of light coming from under the door, but now only the glaring yellow crime scene tape marked the door. A glance, a blink, and I looked away.

Back in my room, clean and wearing fresh clothes if not particularly invigorated, I opened my window and shutters. The sky was light, silhouetted with spires and a dome of the church Ivonna had deemed not important. My room didn't face east, but I imagined a brilliant sunrise would be visible from Sophie's window, above the *piazza*. The image of Sophie tumbling from her window would forever be with me.

It was way too early for breakfast. Yes, I could've eaten something. My stomach felt hollow. Although we had ordered a wonderful meal last night, we had rushed from the café before it was served. I went downstairs to the machine and purchased a coffee. Then I went to the garden. My spirits lifted, for some unaccountable reason, at the sight of several nuns—five, I counted— each apparently meditating privately. I had wondered why we'd never seen the nuns—only Sister Assunta. Now I realized they came out early, before the tourists normally visited the gardens. Maybe I should go back and leave them to it, I thought.

But one of the sisters who sat on a stone bench looked up and smiled, patting the seat beside her. All of the stone benches I could see were occupied, and I thought it might have been rude to go around looking for one of my own, assuming it was all right to stay, so I whispered, "Thank you." She nodded, still smiling, but didn't speak. Likely, we didn't know each other's language, but I suspected that her meditation required silence. She went back to reading from the book in her lap, presumably a Bible. A butterfly landed on my knee, and I remembered the day I'd met Sophie. How innocent she had looked, a butterfly resting on her knee as she slept on the stone bench now occupied by one of the nuns.

The urge to connect with my children overcame me. It wasn't much after midnight in Savannah and Atlanta, earlier in Nashville, and earlier still in Santa Fe. I sent a text—short, just checking in. Making sure my phone was silent, I turned away from the nun so I wouldn't disturb her meditation. Incredibly—perhaps, or perhaps not—I heard from all the children within minutes. Claire, replying from Santa Fe, surprised me. Normally, she was the least likely of all of them to text or e-mail, but on top of that, she asked, "Is everything OK, Mom?" None of the others had read between the lines of my message, which I'd thought was light and meaningless.

"Missing everyone," I replied. "But I'll be home soon. When will I see you?"

And we went back and forth a few times about her plans to come home for Christmas.

I tried to imagine how Sophie's mother might get the news of her daughter's death, how she might react. Sophie had said, "I need to go home to my *Mamma*." She was planning to leave Florence today. What had happened? I could not for the life of me fathom what had happened.

The nun beside me touched my arm. I turned around. She clasped her small, wrinkled hands together in the sign of prayer, pointed to herself and then to me. No words were needed. I understood: *I will pray for you.* Then she closed her Bible and departed.

I WAS WAITING at the doors to the breakfast room when the attendant opened them. Alex came in right behind me. As I stood at our table, set with only two places, he said, "Jordan, it is a sad thing that happened, a terrible thing, but you mustn't think there was anything you could have done. That's what's troubling you, isn't it?"

Alex wasn't far off the mark. But I said, "What's troubling me is that a young woman—a girl of only eighteen—is dead. A life cut short, too soon."

"Let's get our coffee," he said, and we picked up our cups. We went to the coffee machine and on to the buffet.

When we were seated at our table, I said, "Sophie was going to tell me something yesterday at breakfast, but she hurried out of the room. We never talked after that. The last time I saw her, she was going into the chapel with Sister Assunta."

"Do you think she confided in Sister Assunta?"

"She could have."

My dry oatmeal seemed to stick in my throat this morning. I spread a lavish glaze of jam on my toast.

"Eli seemed to think it was an accident," Alex said. "Sophie was upset, perhaps even distraught. You saw her behavior at the Moretti Villa. She could have been drinking last night."

I remembered she said she'd been drunk the night before.

I dug for my phone in my tote bag and checked to see if I had a message from Paul. I was hoping Eli had contacted Paul with information after he'd visited the police station, but it was early morning, maybe too early for Paul, maybe too early for Eli. "I don't know what to think," I said. "There are only three possibilities. It was an accident, or she took her own life, or someone pushed her. And I can't see *any* of those possibilities."

Before we had finished breakfast, my phone rang. Paul said, "I hope I didn't wake you."

"I didn't sleep a wink," I said. "I'm at breakfast with Alex."

Eli had texted Paul on his way back from the police station at about two a.m.

"It was a short text. He can meet us at ten this morning," Paul said.

I was sure I'd be hungry again. "Where did he want to meet?"

"*Piazza Santo Spirito.* At the fountain. Let me come to the convent, and we'll go together."

On another day, I might have said *Piazza Santo Spirito* was not far; I would meet him there. But this morning, without thinking too hard, I heard myself say, "OK."

I told Alex what Paul had said.

"I'm glad you'll be with him today," he said. "I think I'd like to drive out to the Moretti Villa."

My surprise must have shown on my face, for Alex said, with a little laugh, "Is that so hard to imagine?"

"It's not that at all," I said.

"What, then?"

"You don't usually drive—though there's no reason why you shouldn't."

"No reason at all," he said.

Except that those roads were so winding, so treacherous, I thought, the drop-offs so perilous, but I didn't dare say it.

Alex wiped his mouth and dropped the napkin by his plate. "I would like to see Angelica again. The way we left things on Friday, with my episode of angina"—he raised his hands in a gesture of desperation. "Could there have been a more inopportune time for that to happen? Nevertheless, she asked me to come back, you remember, and I think she must have felt as I do. We'll never see each other again."

"Oh, Alex, don't say that."

"I'm simply being pragmatic. Consider that we've not been in touch for fifty years. Nothing has changed, really, in spite of what she told me. She has her life, and I have mine."

"But you think there are still things to settle?"

"No," he said emphatically. "I just think I'd like us to have a proper goodbye."

I finished my coffee, tossed my napkin, and we both pushed back our chairs.

"I'm assuming, of course, that she'll be agreeable to my visit," Alex said. "I'll call her when I'm back in my room."

He went with me to my room and I gave him the car keys. "Just be careful," I said.

I WAS NOT SURPRISED that Ivonna wasn't on duty when I left my key at the reception desk a while later. She may have worked all night, and what a difficult night for her. Knowing how much time she put in at the convent, I suspected she'd be back at work tomorrow, and I would be sure to talk to her. If Sophie had confided in anyone, it was probably Ivonna. Then I thought of Cristiano and remembered seeing him last night, walking away from the convent. *Hurrying* from the convent. Was it possible he had been inside? Could he have been to Sophie's room? Had he seen her just moments before her death? One thing was certain: I would ask him.

No more than two minutes after I went outside to wait for Paul, his car pulled in front of me and let him out. He sent the driver on and greeted me by taking my hands, pressing them to his lips. There was something so sensual about the gesture, the way he gazed into my eyes as he kissed my fingers. "I will not ask how you are this morning," he said, "but one would never know by looking at you that you'd had a sleepless night."

What a charmer, Paul Broussard.

"You don't mind walking, do you?" he asked, as we turned toward *Piazza Santo Spirito*.

"I prefer it," I said. "It's a short walk, beautiful weather, and I need the fresh air."

"I might have walked from the hotel myself, but I was making calls, and it is easier in the car." He responded to my smile with his own. "I am afraid it's true. I am never completely removed from my work." As an afterthought, he said, "I received an unexpected call. An old acquaintance had heard I was in Florence. Salvatore Corsini is an artist I have known many years, and *old* describes his age as well. He will turn ninety this week. He is still working, creating extraordinary mosaics."

"Impressive," I said.

"Indeed. You should see his studio. Perhaps you will. Salvatore's wife—his fourth, I think, a much younger woman—is opening their house for a small party, with wine and cake, on the afternoon of his birthday. Would you like to go to Fiesole on Wednesday?"

"Where is Fiesole?"

"Not far at all. In the hills north of Florence. Half an hour, perhaps."

We stopped at a cross street. Several motorcycles and scooters zoomed past us. Paul took my hand and we hurried across the street just ahead of another gush of traffic.

"Fiesole is much older than Florence," Paul said, as if he had not been interrupted. "Because of the Arno, Florence developed as the greater city, but wealthy Florentine families built villas in the hills around Fiesole. The town itself is quiet, but there are some historical sights worth seeing. The views are magnificent."

He paused, but when I tried to respond, all that came out was, "Nice." Today I just could not think about sightseeing.

"Forgive me if I sounded like one of the tapes from the tours," Paul said.

"You didn't," I said, though he did, a little. "My mind is just—I don't know."

Still holding my hand, he gave a gentle squeeze, as if he could infuse me with his vitality.

"It might be an enjoyable diversion, to spend an afternoon in Fiesole," Paul said.

"You're very persuasive," I said. "I agree. It would be a much-needed diversion. Wednesday, you said?"

TWENTY-THREE

Piazza Santo Spirito was subdued this Sunday morning. A few dog walkers, a few tourists snapping photos of the church with its plain plaster façade, a few of the outdoor tables occupied but it seemed most of the cafés were not yet open for business.

"Alex and I had a pizza over there the afternoon we arrived—exactly a week ago," I said. So many outdoor tables, but I could have pointed out the very table at which we'd sat. Hard to believe we'd been in Florence a week already.

"*Caffe Ricchi*," Paul said. "An old establishment. I have had many pleasant meals there myself."

"How many times have you been to Florence?" I asked.

With an amused frown, he said, "I could not tell you how many times."

We passed in front of the church, and Paul took the opportunity to explain the reason the façade was so simply minimalistic, in comparison to other churches in Florence. Brunelleschi, who designed the grand dome of *Il Duomo di Firenze*, was designing the façade of the *Basilica di Santa Maria del Santo Spirito* when he died, and his plans were never realized.

"One would never imagine the magnificent interior that lies behind the blank face," Paul said. He had cheered me a little, reminding me how fortunate I was to be in this city with the consummate tour guide—not

to mention everything else that was wonderful about
Paul. More than that, I suspected his travelogue was
designed to distract me, and he had succeeded.

I gave him a wry smile. "Have you visited *every*
church in Florence?"

"It would be impossible to visit *every* church in Florence," he said.

And then we turned toward the fountain in the middle of the *piazza*, where a stocky figure in a red shirt
was pacing.

"GOOD MORNING, ELI. We're not late, are we?" Paul said,
reaching out to shake hands.

"*Buon giorno*. No, no, I'm early. Didn't sleep much.
Had my first double espresso two hours ago." He patted
my shoulder and asked in a surprisingly gentle voice,
"You OK this morning?"

"I didn't sleep, either. Probably could benefit from
a double espresso, myself," I said.

"Let's fix you up," he said, walking faster across the
square, to an open-air market.

Fix me up he did, with a scalding hot double espresso
in a china cup. I let the men who knew the language deal
with the menu, handwritten on a blackboard, without
mentioning that I'd had breakfast at the convent. Paul
ordered and pressed several bills into the hand of the
small, dark man with a drooping mustache. The string
of Italian words that came from the man included *grazie* several times, and when the huge plate of breads,
pastries, jam, and butter was ready, he brought it outside, directing us to a table and chairs at a next-door
trattoria. The *trattoria* was not open; all the umbrellas
were down, the chairs leaning against the tables. The

man wiped off the table and three chairs for us, raised the umbrella, and left with another enthusiastic *grazie*.

"Not to worry," Eli said, as my expression surely showed my puzzlement. "Probably his cousin's place—brother-in-law, uncle, some other relative. All in the family."

"I love Italy," I said.

A few shots of espresso, a bite of *brioche* filled with jam, and I was ready to listen when Eli said, "So I went to the *questura*. You understand the *polizia* are not very forthcoming, but I managed to find out"—he used that same gentle tone with me—"they're calling it a suicide."

I SWALLOWED, took a moment for his words to sink in. "I just can't believe Sophie took her own life," I said, finally. "She was going home—today. Looking forward to going home, I think. She said she needed to see her mother."

Paul said, "How can they be sure? It is early in the investigation, is it not?"

Eli raked his hand through his hair, which looked thinner this morning. I'd never seen him in daylight before. I realized for the first time how weary he looked. Caffeine had done nothing for the lines around his eyes—deep creases that his small round eyeglasses didn't hide. "Investigation?" He hunched his shoulders. "Yeah, they'll do an autopsy, but this isn't like they found the girl after she'd been dead a few hours, with no eyewitnesses. Medical examiner was there in fifteen minutes after she fell."

"Or was pushed," I said.

Eli started to say something, but he picked up his cup and took a long drink before he spoke again. "You saw it happen, didn't you, Jordan?" He glanced at Paul, who must have told him about that horrific moment, while we sat in the restaurant across the *piazza*. Eli set down his cup and looked at me again. "Did you see anything to indicate she was pushed?"

"No, but I didn't see her jump, either. It was—too far, too dark. I wouldn't be a good witness," I said.

"Couldn't it have been an accident?" Paul asked.

"Here's the thing," Eli said, both palms on the table now, fingers moving as if he might have been typing on a keyboard. "My source at the station saw the report. He said the window sill is three feet above the floor. I'm sure the one in your room is the same, Jordan. The girl was just over five feet, the report said. She wouldn't have toppled over. If she'd been standing on something, she might've fallen accidentally, but there was nothing there when the police got into the room. She wasn't standing on anything. She had to hoist herself up. It had to be intentional."

"Again—somebody could have done it for her—*to* her." I knew I was sounding impatient but I couldn't help myself.

"The other thing is, her door was locked, and her key was on her bed."

That hit me harder than anything he had told us. Hit me like a physical blow. I took a slow, deep breath, trying to process it all.

Eli explained to Paul about the old-fashioned locks on the door and the keys. I didn't have to be told that each key, attached to a heavy key ring that looked like a six-inch metal barbell, had to be used not just to enter a room, but to lock the room once the occupant exited.

It was impossible to leave the key inside and lock your-self out. The door would not lock automatically.

"Someone must have had another key," Paul said.

"Police would've checked that out," Eli said. "Seems they're satisfied that no one else was in that room."

"So that leaves one alternative. Suicide," I said, "and yet I don't accept it. I can't."

ELI HAD DELIVERED the most substantive news; nothing else seemed to matter. "I'll let you know if anything else comes up," he said, spreading jam on another roll, and we were silent for a minute after that, finishing off the bread and pastries, drinking our espressos.

Eventually, Paul asked, "How long will you be in Florence, Eli?"

"Depends on what I can dig up." Eli leaned back and laced his fingers across his ample middle, where the but-tonhole on his red shirt was stressed. "I told you about the story I'm working on. Jewel thieves. I have some leads about the Camorra that I have to follow up before I leave Florence."

"You were telling us about the Camorra the night of Bella's birthday, and I'm afraid she interrupted you," Paul said, with a trace of a smile. As if she were an ac-tive toddler, and the parent found her mischief amus-ing, I thought—then decided I was being too hard on Paul. "Please tell us more," he said.

I kept a blank expression, but I certainly hadn't for-gotten that night.

Eli explained, for my benefit, apparently—though he needn't have done so because I remembered—that the Camorra was a crime organization based in Sardinia. Small-time jewel thieves worked throughout Italy, and the Camorra moved the jewels through the ports of Naples to the ultimate destination, Nice. "These petty criminals have stayed under the radar because they don't hit the museums or high-end art galleries. They rob a few small shops in one location and move on to another. By the time the local *polizia* get the report to INTERPOL, the crooks are gone."

Paul was looking thoughtful. "INTERPOL is able to connect the small crimes but cannot make the connection to the Camorra."

"You got it. A few arrests have been made, but it's like the mob in the U.S. Nobody wants to risk payback by squealing. It's safer to go to prison."

"The police have been to the convent twice," I said.

"Yeah, two burglaries right here in the Oltrarno district," Eli said, "and somebody at one of the shops, dead. Just a guy in the wrong place, wrong time."

"The first one happened the night before we arrived," I said. "The police were leaving the convent when we checked in. The second time, I woke up to voices and searchlights and police stomping around in the garden. Sister Assunta said there had been a report of someone running to the convent, but the garden has a wall around it that's at least twelve feet high."

"Police were responding to the report they got from a drunk. That's what I heard. Not a reliable witness, but they had to check it out." Eli raised his hands, a *What can they do?* gesture. "And now we have a suspicious death at the convent."

"You think it is suspicious, too," Paul put in, with a sidelong glance at Eli.

"I'm just saying." Eli held his palms out in protest.

"You are saying police are not often called to convents, and here, in one week, they have been to *Convento di Santa Francesca Firenze* three times," Paul said.

"Right. It's unusual. Strange, even. Still, it doesn't mean the girl's death is connected to the burglaries," Eli said.

"It never occurred to me that it *was*," I said. That might be worth considering, but I just couldn't see it.

"Do you know what she was doing in Florence?" Eli asked.

"I don't know the whole story, but I'm going to dig it out if I can," I said.

"You can believe it, Eli. This woman is as tenacious as she is beautiful," Paul said, just as the church bells began to chime.

PAUL AND ELI reminisced for a while longer, and I was content to listen, to be entertained. Some of Eli's stories were hilarious, and it felt good to laugh. The *piazza* began to fill, toward midday. A waiter came out and prepared the tables and chairs as the *trattoria* opened for business. The young man gave us a welcoming smile. No problem that we'd purchased our food next door. Eli was probably right: All in the family. A few minutes more, and we gave up our table.

Unbidden, a thought zipped through my mind, and I wondered why I was just now remembering Luigi, the handyman, who was mugged while taking out trash. "Eli," I said, "did you know about the mugging, just outside the convent walls? Must've been about ten days ago. If the police came to the convent for that one, and I would think they did, it makes *four* times."

Eli's eyebrows shot up. "I didn't know. What's the story?"

I told what I knew, which was hearsay from Alex, but it rang true. "I've seen him around the convent several times since he fixed my sink on Monday. He still has a bandage on his head. I'll try to find out more about it."

"Didn't I tell you?" Paul said to Eli. "Tenacious."

As we walked across the *piazza*, Eli handed me his card. "Paul has my number, but I want you to have it, too. You can reach me anytime. Please, Jordan, if you get a whiff of something rotten, don't put yourself in danger. Call me."

The gravity with which he spoke gave me a jolt. "Whoever mugged Luigi before I ever arrived in Florence is not likely to cross my path. And I can't imagine anything I'd find out about Sophie would put me in danger. She thought her father was having an affair. That's all she ever told me." I didn't mention that she'd started to tell me something else at breakfast Saturday morning. Whatever it was, it couldn't possibly have anything to do with the burglaries in Oltrarno and certainly not with the Camorra. It might have been something about Varinia—or Carlo. *Something I saw when I was going to my bathroom*, Sophie had said. Why had I let the day pass without seeking her out, letting her finish what she'd started to say?

We said goodbye to Eli in front of the church, where we'd seen people filing in for mass. Walking on, with no particular destination in mind, we came to *Via del Presto di San Martino*, the busy street with no shortage of cars and motorscooters, even on a Sunday. As we waited for a break in traffic, I thought of Alex, who might at that moment be on his way to the Moretti Villa. But on second thought, we'd had breakfast before 8:00, and if he'd left Florence by 9:00, he would surely be at his destination already. I explained to Paul that Alex was driving to the villa and I thought I should check on him. Paul's smile was amused. He may have been thinking that Alex didn't need a nursemaid; that's what Alex so often said. But I didn't care.

We stepped back from the street while I texted. I did not expect the immediate reply: I am at the convent.

"I need to call him," I said. "Maybe he didn't feel like making the trip, after all."

But when Alex answered, his voice was strong. "I knew you would be checking on me," he said. "I didn't go to the villa because it was a bad time for Angelica."

I gave a little "Oh."

"I didn't mention my plans to visit, not after she told me what was going on," he said.

"What *is* going on?" I asked.

"Bianca is missing," he said. "They haven't seen her since Friday."

TWENTY-FOUR

PAUL AND I left the Oltrarno district, crossed the bridge—one of several bridges that spanned the Arno—and strolled along the river on the north side. Judging from the crowds—all ages, more locals than tourists it seemed—strolling along the Arno was a highly popular Sunday afternoon pastime. It was another sun-splashed day, with gentle breezes coming off the river. Their leisurely pace and relaxed faces suggested people without a care in the world. I wished for that serenity, wished that here in this amazing city with this amazing man, I could put Sophie's death out of my mind for a few hours—and shake the thought that her death might have had some connection to Bianca's disappearance. Alex was always telling me that I was too nosy, that I involved myself too much in other people's problems. I couldn't help thinking I *should have* involved myself more in whatever was happening with Sophie.

Along the way we paused for Paul to snap a few photos with his phone, with the bridge in the background. A moment later, he showed me his pictures, all of them with me in the forefront.

"I like this one best of all," he said. In that particular shot, my expression as I looked out across the Arno was one of mild preoccupation, but it was not a bad photo of me, in the context of the brilliant setting.

I took out my camera, aimed, and clicked, catching Paul's surprise as he looked up from his phone.

"It's only fair," I said.

And then—not like me to be so spontaneous—I stepped forward, raised my face to his, and kissed him.

Paul Broussard wasn't often taken off guard, so it made me smile to see his momentary astonishment, but he responded with characteristic aplomb. "I am not sure why I deserved that, but I do not need to know."

He knew.

We walked all the way to *Ponte Vecchio*, the covered bridge with its shops known for items of gold and silver. Paul was looking for a gift for his friend who was about to turn ninety.

He asked for my advice. "I cannot buy art for Salvatore. He is an artist, a master in his medium. I cannot give him wine. He has a wine cellar that rivals many fine restaurants. What does one give a man of ninety years? He has everything he needs and desires."

I was no help. In the end, Paul came upon an amazing find. In one of the shops that sold all manner of antique and rare items, he discovered an art book with a section about Salvatore Corsini. "It is a first edition, 1951, and this"—Paul pointed to a photograph on a page full of photos—"*this* is the early work that was, as one says, the ticket to fame for Salvatore. He used glass at that time, not the porcelain tiles that he would later use." Set against a backdrop of a sunset, the mosaic was an old man touching the cheek of an old woman. It was inspired by Salvatore's grandparents, Paul explained. I thought of Norman Rockwell's work, but even in a photograph taken when color photography was still in its infancy, the shimmer of the tiny pieces of glass that made up the design gave the piece an ethereal quality. It was a perfect gift.

The shopkeeper was only too happy to giftwrap the book, but he was by himself and other customers were waiting to make purchases. Though the conversation was in Italian, I could tell that the shopkeeper was worried that he might lose the sale. Paul told him we would return shortly. The man gushed, "*Grazie! Grazie!*" No price tag had shown the price of the book, but that in itself was a sure sign that the first edition cost a fistful of Euros.

As we were waiting, passing the time by window shopping, I noticed Varinia Santoro pushing Carlo's wheelchair. I mentioned to Paul that I knew them from the convent. His prompt remark was that the wheelchair was "quite old fashioned." I had thought the same thing. The wheelchair depended entirely on Varinia's strength to push it. A newer, motorized wheelchair would have been a great advantage. But Varinia seemed strong enough to handle it. She steered the chair into one of the shops, and I was left to wonder, once again, what was the meaning of the exchange on Saturday morning between Varinia and Sophie.

When Paul had his gift, we started back along the Arno, the way we had come. It was just a quarter past two, but I felt myself fading. I'd had no sleep last night, and the mid-morning espresso, however stimulating at the time, was no longer having the same effect. I was delighted when Paul suggested a slight detour that would take us to his favorite *gelateria* in Florence. Because it was a couple of blocks off the street that bordered the Arno, tourists often missed it, Paul explained, but Florentines knew it well.

He indicated a café we were just passing. "Or we can have lunch now and *gelato* later."

I voted for *gelato* now, and Paul agreed.

Ordering was part of the fun. The young woman with a ponytail of black curls spilling down her back let us taste several flavors. I settled on super chocolate—*tartufo*, it was called—and Paul chose some fantastic mixture called *zuppa inglese*, which he described as custard, chocolate, and crème, with bits of cake. The half dozen small tables and chairs were occupied, so we walked on with our cones, north, away from the Arno. Again, not heading anywhere special.

"How far are we from the *Piazza della Repubblica*?" I asked.

"Ten minutes, perhaps fifteen," Paul said.

I told him I'd seen Cristiano outside the convent, just moments after Sophie had died.

"Who is Cristiano?"

"Owner of the tour company, *Vivere la Toscana!*"

"The cooking class," Paul said, with a nod that seemed to say *Ah, yes*.

"And the Vespa tour," I said. "That was why Sophie was at the villa on Friday."

"And she argued with the woman who is now missing," Paul said. "But this man, Cristiano—I don't follow. Why did he go to the convent?"

"I intend to ask him. What I do know is that Cristiano is an ill-tempered man who is much too old to be taking out an eighteen-year-old girl, getting her drunk," I said. "Too old to be involved in any way with Sophie."

Paul raised an eyebrow. "Do you think he had something to do with her death?"

I thought about it and finally decided that I couldn't

imagine how. If he had been to her room, there was still the matter of the locked door. That was a hard one.

We finished our *gelato* cones and threw the napkins in a trash can. "Why were you asking about *Piazza della Repubblica*?" Paul said.

"That's where *Vivere la Toscana!* is located," I said.

"And you want to ask questions of this man, Cristiano."

That was the thought that had flitted through my mind. I reached for Paul's arm. "Cristiano may or may not have something to do with Sophie's death, but whatever he knows—I don't see the police questioning him."

"I believe you are right about the police," Paul said. "If this man can put your mind at rest, we should go to see him now."

TWENTY-FIVE

WE DIDN'T CLIMB the creaky stairs to *Vivere la Toscana!*
Cristiano was at the entrance to the stairwell, replacing
brochures in the wire rack beside the sign. His stringy
hair that he'd managed to tame in a ponytail on Friday
hung loose and looked unwashed. I said, "Hello, Cristiano," and when he turned my way, it occurred to me
that he'd had a worse night than I'd had, not just a lack
of sleep, but probably a swim in a sea of alcohol, too.

"Good afternoon," he said without enthusiasm, but
as Paul moved in beside me, Cristiano put on a different face, straightened his shoulders, and spoke with a
lilt in his voice. Paul Broussard did have a certain effect
on people. "May I help you?" Cristiano said.

"I believe you can," Paul said. With a nod toward me,
he made his meaning clear.

"Ah, you were in the cooking class at the Moretti
Villa," Cristiano said, raising his forefinger as if the
thought had just struck him. "Forgive me if I do not remember your name."

I suspected that he remembered me as the presump-
tive thief of Bella's sapphire bracelet, but I was not there
to reminisce. I supplied my name and said, "I suppose
you know about Sophie Costa."

He caught his breath, didn't speak for a moment. I
sensed he'd started to deny knowing her at all but decided
against it and was trying to figure how much to admit.

"The two of you were talking at the villa on Friday. Sophie told me you were with her that night, the night she got so drunk. Then I saw you at the convent last night—a few minutes after Sophie died." I paused, but he remained silent. "I'm sure you knew her," I said, "and you must know she's dead."

He darted a quick glance at Paul, who had picked up a brochure and moved aside. One might guess he was entirely absorbed in whatever he was reading.

"I know nothing about that," Cristiano said. His gaze shifted again to Paul. "What authority do you have?" To me, Paul looked nothing like the *polizia* or *carabinieri*, but that might have been what Cristiano was thinking.

"No authority at all," I said. "I was Sophie's friend. I'm just trying to understand what happened to her."

"And you believe I can tell you?" He gave a nasty laugh and went back to shoving brochures in the rack. "You are wasting your time."

"But you were there, at the convent. Did you see her before she died?"

He jerked his head, glaring at me. "No! What do you want? Why do you accuse me? You have nothing to bring against me!" His eyes were wide with something akin to panic. I remembered what Marisa had said about Cristiano's trouble with police when he was young. He wouldn't want to deal with the police again.

"I'm not accusing," I said. "I'm just wondering why you were at the convent."

He blinked a few times. His expression altered, a decision made. He seemed more annoyed now, rather than fearful. "She asked me to meet her." He gave a bark of a laugh. "It is true! We had a few drinks the night before. Maybe she liked me. In the afternoon she sent a text and said she wanted to tell me something. I said I would meet her outside the convent because I did not know what time I could close. Saturday night is a busy time! And if she is waiting here for me, I cannot change my mind! So I went to the convent. I was late. The streets were full. You were there? You saw the festival? I could not get through. And then I saw the *polizia*." His voice had modulated, but now, after a pause in which the scene may have been replaying in his mind, a reminder of police authority, he assumed a scornful tone again. "I left as soon as I could pass through the crowd. That is all. That is all I know."

He turned to go into the stairwell.

"Wait—please," I said. "Just one more minute. Please."

"I have answered your question," he said. "Why do you make trouble for me?"

"Did you exchange calls with her? The police will surely check out the last calls and texts that she made." I saw in his eyes that I'd hit the mark. Probably police were not going to investigate at all. That was what Eli had implied. But Cristiano didn't know that.

He took a step back and, for the first time, sounded a little vulnerable when he said, "People in the crowd were talking about what happened. I tried to call Sophie. I sent a text. Nothing. Some women who were staying at the convent were—shocked. I asked—they spoke French, but I do, as well—and they said the girl's body fell very close to them. They saw her die. And they said her name was Sophie. That is all I know. I must go to my work now." He headed up the stairs, taking two at a time.

"Do you think his story rings true?" I asked Paul.

"Yes," Paul said. "But he left one important question unanswered."

"I know," I said. "What was it that Sophie wanted to tell him? I wonder if it was the same thing she had wanted to tell me."

THE AFTERNOON SLIPPED AWAY. Our mid-morning breakfast was hours ago, and the *gelato* had not taken the place of a meal. It was much too late for lunch, too early for a proper dinner—but in Paul's words, we were both *waning*. As we were contemplating an early dinner, I received a text from Alex: Reporting that I have been to Santa Maria Novella Church.

I texted back: Very funny. Thank you for keeping me informed.

"You should invite Alex to meet us," Paul said. He suggested a café in the *Piazza Santa Maria Novella*, just across from the landmark church, and Alex accepted the invitation. Apparently, he was already in sight of the café when he texted.

Not being entirely familiar with the layout of Florence, I had thought Paul and I were a long way from *Santa Maria Novella*, but within five minutes, we saw the pointed Gothic arch up ahead and, momentarily, the magnificent façade. Alex was waiting at an outdoor table. Once seated, Paul said, "Among the places to eat in Florence that cater to tourists, this is one of the nicer ones. It seems to suit our purposes this evening."

Alex and I agreed that the café was perfect. Like Paul and me, Alex needed a meal. He had munched on fruit as his lunch, and from what he told us about his day, I gathered he'd more or less forced himself to get out of the convent. He had taken a tour of the church, made numerous notes, and he insisted that it would be worth my time on another day, but he didn't elaborate on every intricate detail of the site. That was not like Alex.

Paul selected a bottle of wine, and when the waiter was gone, I said, "What is this about Bianca?"

"She hasn't been seen since Friday. I'm not sure anyone saw her after you and I left that evening." And then Alex added, as if the thought had just struck him, "You may have been the last one to see her, Jordan—when she and Sophie were having that row you witnessed."

All of us seemed to take a moment for that to register.

"Apparently no one realized Bianca's car was gone until later that night, and no one worried until Saturday," Alex said. "Angelica implied that Bianca had left like that before." It occurred to me that if Sophie was right about her father and Bianca, maybe Bianca had gone to him, wherever that might be. Sophie must have been making those very accusations when I overheard the argument, but they argued in Italian. All I knew was that there had been a lot of rage. If Bianca realized that Sophie had figured out about the affair with Sophie's father, she probably knew the whole truth was about to come out. Raff would know; the Moretti family would know. Her life there at the villa was about to unravel.

"On Saturday—yesterday—a photographer came to take pictures of the family, for advertising the *agriturismo*," Alex said. "Angelica said they'd all believed Bianca would return for the photo session. She knew how important it was for the family. The family business."

"I had the impression she didn't care too much about the family business," I said.

"So it would seem, now," Alex said.

"You assume that the woman could have returned, that she chose not to," Paul said. "Are you sure that is the case? Something could have happened to her. Perhaps a car accident."

I thought about the treacherous roads, hairpin curves, and deadly drop-offs in the Tuscan hills. Paul had a point.

The waiter returned, opened our bottle of wine, and poured. He and Paul conversed about the menu, and he left us to make our choices. When we had decided, Alex picked up the thread of conversation again. "I asked Angelica if they had contacted the authorities. She said no. She had come to believe they should, but Raff refused. Apparently he went somewhere early this morning to look for Bianca. Angelica thought he must have had an idea where she'd gone." Alex turned the stem of his wine glass around and around. "I can imagine it's awkward for her. She's the matriarch, but this time she's not the one calling the shots. It's up to Raff."

Dinner stretched out longer than we might have thought, but none of us seemed to be in a hurry. Our simple first-course choices were perfect. We managed easy conversation about the pleasures that Florence offered. No more about the Morettis' problems. No more about last night's tragedy. We watched children play on the carousel, with its calliope music. Night fell; the air was cooler but still mild. By the time Paul called for the check, darkness had settled. Alex and I didn't have to be coerced to take a taxi back to the convent. Paul insisted that the Westin was very close, and he would enjoy a brisk walk. We had no trouble finding a taxi in the *piazza*.

As Alex got into the back seat on the driver's side, Paul opened the other door for me. "Some say the rooftop of the Westin at twilight is magical," Paul said, just above a whisper, his smile playful. "Shall we try again tomorrow night?"

I said yes. We should definitely try again.

As the taxi let us out in front of the convent, someone on a motorscooter pulled up to the high wall, about thirty feet away from us, hopped off, and led the scooter around the corner. The rider hadn't taken off her helmet, but her hair, shoulder length, caught the convent's lights, and her form-fitting pants made clear it was a female's body.

"You go on in. I'll see you at breakfast," I told Alex.

"Jordan—where are you going?" he protested.

"Just over there. I'll be fine. I'm coming in soon."

The stone wall that surrounded most of the convent extended almost to the adjacent building, a two-story structure that looked like offices. But when I reached the corner, I saw there was a rough path. The rider walked her scooter all the way to the back, past an area of untended, overgrown foliage, and around another corner. I followed. A security light gave off a weak glow. The young woman stopped at a gate, removed her helmet, and put a key in the lock.

"Ivonna?" I said.

TWENTY-SIX

HER HEAD JERKED, and she gave a little squeal.

Hurrying toward her, I said, "I didn't mean to startle you."

She put her hand on her chest, spreading her fingers. "*Signora!* I am glad it is *you*!"

I didn't ask who she'd thought it might be. With burglaries in the neighborhood, a mugging, and now a suspicious death there at the convent, her skittishness could be excused.

"I saw someone coming around this way, and I was curious," I said. The wrought-iron gate was built into the stone wall. I shouldn't have been surprised that there was a gate. The Sisters in the Nunnery would use it to enter the gardens. The trash bin was nearby, on the edge of the lot where we parked the car, and this was the general vicinity in which Luigi was mugged.

"Sister Assunta lets me bring my Vespa into this place, where it is safe. Come with me."

I followed as Ivonna maneuvered her motorscooter through the gate. She locked the gate behind me. This was part of the garden I hadn't seen, a stretch of mowed grass, far back from the building, the fountain, the flowering bushes, and the maze of hedges.

She parked the scooter and retrieved a backpack from the carrier.

"Do you always ride a motorscooter to work?" I asked.

"I cannot buy a car. The busses are slow, but I take the bus if it is too cold or too wet."

I'd thought she might take a little time off from work, given how difficult last night must have been. When I told her I hadn't expected her back so soon, she said, "I need to work." We made our way through the garden, past the fountain, to the French doors. Inside the convent, she said, "I must put on different clothes." She pointed to her high boots and tight leather pants.

"Ivonna, just one question—please," I said. "Did Sophie give you any indication—any hint or clue—that she might take her own life?"

"*No.*" Ivonna kept her voice low, an awareness that someone might be nearby, but the word was emphatic. "Is that what you think, *Signora*?"

"That's not what *I* think. Did the police ask you anything about another key?"

She hesitated, then said, "The *polizia* had many questions last night. Now, I am sorry but I don't want to be late for my work."

I'd promised one question and had asked two. I had more. "Can we talk again about this later tonight? I know you were Sophie's friend. So was I."

She gave a dismissive wave. "I will take a break at ten o'clock," she said. "We can meet in the garden."

I HAD THOUGHT I might have trouble staying awake until ten, but I didn't. I took my second shower of the day and made a mental list of questions to ask Ivonna. Lying on my firm bed, I exchanged texts with Julie, mostly about Winston, my dog, who was not as well behaved for her as he was for me. Julie was the daughter who lived with me in Savannah, putting her expensive Cornell education to work as a minimum-wage-earner at a bicycle shop. It was a temporary arrangement, I assumed, and I had anticipated the day she might move out. Now I wasn't necessarily thinking along those lines. Each time Sophie's words echoed in my memory—"I must go home to my *Mamma*"—I breathed a prayer of gratitude that I was not that mother today.

Just before our arranged meeting time, I went by the office to ask Ivonna if I could buy her something from the vending machine. She was locking the office door. The key ring was simply a ring, not a metal barbell, and I could tell there were only a few keys on it. She attached the key ring onto a loop at her waist band. "I was going to buy an espresso," she said. "It helps me stay awake in the long night."

"I'll get it," I said.

"*Grazie*, you are kind," she said.

We left the vending machine with her espresso and my sparkling water. No one else was in the garden, not that we could see. Ivonna lit a cigarette as soon as we were seated on one of the stone benches.

"I'm not sure what I can tell you about Sophie," she said. "I knew her just one week. It was just one week, today, that she arrived at the convent. The same as you."

"She told me her parents thought she was in Rome, visiting a friend," I said.

Ivonna nodded as she blew out smoke. "She was much more—adventurous—than I am. And she is just eighteen. I told her she should not lie about a thing like that, but she laughed."

Was eighteen, I thought, and perhaps Ivonna thought the same thing, because her eyes met mine briefly, and then she lowered her gaze.

"Were you in the office when Sophie came back to the convent on Friday night?" I asked. "It was probably very late, and she had been drinking."

"It was very late, yes. She came in just before the one o'clock curfew. You know about the curfew, don't you?" she said, smiling.

"I know about it, but most nights I'm in my room much before the curfew. Last night was different, of course. I'm not sure what time it was when the police allowed us back in."

"A terrible night," she said.

I nodded. "Do you know why Sophie came to Florence?"

Ivonna inhaled again and exhaled slowly.

"She told me she had first contacted a family that owned a villa, somewhere in Tuscany, but for some reason, they were not taking guests at this time. Someone at the villa suggested the convent. Someone who knew Sister Assunta."

The story made sense. I didn't know how Sophie had found out about the Moretti Villa, but she'd learned about Bianca, so it probably was not a great leap to discover the villa. Maybe just a few clicks on Google.

"That's exactly how my uncle and I wound up here," I said, and I gave Ivonna a little background about the Moretti Villa, how Alex and Angelica had known each other years ago.

Sophie hadn't told Ivonna any more about her family than she had told Alex and me. "When she talked about her village, her face was very—beautiful," Ivonna said. *Radiant* was probably the word she was looking for. "I don't like to believe she was so sorrowful that she took her own life, but if she died by accident, do you think there will be trouble for the convent?"

"I have it from a good source that the police don't think it was an accident," I said.

Ivonna sipped her coffee, looking thoughtful, her brow a little furrowed, but I couldn't tell whether she was thinking about the third possibility.

I looked at the key ring. "Is one of those a master key?"

"They are all master keys," she said. Holding her cup in one hand, she had her cigarette between two fingers of the other hand, but she used her pinky to point. "This one for rooms on *il primo piano*, this for rooms on *il secondo piano*. This is for the office, breakfast room, and *cappela*—the chapel—on *il piano terra*."

"Are there other sets of master keys?" I asked.

"Sister Assunta has a set that she keeps with her at all times. The housekeeper comes to the office each day to get a master key for the rooms, and she returns it at the end of the day."

"What about Luigi?" I asked, and when her expression turned a bit sheepish, I said, "I know what happened to Luigi—out there, at the trash bin. I understand why you didn't say anything about it. But he must have keys, too."

"Not keys to the rooms of the guests. No, *Signora*. Sometimes I myself unlock a door for him, or the housekeeper uses her key if he must go into a room. Sister Assunta is very careful about the keys, you see. But Luigi is very trustworthy."

"And you're very protective of him," I said, with a smile.

She returned a weak smile. "Luigi is my mother's

uncle. It is not a secret. Sister Assunta knows this. But there is something else."

I felt a stitch in my chest, as Sophie's words came back to me. Almost the same phrase—*something else*—but she never got the chance to say what it was.

"You can tell me," I said.

"About the night he was hurt. The night someone attacked him at the trash bin," Ivonna said. "It was not just his wallet that was taken. His keys were taken, also. But he begged me not to tell Sister Assunta. He was afraid she would be very upset."

"What keys did he have?" I asked, trying to follow.

"Only a key to this gate and keys to places of storage, keys he must have to do his work—but not the guest rooms!" She paused, as if gathering her thoughts, and finished off her espresso. "The next day I had new keys made for Luigi, to have when he came back. Sister Assunta does not know!"

"Did you tell the police?"

"No! Only you, *Signora*, and I am not sure why I have said anything now. You will keep this secret, I beg you. Please?"

"It's not my place to tell," I said. "I want to know—know for sure—what happened to Sophie, if I can find out. That's the only reason I was asking about the keys. I don't intend to make trouble for you or Luigi."

"The *polizia* also asked questions about keys." An anxious note came into Ivonna's voice as she said, "They asked, 'Are you certain you did not go to room twelve with the master key?' It was a good thing a man and woman from Madrid had arrived. Their flight was delayed, and I had just checked them in. They said, 'No, no, she has been with us.' I don't know what the *polizia* thought I had done. I had been in the office all evening!"

"Just making sure no one else could have entered the room," I said.

Ivonna nodded and said, with resignation, "I know that Sophie's key was on her bed. I heard the *polizia* say it." She didn't say *suicide*, nor did I, but the word hung between us. She dropped the cigarette butt into the empty cup.

Maybe there is something else, something we will find out, I wanted to say, but I couldn't yet say it with confidence.

TWENTY-SEVEN

IT TOOK A WHILE to get to sleep, as I thought about what I had learned from Ivonna. Not much. Her explanation about the keys was reasonable. It eliminated the likelihood that someone had been in Sophie's room and used another key to lock the door behind him—or her. I couldn't help thinking about Bianca, wondering why she'd disappeared, but I had no reason to believe she had come to the convent to continue the fight that started the day before Sophie's death. Cristiano had been *outside* the convent. Not that his character was sterling, but it seemed logical that he would've met Sophie there and taken her somewhere else if he'd had evil intentions.

Aside from the problem with the key, who would murder an eighteen-year-old girl? And why? I needed to know more about Sophie. One person I might talk to was Sister Assunta. Sophie had gone into the chapel with her after she'd left the breakfast room on Saturday. If Sophie was, indeed, as troubled as she would've had to be to commit suicide, or if she was afraid of someone, Sister Assunta might provide insight. And then there was Varinia Santoro. Somehow I needed to find out what was behind the exchange between her and Sophie on Saturday morning. With that thought, I drifted off into a restless sleep.

I woke early to sounds in the hall. Opening my door a crack, I saw someone had removed the crime scene tape across the door of Sophie's room and Ivonna was using her key to admit two men into Sophie's room. One, a policeman in uniform, and another in plain clothes that I judged to be a detective. Quickly I pulled on my clothes and went down the hall, locking my door behind me.

"Ivonna—*Buon giorno!*" I called, as she followed the detective into the room.

I was afraid the uniformed policeman would close the door behind them, and though I'd knock if I had to, I preferred to make my appearance seem spontaneous, not so deliberate.

Ivonna, more pleasant than one had a right to expect after she'd been in the office all night, returned my greeting. She made no formal introductions with names, not theirs, not mine, but, as she unfolded a large brown paper sack with paper handles, she explained that the *polizia* had told her she could gather Sophie's personal items. A final look-around, and they would release the crime scene, I presumed. To them she explained that I had known Sophie, that I had a room at the end of the hall. I expected to be sent away, but the long-haired detective, dressed in jeans and leather jacket, wearing fancy sharp-toed boots—surprisingly casual—simply asked, "Were you in your room when this happened?" I said no, not in my room, not in the convent. The younger man in uniform eyed me with skepticism, but he turned on an admiring smile for Ivonna before he responded to an order the detective gave in Italian. Both men got down to their business, leaving me standing at the door.

I took a few steps into the room, willing myself to note as many details as possible, using my mind as a camera, making a snapshot that would document everything. In the corner, left of the door, was the small bed, just like mine, even down to the blue coverlet. Above the bed hung a crucifix. Closer to the window was a dresser with three drawers, a little more ornate than mine. The window was shuttered. To the right of the window were a desk and matching chair. The policeman opened the closet. He touched each of the four shirts on hangers and examined a pair of sandals that had been tossed into the corner. He motioned to Ivonna and dropped the sandals in the paper sack. She gathered the shirts and folded them before putting them in the sack.

Sink with mirror to the right of the door. Old-fashioned radiator beside the sink, with a lacy top on it, as if Sophie had laid it there to dry.

My guess was she'd spilled something on it—the night she went out with Cristiano?—hand-washed it, and spread it out on the radiator. Not important, just poignant.

With the windows closed, the room was stuffy. I looked up. The transom was open at what seemed to be the standard angle, about forty-five degrees, like the one in my room. Without the cross-ventilation between transom and window, there didn't seem to be a purpose for it to be open, but likely no one had bothered to find a ladder, to push the glass closed. I stared a little longer. No one could get up there without a ladder, and no one could squeeze through that space.

The detective had opened the dresser drawers and closed two of them that must have been empty. The policeman went to the dresser, and Ivonna followed. He grabbed up a couple of bras without paying much attention but took out each small colorful bikini, one by one, and gave it a closer look before dumping it into the sack. He gave a huff after examining a black thong and seemed to try with raised eyebrows to get a reaction from Ivonna. She looked away. The detective might have been more professional, but he was inspecting a plastic bag filled with what must have been the underwear Sophie had worn during the week. He actually picked up a flowered bikini and sniffed before handing the plastic bag to Ivonna. My face burned. I wanted to say, *Show some respect! This young woman is dead!* but I bit back the words, knowing they would get me thrown out of the room for sure.

The detective examined a few items on top of the dresser—nail polish, deodorant, travel-size bottles and articles I couldn't identify from my vantage point but I knew what a girl would use on her face, her eyes, her skin, her hair. Apparently satisfied that there was nothing of importance in the cosmetics, he gestured, and Ivonna cleared away everything. He went to the desk, opened the drawers, and finding nothing, he slammed them shut.

"Where's her sketchbook?" I asked the detective. "And her rucksack? Her wallet?"

He seemed to consider whether I merited an answer, and then, with a note of annoyance, he said, "Some items are already in evidence."

The police would have taken anything that seemed pertinent that first night, I thought, noting that Sophie's toothbrush should have been on the shelf above the sink, maybe standing in the empty glass. Maybe her hairbrush, too. Not much was left in this sad room. Sophie hadn't brought much to the *Convento di Santa Francesca Firenze* in the first place. Everything had to fit into her rucksack.

The last item the detective pointed out to Ivonna was the lacy blouse, from the radiator. She picked it up, folded it, and laid it on top of the other personal effects. The paper sack was full. The detective scanned the room one last time, a slow, clockwise inspection, and said to Ivonna, "We are finished."

"What happens to these personal items?" I asked.

"We have no use for them," the detective said.

"Her family will want these things," I said, "but they're in Casa Vittoni."

The detective regarded me with a mocking smile that seemed to say, *You don't know as much as you think.* And then he said something in Italian. Ivonna gave the paper sack to the uniformed officer, and the two men departed.

"What was that about?" I asked Ivonna, as we moved into the hall.

She locked the door. "Sophie's father is coming to the *questura* today. The *investigatore* said the father should not have to make a trip to the site of the suicide."

SISTER ASSUNTA WAS busy with the altar flowers when I found her in the chapel. The small white flowers had a strong, cloying fragrance, like the scent inside a funeral parlor. I was sure that was not intended, but it struck me as sadly ironic. An amateur—not an expert—gardener, I asked the name of the flower, after we had exchanged greetings. She said the name in Italian and then, "I do not know what you call it."

"Clematis? But the fragrance is stronger, sweeter."

She made a little dismissive gesture, held my gaze a moment longer, and went back to arranging the stems in the large glass vase. Clearly she knew I had not come to discuss flowers.

So I got to the point. I knew Sophie had talked with her. The police were saying Sophie had taken her own life. I didn't believe it. Did she? Sister Assunta kept working steadily, not looking at me. "I would like to think it was a terrible accident," she said.

"The police don't believe it was an accident."

That dismissive gesture again, this time suggesting that the police didn't always know.

I groped for the right words, not to offend. "If she confided in you, I understand about betraying a confidence, but it wouldn't be the same as a confession—to a priest."

She turned to me, with a hard gaze, and said, "You do not need to instruct me on the sanctity of the confessional."

I hurried to say, in all earnestness, "I'm sorry. I didn't mean to be disrespectful, Sister. Please—just help me if you can. Anything you can tell me about your conversation with Sophie."

She went back to arranging flowers, placing another stem, strategically. "It was not a conversation in confidence, as you say. We talked about forgiveness. It was more—more philosophical than personal. She did not say whether she needed forgiveness from someone."

Or who she might be trying to forgive, I thought.

"Do you think she was afraid of someone?" I said.

"Afraid? No." Sister Assunta put in the last flowers and stepped back from the altar. "I will tell you this. She asked what I knew about someone here at the convent, and I answered her truthfully. My only source of information is the registration form that our guests complete."

I could guess who the someone was.

Only then did Sister Assunta look at me with sadness, not the guarded expression she had maintained. "Sophie had come to Florence for a purpose, to find truth."

"Truth?"

"That is exactly what Sophie said: 'I came here looking for truth.' Even as we spoke, it seemed to me that she had found the truth and it was not what she had hoped it would be. But nothing the girl said—*nothing*—prepared me to hear that she had taken her own life."

Sister Assunta made the sign of the cross. It seemed like a sign of finality, and so I turned to go. But another question begged me to ask, and I didn't expect I'd get another audience with Sister Assunta.

"Sister, did you know Victor, Angelica's husband?" I asked.

If she was surprised by the sudden question, she didn't show it.

"I was invited to the wedding," she said. "That is the only time I ever saw her husband."

"What was he like?" I asked.

"He was a kind man, I believe. I could see he was deeply in love with Angelica." Sister Assunta smiled with such warmth that I wondered if she ever thought about what she'd missed, choosing a life without marriage.

"And was Angelica deeply in love with him?"

She hesitated, just one beat, but it was significant. "She was marrying him. Marriage is sacred. I have to believe she loved him. Angelica and I did not keep in touch as we should have, but from time to time she would come to the convent. Sometimes we sat in the garden and talked for hours. I am sure that she came to love Victor very much in their long years together."

Without answering my question head-on, she had answered it.

"My uncle knew Victor very well," I said. "They were traveling together when they met Angelica."

"I know about your uncle," she said. Then she gave her flowers one last loving touch with both hands and said, "I must get ready for morning prayers now."

"Thank you for your time, Sister."

"I was glad to talk with you, though I am sure I was no help."

"Oh, but you were," I said.

TWENTY-EIGHT

IT WAS NOT YET seven-thirty. I was the first in line for breakfast. Actually, there was no line. I was the only one waiting when the woman I had yet to see smile opened the doors to the breakfast room. But others were not far behind, and Alex arrived by the time I had my food.

I reported the highlights of the conversations I'd had with Ivonna and with Sister Assunta and told about seeing Sophie's room earlier this morning when the detectives cleared out her personal belongings. "But I still have nothing definite," I said, "nothing to prove or disprove suicide."

Alex's expression was kind, but concerned. "And why must you, Jordan, be the one to prove or disprove suicide? Isn't that the job of the police?"

"But Eli said—you weren't with us yesterday when he was telling Paul and me that he didn't expect much of an investigation by the police. This morning the detective said they were finished with Sophie's room. If they'd suspected foul play or entertained the notion at all, don't you think they would be back dusting for fingerprints, that sort of thing?" I could hear myself becoming a bit strident. With an effort to modulate my voice, I said, "If this was murder, Alex, the killer should pay. And that means someone should find out the truth."

I thought about what Sister Assunta had said about Sophie's search for the truth. Had her discovery, the truth about her father and Bianca Moretti, led to her death? I took a long time, buttering my roll, thinking of the father who would be at the *questura* today. Would he contact Bianca? Alex went back to the buffet. The attendant had put out a fresh bowl of cut-up fruit. When he returned, he was quiet, as deep in his own thoughts as I was in mine.

"For a week's worth of research, I don't have a lot," Alex said, after a few minutes.

"Things seemed to go well at first, don't you think? We took in the must-see sites, the *Duomo*, *Uffizi*, the *Accademia*," I pointed out. "Granted, things have come up that we didn't anticipate."

"Certainly those were on the must-see list, but every travel guide has information about the big museums, the main churches, all the tourist spots. I was rather excited when I learned that the Morettis were running an *agriturismo*." Alex leaned in a little, his face earnest. "Jordan, I do need to spend more time at the villa. For my research."

I gave him a wry smile.

"And I won't deny that I'd like to see Angelica again. As I told you, I feel we didn't get to say a proper good-bye." Alex's brow furrowed. "But I'm not sure what to do. Angelica is caught up in her family's troubles. I don't want to intrude. On the other hand, she might be needing a friend."

Alex usually had definite opinions and rarely asked for my advice. He hadn't actually asked for my advice this morning, but he'd said he wasn't sure what to do, and I couldn't remember another time *ever* when he'd confessed that he was in a quandary and was having trouble working through it. I was about to give a piece of advice when he said, "I think the best course is for me to call Angelica again and just ask. I'll tell her exactly what I've said to you. I have no doubt that she'll extend an eager invitation, and I think I can judge whether she's just being kind or if it would actually be useful for me to visit."

"That's what I was thinking," I said.

"Yes, that's exactly what I'll do," Alex said.

ALEX MUST HAVE made the call the moment he returned to his room. I hadn't been back in my room more than twenty minutes when there was a knock at my door, and Alex was there, carrying his duffle bag, telling me in a most cheerful voice that he was on his way to the Moretti Villa. He wanted to be sure that I wouldn't need our rental car today—or tomorrow, if he stayed over, which Angelica had suggested. "Most importantly," he said, "I urge you to *be careful*, Jordan. You have a tendency to get yourself into situations"—he raised his eyebrows—"I don't need to recount, I'm sure."

"No, you don't," I said. "I will be careful, and you be careful, too."

I gave him a big hug, which he returned, lingering, in fact, for an extra moment.

"It's my hope that Paul will keep you in line," he said, before letting go.

"Alex—really! Please just get on your way and have a wonderful time."

I had forgotten to ask him if there was any news about Bianca, but I was sure that if he knew of any developments, he would have told me.

I WAS A little ashamed of the relief I felt when Alex was gone. I wouldn't have to worry about him, once he'd arrived safely at the villa. Angelica would watch over him. More to the point, I wouldn't have to worry that he was worrying about me! He probably wouldn't think of me at all, and I could do what I needed to do.

I was wondering if I could put Paul off until this afternoon, when he called.

He reminded me that today was the other business meeting he'd scheduled while he was in Florence. He'd told me, the night of Bella's birthday party. I remembered, once prompted, though I wasn't sure that he'd said the meeting was Monday. One had been on Friday, the day of the cooking class.

But—no matter. This would work out well. I may have sounded overly enthusiastic when I said, "Not a problem. I'll find something to do."

"You don't seem at all disappointed," he said, and I could tell he was smiling, but I also caught a note that made me think he was not altogether teasing.

"You have work to do, and I haven't bought any souvenirs," I said. "So we'll just see each other at the Westin. What time?"

He laughed that rich laugh of his, and I think he was satisfied. We made our plans for tonight. I assured him that he needn't send a car for me. I could get myself to the Westin.

"It will be a special evening," he said.

"I know," I said, and I meant it. I remembered the word he'd used: magic.

But before then, I had things to do. And my plans began with a call to Eli Schubert.

I HAD TO leave a voice mail. Eli had made a big deal out of giving me his number, instructing me to call if I sensed any danger—smelled something rotten, he'd said. A good thing I wasn't in danger since I couldn't reach him. My message made it clear that there was no emergency. I just needed information. Waiting for his call, I did exactly what I told Paul I'd do. I went souvenir shopping.

Not far from the convent, on *Via Romana*, was a shopping district that I'd noticed the day Paul and I had toured the Pitti Palace. The modest shops were a far cry from the gold and silver shops at *Ponte Vecchio* where Paul had bought the first edition for his friend. If I'd looked around the *Ponte Vecchio* offerings I might have found something besides fine jewelry and antiques, but shopping, which consisted of a lot of browsing in my case, was an activity best accomplished by myself. Ninety minutes after I entered the first of the artsy shops, I left the district with an assortment of small ceramic items, leather bound journals, and pashmina shawls, all easy to pack. I'd decide later which I'd give away and which ones I'd keep for myself.

Back at the convent, I had just returned to my room when my phone rang. It was Eli.

"What's up, Jordan? No trouble, I hope. You didn't sound like it was trouble."

"No, nothing like that." I dumped the plastic bags on my bed.

"I'm in Pisa," Eli said.

"Visiting the leaning tower?"

"Not hardly, but I did see it at a distance. It's still leaning. I've been meeting with an investigator from *Squadra Mobile*'s organized crime team."

"*Squadra Mobile*?"

Eli chuckled. "Yet another of the many branches of Italian law enforcement. Pisa had a string of burglaries this summer, much like we're seeing in Florence, and they've just made an arrest. May be just a lowlife, no connection to the Camorra, but I plan to stay for the preliminary hearing this afternoon." He took a noisy breath. "So. What was it you wanted, Jordan? You said you needed some information."

I asked him the name of the Chief Inspector, the woman that we saw at the convent Saturday night.

"You mean Eleanora de Rosa?"

"That's the one. Do you think she'll talk to me?"

Eli's laugh this time was more of a bark. "I can tell you there's one way, maybe only one, that she'd talk to you. Do you have information to give her?"

"Not exactly. But I hope I can convince her to investigate Sophie Costa's death as a murder, not just call it a suicide."

A pause. "Jordan—look, Jordan, I can appreciate your point of view, but you can't just walk into the *questura* and tell the Chief Inspector how to work her case."

"Sophie talked to Sister Assunta, too," I said. "The Sister had no indication that Sophie was suicidal. Sophie had told her, as she'd told me, that she was going home on Sunday, and she was looking forward to seeing her mother. I've spoken to a couple of other people, too, and they had no clue that she was suicidal. Seems to me someone may be getting away with murder."

A long pause on Eli's end. Then, "How can I help?" Sure, he was placating me, but I didn't let that stop me.

"You have contacts at the police station," I said. "Where is the *questura*, by the way?"

He gave me directions to the location on *Via Zara* where I could find the Chief Inspector.

"If you want to wait until tomorrow, I'll go with you,

for what it's worth," he said, "but I won't be back in Florence until tonight. Maybe you ought to take Paul with you."

These men! I thought. "He has a meeting. Besides, he'd try to talk me out of it."

"Yeah, I think he would. Maybe I should try to talk you out of it."

"You can't," I said.

"I figured as much." I heard him take a deep breath. "I know a couple of the desk sergeants. I can make a call. Maybe you can get in to see de Rosa. That's about all I can do."

"Thanks, Eli. That's all I want, just a foot in the door."

"Eleanora de Rosa is tough," he said. "Nothing soft about her. You won't get sympathy from this woman just because the victim is a young girl. She may toss you out on your ear."

"If that's the worst that happens, it's worth taking the chance," I said.

TWENTY-NINE

VARINIA SANTORO WAS pushing Carlo's wheelchair into the hall as I was leaving my room. On my mental list of people who might know something about Sophie, Varinia was the only one left—except for Bianca Moretti. I'd like to talk to her, too, but I had no idea where to find her.

I called to them: "*Buon giorno!*" Varinia gave a smile and a nod, nothing in her manner that invited me to join them, but I did. I caught up with them, and we went to the elevator together. The tiny elevator would have been too crowded with all of us, considering how much space Carlo's wheelchair took up, so while we waited—the elevator was always slow—I said, "Are you going out? I'll walk with you."

Varinia said, "Carlo and I did not have breakfast this morning. We are going for an early lunch."

And then the elevator arrived. The door opened, they entered, and Varinia pushed the button for the ground floor several times, as if that might make the elevator go faster. I didn't wait for the long, drawn-out process to repeat itself. I entered the corridor that led to the staircase, a rather grand staircase, with marble treads twelve feet wide. It curved to a landing on *il primo piano* and then on down to *il piano terra*. I made it to the ground floor ahead of the sluggish elevator. Varinia and I turned in our keys at the same time to the young woman in the office whose name I had not learned.

Varinia had conveniently ignored my comment about walking with them, so I didn't ask again. I remained beside her, working to keep up, as she expertly maneuvered the wheelchair along the uneven surface of the *piazza*. She looked straight ahead, focused on her task.

"I haven't talked with you since Saturday night, since the young woman named Sophie died," I said. "Did you know her well?"

"Know her? Not at all." Varinia made a face. "She had breakfast at your table each morning. I thought she was your friend."

I didn't know exactly how to answer. I should have tried harder to be a better friend, but I declared, "We had only known each other a few days."

"Do you think she was drunk when she had the terrible accident?" Varinia said.

That came out of the blue—but it made sense that guests of the convent were still thinking *accident*. Before I could reply, Varinia said, "She was *very* drunk the night before."

"You said something to her about that. The morning—Saturday morning—the day before she died." I waited, hoping she'd fill in the gaps. But Carlo said something, and she stopped, leaned down, and straightened the blanket on his legs. It was thin but was surely uncomfortable, considering this warm September weather.

"Carlo says I should not go so fast," she said.

"It must be bumpy," I said. The wheels were small, but I didn't go into the specifics of his wheelchair. "You were saying—about the night Sophie came in drunk."

"Was I? I only said that I saw her when she was going

to her bathroom. Our bathroom is *en suite*, of course, but I had gone down for a mineral water from the vending machine. I was having trouble sleeping. I heard her *retching* and waited in the hall until she came out of the bathroom. She was very pale but not in need of assistance. So we both went to our rooms." Varinia gave a dismissive wave. As she maneuvered the wheelchair with one hand, bumping along, I could tell that Carlo was using his feet to brace himself. "On Saturday night, Carlo and I went to sleep early, as we often do. I didn't know what happened to the girl until the next day."

I had assumed they were outside the convent watching the festival. Remembering how many guests were trying to get back in while the police were investigating, I had made a wrong assumption. *Everyone* had not left the convent during the festival.

"You didn't see the *Festa della Rifocolona*?"

She gave a little twitch of her shoulders. "As you might imagine, by the day's end, we are very tired."

"I can imagine," I said, thinking, But sometimes you have trouble sleeping, right?

"Where are you going?" she asked. We were at the other side of the *piazza*.

"*Via Zara*," I said, pointing left.

"So we will say *Ciao*." She turned the wheelchair to the right.

I wasn't sure what I'd hoped I would learn from Varinia. Whatever Sophie had seen or thought she'd seen that night, I was afraid I would never know.

ELI KEPT HIS PROMISE. The desk sergeant at the *questura* nodded when I identified myself, a sign he knew who I was, recognized the name Eli had given him. He was pleasant, though unsmiling, about my age, with the kind of middle-age spread that often comes with a desk job. He gave me a visitor's badge and said, "Please, sit. I will let you know when Chief Inspector can see you."

I took a seat in a black molded plastic chair. A few seats down from me, a young—thirtysomething—man and woman waited, fidgeting, scowling, whispering to each other. Whether in Italian or some other language, I couldn't tell. After ten minutes or so, a detective, I presumed, appeared at the entrance to a corridor and motioned to them. He opened a brown folder and glanced at it before leading the couple down the hall. Tourists, I thought. Probably a pickpocket or a mugger had targeted them.

Making up the scenario was something to occupy my mind while I waited. I saw no newspapers or magazines, not that I could have read them.

Though I was the only visitor in the waiting area now, there was considerable activity. Several men and women, some in uniform and some in plain clothes, passed by me, going one way or the other, no one paying much attention to me. Two young uniformed *polizia* brought in a man who might have been homeless, from the looks of him. They conferred with the desk sergeant and took the man, in handcuffs, through another door. It seemed that as soon as the desk sergeant finished one call, his phone would ring again. Thirty minutes passed, as I contemplated how much the *questura* looked like other police stations in France and Ireland. I'd seen a few. Ironically, I'd never been inside a police station in the United States.

Forty minutes passed, then forty-five, and fifty.

I wasn't sure the Chief Inspector was going to see me at all.

But she did. The phone rang at the desk, the desk sergeant answered, and he called out to me in a much louder voice than was necessary, "Chief Inspector will see you. End of the hall." He pointed to the corridor into which the other visitors—and the detective who had come to meet them—had disappeared. No one was coming out to meet me.

The corridor ended at the door of the Chief Inspector's office. She sat behind her desk, straight ahead, with a medium-sized window behind her that framed the street life beyond. It was a modest office, but her desk was huge. She stopped working at her computer to extend her hand across a mound of papers. "I am Chief Inspector Eleanora de Rosa."

"I'm Jordan Mayfair. Thank you for seeing me," I said. I noticed a half-eaten sandwich, almost hidden by a stack of files. "I apologize for interrupting your lunch. I won't take too much of your time."

She motioned to a wooden chair that looked a little nicer but no more comfortable than the ones in the waiting area. She looked back at her computer for a final tap on the keyboard. *Send? Submit?* "I don't have much time to give you," she said.

Right to the point. That was fine with me. I got right to the point, too. I said, "I'm staying at the convent where Sophie Costa died Saturday night. I don't think she took her own life."

Now I had the Chief Inspector's full attention. Her dark eyes, almost black, fixed on me in a hard gaze. "Do you bring new information?" she said, and I remembered that Eli had asked me almost the same question—did I have any information to offer?

I had nothing that qualified as solid evidence, but I took my best shot. Sophie was eager to be going home on Sunday, I explained. Sister Assunta would back me up on that. Sophie was also expecting to meet a friend that night. I felt a little twinge, bringing Cristiano into it, but the date they had planned was relevant. If he'd told me the truth, Sophie's phone, with his texts on it, would prove his truthfulness. "You took her phone, didn't you?"

"Who was the person she was meeting?"

"Expecting to meet. Someone from a tour company."

"Name?" She picked up a pen.

"Cristiano—something." I could not remember his last name at that moment. "His tour company is *Vivere la Toscana!* in *Piazza della Repubblica.* His number will be on the phone."

"He may have been contacted already if what you say is true. I will give this to one of the detectives. I do not handle every aspect of every case, Signora Mayfair. Have you been interviewed by the detectives?"

"No, it wasn't an interview." De Rosa didn't seek an explanation. She glanced at the heavy gold watch on her wrist, like much of the jewelry I'd seen at *Ponte Vecchio.*

"The detectives that came to the convent this morning said they were finished with Sophie's room." I tried to choose my words carefully, though I was certain I was about to be dismissed. I hadn't made any progress, except to throw Cristiano under the bus. "Could there still be evidence that someone else was in the room with her? Someone who might have had another key? Maybe if others in the convent were interviewed—and what about fingerprints? It hasn't even been forty-eight hours. I hope you'll keep investigating." I felt my words just tumbling out, and I could tell from de Rosa's deeper breathing pattern that her patience was wearing thin.

"Who *are* you, *Signora*, that you have such interest in this case? Such knowledge of what the *polizia* should do, in a country that is not even your own?"

Her words stung, but until she kicked me out of her office, I wasn't going to give up. "I mean no disrespect, Chief Inspector. All I want is justice for this young woman. There is one other thing. I think Sophie saw something that frightened her, the night before."

De Rosa's phone beeped. It was one of those desk phones with many lines. She answered, said something, and pushed her chair back from the desk.

"Do you know why the girl was frightened?" she asked, as if we hadn't been interrupted.

I hesitated, trying to find the right words to explain what had seemed suspicious to me. The impatient Chief Inspector stood up. She was a good six feet, shapely, a little busty. The jacket of her gray suit was belted around her waist, which was small for the rest of her torso. My tentativeness spoke for me and de Rosa said, "You have nothing, *Signora*. This is the business of the *polizia*. Now I must ask you to leave. Leonardo Costa has arrived. I will personally give him his daughter's things. He has been with the medical examiner at the morgue. It is not a good day for Signor Costa."

The first sign of any *softness* from the Chief Inspector.

Standing, too, I said, "What will you tell him?"

De Rosa stiffened. She was right. My question was out of line. I raised my palm and made an apologetic face.

"I will tell him what I know," she said. "What I know to be fact, not speculation. And now, *arrivederci*, Signora Mayfair."

I thanked Chief Inspector Eleanora de Rosa for seeing me and started back down the hall. De Rosa came to her door to meet this visitor. I heard her voice behind me: "Signor Costa."

My breath caught. I was frozen in place, but as Sophie's father came toward me, I was able to whisper the name I knew.

"Raff?"

THIRTY

RAFFAELE MORETTI'S SHOCK was as great as mine. There may have been an instant when he groped for a story, but the moment passed like a flash of lightning, and the transformation was complete, with a long exhalation, with his *game over* expression. Silence, and then, his voice thick with defeat, he said, "Jordan. Will you wait for me in the *piazza*?"

I said I would.

I went to a nearby outdoor table, one of the few that was empty. A waiter appeared after a few minutes. I ordered a bottle of water and an *espresso*. He laid a menu before me to study, one laminated sheet. It was lunch time. I shouldn't take up a table just to drink water and coffee. I pointed to *bruschetta* on the menu and handed it back to the waiter. Around me, typical tourists were laughing, drinking wine, taking pictures of each other. My visit to Florence was supposed to be just as carefree.

A text came in from Alex while I waited. Safe and sound at Moretti Villa. I couldn't bear to think of Angelica, of the truth she didn't yet know.

Raffaele—Leonardo Costa, Sophie's father, whoever he was—didn't stay long with Chief Inspector de Rosa. Fifteen minutes, tops. She was not the one breaking the news about Sophie, not even the one delivering the medical examiner's verdict, so what was there to say?

The waiter had just delivered my *espresso*, bottle of

water, and glass when the grief-stricken Raff came out of the *questura*. He was wiping his eyes, managing in spite of the white cardboard box he balanced on his hip, his arm around it. The size of a banker's box, it was probably the standard type of container that the police used for evidence from a crime scene. Raff saw me, put away his handkerchief, and came to the table, stopping the waiter on his way. The waiter nodded.

"How did you know?" Raff asked. He set the box on the ground and pulled out the chair across from me.

"How did I know about *you*? I didn't, not until now. But I knew Sophie."

He leaned in a little, waiting for more.

"You and I talked about the convent, and you asked if I'd met Sister Assunta." I smiled. "I met Sophie at the convent. She was a sweet girl."

He ran both hands through his thick hair and shut his eyes tight for a minute. "Oh, my Sophia," he said, in a soft wail. "*Il mio piccolo gattino.*"

"Little kitten," I said. "She told me that's what her *papa* called her."

He let his hands fall into his lap. I could only imagine the pain that contorted his face. After a minute, he said, "I thought she was in Rome, visiting her friend at *universita*. I thought the visit would make her want to study at *universita*, also. Why was she in Florence, Jordan? Did she tell you why?"

"She said she came here to find the truth," I said.

I poured water into the glass and pushed it over to him. At first he looked at it as if he wasn't sure what it was. Then he reached for it and took a big swallow. The waiter was back in another minute, setting a glass of red wine before him, and he took a big swallow of that, too.

"Sophie was at the Moretti Villa on Friday," I said. "She was on the Vespa tour."

"No! I would have—" He groaned. "Rob and I were going over accounts, in the winery."

I drank some of the strong, black *espresso* before I started explaining. "Something happened with Sophie and Bianca. I overheard a loud, rather fierce, argument. I couldn't understand what it was all about, but Sophie threw some of the Moretti family photographs at the wall. Until then, she believed that her father was having an affair with Bianca. That much, she told me. She'd come to Florence, then to the villa, I think, to confront Bianca."

Raff turned the stem of the wine glass around and around in his hands, staring into the dark red liquid, as if trying to find answers. His eyes grew glassy, and he whispered, "*Dio mio!* She *did* take her own life. Because of me."

"Is that what you were told?" I asked.

"The medical examiner said he had ruled out an accident because of something about the window, how it was necessary for her to lift herself up, and she was in a locked room, with nothing to suggest anything but suicide." His expression was earnest, almost pleading, as he said, "How well did you know her, Jordan? Do you believe Sophia could take her own life?"

My thoughts on the matter had taken an entirely different turn in these past few minutes, knowing now that the *truth* Sophie had learned was much more devastating than she'd imagined. Her father wasn't just cheating on her mother; he had a whole other family at the Moretti Villa. Maybe she simply could not wrap her mind around that information.

"I didn't know her well—just for a week—and I honestly don't know what to think, Raff." I was glad to see the waiter reappear at that moment. He brought the *bruschetta* and an extra plate, as well as another empty glass. He poured water for me and replenished the water in Raff's glass. Raff threw back the last of his wine and gestured for another.

I cut a slice of the *bruschetta* for Raff. He shook his head, but I pushed the plate in front of him anyway. I hadn't ordered to satisfy hunger, but the toasted garlic bread with olives, tomatoes, and mushrooms hit a spot. "Raff, you seem like a decent man," I said, after a couple of bites, another drink of water. "But—two families? Surely you knew someone would get hurt."

He considered before he answered. "I suppose there is no defense except to say that twenty years ago I made a choice, and I could never go back."

"Twenty years?" The idea of a deception that had lasted twenty years seemed incredible.

He nodded. "I met Carmina at a sales meeting in Naples. She had a past, no contact with her family. It was easy to be with a woman like that, and I continued to see her when I could. And then Sophia was born."

I did the math. A couple of years, and then the situation had become far more serious. "When did you become Leonardo Costa?" I asked.

He managed a weak smile. "It was a time in my life when I was ready to be someone besides Raffaele Moretti. We went to Casa Vattoni, a very remote little village, and made a home as Leo and Carmina Costa, and we raised our child. No one suspected we were not married."

"So the Moretti family knew nothing, but Carmina

knew everything?" I said, trying to get it all straight in my mind.

"I could not leave my life in Tuscany, and I could not leave Sophia and Carmina," he said. "She—Mina—she took what I could give her. That was how it had to be. That is how it has always been." He took a long drink of water.

I had a hard time with his choices, but it was not my place to judge. So I waited, as Raff found his own way through the extraordinary story.

"AT FIRST it was not as difficult as you might imagine, before technology became so advanced," Raff said. "Casa Vittoni was a place one could"—he made a gesture, grasping for the expression.

"Lay low?" I suggested.

"Yes, one could lay low, retreat from the world." He cast a wistful gaze across the *piazza*, but he seemed to be looking back in time. "All has changed, with tourists in every tiny spot on the map, the Internet in every village. Sophia as she grew up, she was always using her computer."

"She told me her father worked for a company that produced olive oil, based in Sicily. Was that a fabrication also?" I raised my hand in an apologetic gesture. "I'm just trying to understand how you did it. It seems—astonishing."

His smile showed a hint of irony, but mostly it was just sad, wistful. I suspected he was thinking, *If only I could go back*. "You are trying to imagine how one would keep up such treachery, not just satisfying two families, but satisfying two employers."

I gave a little shrug and a nod.

"It was—commission, as you say—some income but not much. Sophia believed it was my only work, but I managed orders on computer. That was all." He let his gaze wander off as he said, "I was in Tuscany during all those times she thought I was in Sicily."

The waiter delivered Raff's wine, and he raised the glass to his lips. Not so much in a hurry, as he'd been with the first. The waiter poured more water for us, draining the bottle, without seeming to intrude. The tip in Italy was usually small, if given at all, because the check always added a service charge, but this waiter deserved a good tip for being so intuitive.

Raff, once into his story, continued without encouragement. "I knew Sophia had seen my phone, the one I always said I kept for business. The same when I was at the villa. Two phones, one that I used secretly. I tried to be careful, but it was difficult, as Sophia grew up. Not so difficult at the villa. No one gave my personal business much concern at the villa." He finally took a bite of the *bruschetta*. "*Grazie*, Jordan. I haven't had much to eat since yesterday."

"Where have you been, since you left the villa?"

He had been in Florence, he explained, looking for Bianca. He knew a bed and breakfast run by friends of Bianca, but they said she wasn't there. "I didn't believe them, not at all, but I went to other places she might have gone, the fashion houses near *Via de' Tornabuoni*—Gucci, Ferragoma, the designers she favored—the places she would go to eat, to have drinks," he said. "Bianca sometimes went away after we had a fight—a disagreement, I should say—but this time it seemed more urgent. *Mamma* said Bianca and someone from the tour group had screamed at each other. She didn't know why. *Dio mio!* I never thought of Sophia! Never!"

He had received the frantic call from Sophie's mother late in the afternoon on Sunday.

The strain had been showing in his face, but as he recalled the hours since that news, his color went from pale to gray. The *polizia* had contacted authorities in Casa Vittoni, and they had gone to tell Carmina that a girl who carried identification as Sophia Costa had died in Florence.

"I did not believe it!" Raff said. "I told Mina that it could not be true. Sophia was not in Florence! But we were not able to reach Sophia on her phone—or her friend in Rome. I made calls to the *polizia*, but it was Sunday. I could not get information about Sophia and no one would see me. At last I spoke to someone who gave me a number to call this morning. It was the medical examiner's office at *il obitorio*, the morgue." He said in a mournful voice, "I took a room and spent the night praying that there was a mistake, but my prayers were not heard."

I contemplated the unbearable guilt that was so apparent in Raff's haunted eyes. Would it make any difference if he believed Sophie *didn't* take her own life? I couldn't say that with authority. It would be irresponsible to mention my suspicion that she might have been murdered. Nothing could bring back his daughter, and he would always know that the reason she was in Florence was to find the truth about her father.

We finished the *bruschetta* and the water. I drank my *espresso* and Raff drank his wine.

THIRTY-ONE

"JORDAN," HE SAID, after a long space of quiet, "I don't know if you will go back to the villa or see *Mamma* again, but I must ask you to let me handle this in my own way."

"It's not my place to tell," I said.

He smiled, another one of those sad smiles. "Thank you. It is easy to talk to you. I think I can trust you."

"You can," I said, returning the smile. "I doubt I'll see Angelica again. My uncle is at the villa today, saying goodbye."

"You must not speak to your uncle about this—please, Jordan. He would feel obligated to tell *Mamma*, don't you think? Promise you will not say anything to him."

That would be hard. I didn't promise. I asked, "What are you going to do about your family—the Morettis—and Sophie's mother? Where do you go from here?"

"I need time. I must go to Casa Vittoni to bury my daughter, *il mio piccolo gattino*. To *Mamma* and Roberto, I will plead some urgent business matter in Naples, where we have many accounts for our wines." He'd said it all in a breathless rush.

"And Bianca?"

He touched his temple, rubbing in small circles, as if he had a headache.

"I have ruined many lives, haven't I, Jordan? I will go back to the bed and breakfast that her friends own and try to persuade them that I must see her. I will try to explain. Not to seek her forgiveness, because I cannot expect forgiveness, but to promise her—give her whatever she wants. She does not want *me*, I can tell you. Bianca and I have not been good for each other for a long time." He took a deep breath. "But I cannot stay in Florence today. Mina needs me now. If Bianca continues to hide"—he ran his hand through his already-mussed hair—"I don't know. I will have to leave a message on her phone."

I didn't know who deserved pity most.

I asked the name of the B&B. Raff gave it to me, *Residenza Eduardo*, and I wrote it on a napkin. "Would you mind if I tried to see Bianca tomorrow?" I asked.

"Tomorrow? I will be in Casa Vittoni. Speak with Bianca if you like. If she is still there."

He didn't ask why I'd want to see her, which was a good thing because I didn't have a plausible story. For my own curiosity, I thought I should talk with the last person on my list. If Bianca had been in Florence since Saturday, she could have been in contact with Sophie. She could have been at the convent, at some point.

Raff insisted on paying the check, and I insisted, and in the end I think he was just too tired to argue. He scooted back his chair, picked up the box, and set it in his lap.

"I hope they gave you her sketch book," I said. "I saw some of her sketches. She had talent."

The box was not sealed. He took the lid off and rummaged in the box, among clothes that had not been folded. Her rucksack was on top of everything. I suggested that it might contain the sketchbook, and it did. Raff took it out and thumbed through it, his expression a mix of pride and sorrow.

"How about her phone? Did they give it back?" I asked.

"Not yet," he said. "The Chief Inspector promised I would get it eventually, but she wanted to go through the calls and texts again."

Maybe my visit to Chief Inspector Eleanora de Rosa had not been all for nothing.

I WOULD HAVE SHOWERED, anyway, getting ready for the evening with Paul on the rooftop of the Westin—wasn't this supposed to be magical?—but as I turned the water on full force, as hot as I could stand it, I was trying to wash away the stress that tightened my muscles and set up the drumbeat in my head. This time of day, five p.m., was not a time that most guests of the convent were taking showers, so I had plenty of hot water. I adjusted the shower head to direct the surge of water onto my eyes, then the back of my neck, all the way down my spine. After ten, maybe fifteen, minutes, the water began to cool. A little less tense now, I dried off, wrapped in my robe, and returned to the room. I checked my phone, first thing.

Paul and I had exchanged a few messages as I'd walked back to the convent. He'd be waiting for me in the lobby of the Westin. A text from Alex had come in while I was in the shower: Did you get my earlier message? I'm fine. Are you? I had not answered the text I'd read while waiting at the outdoor table for Raff, a.k.a. Leo Costa. Alex deserved a call, I thought.

"When you didn't check up on me—or reply with some witty remark—I wondered what had happened to you," he said.

"Sorry, Alex. I got caught up in this and that." What a lame excuse! I should have created a story for myself. I couldn't tell him where I'd been. At some point I'd give him the details of my visit to the *questura* and my conversation with the Chief Inspector, but I didn't know if I could ever reveal to Alex what I'd discovered today about Raffaele Moretti. And Alex would know I was hiding something. He was that good at reading me.

But I didn't give him a chance to ask more questions. I did the asking. Had he gathered some great information for his book about the *agriturismo*? How was Angelica? Had they heard anything about Bianca?

"Yes. Angelica spoke to Raff about an hour ago, and apparently he found Bianca in Florence," Alex said. "She's—shall we say, cooling off? Raff said she was staying in Florence for now. Angelica didn't seem too surprised. I take it that this sort of high drama has characterized Raff and Bianca's marriage for some time."

"What about Raff?"

"What do you mean?"

"I suppose he's on his way back to the villa," I said, knowing full well that he was not.

"Actually, I think Angelica said he had to take care of some business matter. I didn't pay much attention to that, after I heard that Bianca was no longer missing." He paused. "Jordan, is everything all right?"

I was never good at being evasive.

"Sure."

"I don't suppose your *investigation* has shed any new light on Sophie's death."

I had to get off the phone. "No proof that anyone else was in the room. But tonight I'm meeting Paul at the Westin, so that's what's on my mind right now."

It was clear that my uncle suspected something was

not quite right when he said, "Maybe I should come back to Florence early in the morning."

"Don't even think of hurrying back!" I said, trying to sound breezy. "Stay as long as you need to stay. I'll let you know if anything comes up—but I can't imagine what it would be!"

"I'll take that as a promise," he said, letting it go at that, letting me off the hook.

PAUL HAD PROMISED to meet me in the lobby. He was waiting in front of the hotel. As my taxi approached, I saw him conversing with the doorman, and it made me smile to think that he was so sure of himself, unlike some men who were still doing the "play hard to get" thing, afraid of appearing too eager. Not Paul Broussard, a man who—I was sure—did not have to do anything to have women swarming around him, if that's what he wanted.

Why me? I wondered tonight, as I often did. But that question was for another time.

When the taxi pulled to the curb, Paul was there, handing bills to the driver while the doorman—quite young, I realized—opened my door. And then Paul's arms were around me. Not too insistent—nor was our brief, sweet kiss too showy. "I have missed you today," he said, tilting my chin as if to get a better look. It was enough. The young doorman, whose large cap made him look like a kid playing dress-up, was smiling faintly as we passed him, and I imagined he was thinking: *There's a man who knows how to treat a woman.*

Someone was playing jazz at a grand piano in a lounge, adjacent to the lobby. Paul said, "I think the pianist is very good. He seems to have an extensive repertoire, and he always has an audience. Later tonight, some will be dancing." He was smiling, and I wondered if he was remembering the night we danced in Paris, and the roof rolled back. Like a dream now.

We got on the elevator with several others. Silence prevailed, as it tends to do on an elevator. At two stops, people got off. An attractive couple, much younger than we were, rode to the rooftop with us. They rushed ahead of us to see the hostess. Paul and I exchanged a look of mutual amusement.

"I'm in no hurry," I whispered.

"Nor am I," he said. "You are here. I am happy."

The hostess, one of those stunning young women that seemed to be everywhere in Florence, greeted us, calling Paul *Signor Broussard* without checking any list for his name. No doubt he had gone in person to reserve our table on the terrace, and he was not the sort of man she would have forgotten. She led the way to the outdoor seating, every table with a grand view, but I suspected ours was the best. Breathtaking!

"Is it what you expected?" Paul asked.

"Everything you promised, and more," I said.

THIRTY-TWO

WE LOOKED DOWN on the twisting Arno, the bridges, the Oltrarno district just across from us, the spires and domes, the western sky with fading streaks of pink, where the sun had set, and gentle hills silhouetted against the sky in the east.

The server, another Italian beauty, brought a wine list.

"We should start with champagne," Paul said to me. He looked at the wine list for a moment and handed it back to the server. They exchanged a few words of Italian.

I brought out my camera, and we stood at the rail beside our table. I took photos, as others were doing. The Westin's rooftop bar was touristy, yes, but I couldn't imagine a more spectacular view. The breeze was stronger up here than it was on the street. Paul touched my hair that kept blowing into my face. He pushed a strand out of my eyes and let it slide through his fingers. "Did I ever tell you that my first love was a girl with titian hair? She was eleven. I was ten." He laughed. "To be truthful, it was a one-sided infatuation—my infatuation with her. She did not reciprocate."

"Foolish girl," I said.

The server was delivering champagne when we returned to our table.

We clinked glasses. The fine crystal chimed like a bell.

We sipped the champagne, and just looked at each other for a long moment. A smile played on Paul's lips, as he studied me. He asked, "What are you thinking, Jordan?"

"I'm thinking that you said it would be magical, up here, and it is."

"I never lie to you," he said.

AND SO BEGAN the evening. Soft laughter, sparkling champagne, our fingers touching across the small table, entwining, caressing. Night settling, ribbons of light glittering on the dark water.

The wait staff set up a long table with an array of chafing dishes at one end of the terrace. After a while, as I began to feel the champagne's bubbles, I said, "Wonder what's on the buffet," trying to make it a casual comment.

"Ah, we must find out," Paul said, and he motioned to our server. At his request, she went to the table where others were serving themselves and filled two small plates for us. Her selections were perfect, a sampling of traditional antipasti choices—meats, cheeses, olives, and such—as well as items Americans tended to expect on a buffet—shrimp, meatballs, and canapés with a variety of fillings.

She replaced our empty champagne flutes with tall wine glasses, each of which might have held a quart in its broad bowl, but the proficient server poured the standard two fingers worth. Paul gave a little lesson in wines as I studied the elegant label. This was a Tignanello 2012, produced in the Chianti region of Tuscany, made from the Sangiovese grape, the native grape of Italy that was found in most Italian blends. "The vineyard, you see, is the Antinori estate," Paul said. "I would like to have surprised you with a Moretti wine if one had been offered, but perhaps the Moretti winery markets to smaller venues."

I hadn't mentioned to Paul that Alex was at the Moretti villa for a couple of days, so I told him now. We talked about Angelica's family, and when I spoke of Raff, my expression must have betrayed me because Paul said, "What is it that is troubling you?" I wanted to tell him everything I'd learned today about Raff's double life when I went to see Chief Inspector de Rosa. I'd managed to put Sophie's death out of my mind, but it all came back now.

I gave a long, deep sigh. "I am so sorry, Paul. The Moretti family and all of their problems have been too much on my mind. I'm not going to let the Morettis— or anything—intrude on this night."

He took my hand in both of his and fixed me with his earnest gaze. "Jordan, you must never apologize for telling me what is in your heart."

That was Paul, being a charmer. But I knew he didn't really want me to talk about duplicity and murder tonight. I realized that my bubbly feeling was probably not due to one glass of champagne. It was the intoxicating effect of Paul Broussard.

As the night went on, the server asked if we wanted to see a menu. "Perhaps later, *merci*," Paul told her. Perhaps later I would be hungry again, but the small plate with its variety of delights had been a meal in itself. I rose from the table and took more photographs of the city that lay before us like a tapestry covered with diamonds, under what was now a dark sky. Paul, standing near me, just back from the rail, took a photo of me. "I thought nothing could improve on the ones at the bridge, but this one—ah, even more lovely. I shall treasure it," he said. As he showed me the photo on his phone, our server offered to take a picture of us together. I handed her my camera. I looked up at Paul—a little embarrassed by the attention—and Paul was looking at me when she took the shot. I knew without checking the viewer that I would treasure this one.

The wind began to kick up, and Paul studied the sky. "I hope the rain, if it comes, will be tonight or tomorrow, not Wednesday, our day in Fiesole."

"Are you a weatherman, too, along with all your other talents?" I said.

"I am simply an observer," he said. "You see the moon and stars are hiding behind clouds."

"A poet, too," I said.

"Ah, Jordan, you must stop," he said.

And then a puff of wind sent a glass on another table crashing to the floor. The wait staff scurried to secure flapping tablecloths. We returned to our table and picked up our glasses. Paul might be right about the rain, I thought. It might even storm.

But the gusty breezes didn't cause alarm on the terrace. The air was more exhilarating than threatening. After a while the wait staff removed the buffet, probably no earlier than usual. Tables that emptied were soon occupied again. Eventually Paul and I ordered coffee and shared an Amaretto Tiramisu. I could not have said what time it was when Paul asked, "Do you smell the rain?"

I smelled the rain. I felt the electricity in the air.

With the wind whipping, we made our way inside, where the server had told us she would finish checking us out. Waiting, I smoothed my hair. Paul straightened his jacket. Soft piano music was piped in, so soft it was barely audible, but Paul said, "Music from the lounge."

And we found ourselves minutes later on the crowded elevator, headed downstairs for the music. Pressed close to Paul, I still felt the electricity. I may have imagined the scent of the wind on his clothes, mixed with the clean smell of good soap coming from his skin.

The lounge was crowded, too. All seating taken, likely, but I didn't check for a seat. Paul led me straight to the dance floor and took me in his arms, and we began to dance with an ease that felt as if we'd rehearsed for a long time. The pianist finished "Unchained Melody" and began to play "Music of the Night" from *Phantom*. Serendipity, I thought, as I leaned into Paul, my forehead touching his cheek, and I remembered some of the lyrics about surrendering to dreams, senses abandoning their defenses, fantasies unwinding.

If I hadn't known before how the night would end, I knew it now.

The rain came in before the song was over. It did not start as drops. It came suddenly in sheets, torrents that struck the windows with astonishing force. When the music ended, Paul was still holding me tight against him, and I could feel our heartbeats between us drumming like the insistent rain that beat against the glass.

"Will you stay with me tonight, Jordan?" Paul whispered, close to my ear.

I let my hand slide down his sleeve and pulled him away from the crowd, couples who were waiting for the next song. I led him away from the dance floor. That was my answer.

THIRTY-THREE

UNACCUSTOMED TO SHARING a bed, I would have expected a restless night, waking often, wondering in the first instant of alertness whose arms were around me. But it wasn't like that at all. Sometime in the wee hours Paul and I settled into sleep, sweet oblivion, skin to skin, and I did not wake from my deep, velvety slumber until morning.

Paul was already dressed, crisp white shirt, dark pants—signature Paul. Already wearing shoes. Jacket neatly draped on the back of a chair. My clothes neatly folded on the chair. He had done that this morning, picked up my strewn garments from the floor. Paul was fastening a cufflink without looking. He was gazing at me from the foot of the bed. He looked so put together that I wanted to hide under the covers. Ever so intuitive, Paul must have known that what I wanted most of all was to make myself presentable. His smile was amused as he came forward. "You are awake. I will get coffee for us, and pastries." He gave me a light, tender kiss.

"Coffee? Yes, please! A pastry, too," I said—or something equally inane.

He put on his jacket. Monsieur Broussard would not go out without his jacket.

At the door he turned and said, "Waking up with you beside me was everything I had dreamed." And then he was gone. And I thought I was surely dreaming, myself.

HE HAD PULLED the curtains back a little, just enough to let in a beam of sunlight. Yes, sunlight. No more rain. Maybe I had imagined the storm, or was it the lovely storm in our room that I remembered? I let the delicious night replay in my mind. It was everything I had dreamed, too, and more.

I hopped into the shower for a minute and slipped into the terrycloth robe that hung in the bathroom instead of my little black dress from last night, which was all I had. Good thing that I hadn't opted for a tiny little evening purse, which would have been attractive, but not practical. My tote bag was always with me in Florence. One of the items in it was a cosmetics zip-bag, with toothbrush, comb, deodorant—the essentials I was glad to have this morning.

I was preparing to use the hair dryer on the wall when I heard Paul return. I came out of the bathroom to meet him. He had set the coffee and paper bag that apparently held our pastries on the low table at a sitting area. "*Bonjour, ma cherie*," he said, reaching for me. A few moments of slow kisses and lingering embraces, and we sat down to real American coffee and real French croissants.

"The rain must have brought autumn to Florence," he said. "It is very cool today. I can imagine that the rooftop bar might not be so comfortable tonight."

"So we were just in time last night," I said.

"Perfect timing," he said. "From my point of view, everything was perfect."

"From my point of view, as well," I told him.

I loved that wry smile of his that said everything he needed to say.

The croissant was a flaky, melt-in-your-mouth pastry, the most wonderful pastry I had ever tasted. And the coffee, a full eight ounces, much like what I might have brewed for myself at home. At the convent, I would have needed to go to the coffee machine four times for this much. It felt like a good time to tell Paul what I'd learned about Raff's two families.

"I understand now," he said, "when you spoke of the Morettis' problems last night, there was more to it than you wanted to say."

"I can't tell Alex," I said. "He's too close to Angelica. But you don't know these people."

"And it is important to you, to find out whether this was the reason for the young woman's death. Whether this knowledge about her father was so upsetting that she took her own life, or whether it was murder." He said it as a statement of fact, but I nodded, confirming.

If Paul thought I was on a fool's errand, he didn't show it. He asked what my plans were for today. All I had in mind was to talk with Bianca, if I could. Raff had given me the name of the bed and breakfast where he believed she was staying, and apparently he had located her there. I found in my tote bag where I had written *Residenza Eduardo*, and Paul looked up the address on his phone. "Not far from *Piazza della Repubblica*," he noted.

It wouldn't be a bad idea to see Marisa, too, I thought. I couldn't remember whether Sophie had dealt with her or someone else when making her reservation for the Vespa tour—or maybe she had arranged it online, but she said she'd met Marisa. Cristiano wouldn't be happy to see me. Marisa might not even be at *Vivere la Toscana!* today, but it would be worth my time to drop by. It was possible Marisa knew something about Sophie that I hadn't even considered.

"Shall I go with you? Or perhaps you want to make these inquiries by yourself. Whatever you wish," Paul said, just as his phone jingled.

He said, "Ah, Bella, good morning." It was a suitable time for me to pick up my little black dress and underwear and retreat to the bathroom. It struck me that I had no uneasy feelings about Bella today. She was Paul's daughter and it was only right that they should be forging the relationship they'd never had. It might take a while for me to forgive what she'd done to me at the Moretti Villa, but this *difficult* young woman—the word Paul had used—seemed desperate for her father's approval and attention, and desperation forced people to do desperate things.

Today it didn't matter so much. Something had changed. Much had changed since last night. Though my hair was almost dry, I used the hair dryer, and the noise drowned out Paul's conversation. But the call was short. Three or four minutes—and Paul gave a gentle knock on the door. I turned off the hair dryer.

"I told Bella that you were with me, and I would call her later," he said.

I imagine he could tell I was pleased that he hadn't kept my presence a secret. "I hope you didn't think I minded her call," I said. "I didn't. Really."

"I am glad," he said. "She wanted to speak about our schedule, when she should return to Florence, when we will return to Paris. But it is not a good time this morning to speak of leaving." He took a step closer, touched my skin at the collar of the robe, and traced the neckline to where the robe overlapped. I fumbled with a button on his shirt.

"I can't think about leaving, either. Not this morning," I said, as he tugged at the belt of my robe.

IT WAS MIDDAY before I left the Westin in a taxi, my strappy sandals not suited for a thirty minute walk. Paul opened the door of the taxi for me. "Tonight?" he said, and I said yes. He could have just meant dinner, but I knew what he meant. It was chilly outside, as Paul had said. The mild weather had been wonderful, but I didn't mind the crisp, bracing air. I was wearing a sweater I'd dug from my tote bag that would suffice until I could change clothes at the convent, and then I thought I would enjoy walking to the *Piazza della Repubblica*.

Ivonna was not working. I asked the other young woman for my key and went to the elevator, which was just opening to let Varinia Santoro out. She was carrying what looked like a laundry bag, filled and fastened with a drawstring.

"Going out to do laundry?" I asked.

"Yes. It is difficult to bring enough clothes for both of us without washing," she said.

She hurried by me. I got the feeling she was trying to hold the bag away from me as if she thought I might grab it—or want to look inside. Alex was right, of course. I did tend to be a nosy sometimes, but I had no interest in Varinia's dirty clothes.

I had just reached my room when my phone rang. It was Eli Schubert. "How'd it go yesterday with the Chief Inspector?" he wanted to know.

"She didn't exactly toss me out of her office, but I didn't get far with her," I said.

"Sorry I couldn't be much help. I did what I could."

I thanked him for running interference with the desk

sergeant. Otherwise, I doubted Eleanora de Rosa would have spoken with me at all. "I may have convinced the Chief Inspector to check out the texts and calls on Sophie's phone, and they may prove that Sophie was planning to meet someone that night. A date, of sorts. That might indicate she wasn't planning suicide. The police kept her phone." I hoped Eli wouldn't ask how I knew that.

"Not bad work, Jordan! More than I expected you'd get out of the Chief Inspector—but Paul said you were tenacious."

I asked him about the preliminary hearing he'd attended in Pisa yesterday.

"The kid was bound over on all charges," Eli said. "Thing is, he admitted to breaking into a house to steal some electronics but he denied the other crimes. They had nothing to connect him with the burglaries of the shops. Doesn't sound to me like that kid is the cat burglar that stole jewels for the Camorra, but it wasn't my call."

"Cat burglar?" The first I'd heard of that.

"He enters through skylights or high windows that aren't wired for alarms, so, yeah, cat burglar. Same M.O. in Florence. My source at the *questura* finally gave up that little detail. There's nothing to suggest the kid in Pisa had been stealing jewels in Florence, but *il pubblico ministero* didn't get into that. He wasn't trying to tie the crimes in Pisa to the Camorra. He just wanted to show he'd made Pisa safe for tourists." Eli's laugh was sardonic. "Good lesson, Jordan: Don't get yourself arrested in Italy."

"I won't get myself arrested unless they haul me in for being nosy," I said.

"Still on the trail, then?" He chuckled. "Maybe you're in the wrong business. Ever think of giving up architecture for investigative reporting?"

"Nope," I said. "I just want to know what *really* happened to Sophie."

Eli said he'd checked out the story about the mugging at the convent. Police had the report, but no leads. That wasn't unusual, Eli said. Muggers and pickpockets in tourist hotspots most often got away with their crimes. I reminded Eli that Luigi wasn't a tourist, wasn't even in a touristy part of the city when he was mugged.

"I know, and counting the mugging, that makes four times the police have been at the convent in a couple of weeks." Eli paused, maybe trying to work something out in his mind. "You need to be careful, Jordan. I learned this morning that police think they thwarted two more robberies in the Oltrarno district, one last Friday night and one just last night." The *polizia* had made a greater effort to watch the artisan shops in Oltrarno, Eli said, and they'd seen somebody they believed was trying to break in. Two different shops. Both times the suspect got away.

"And the first time was Friday night," I said, almost to myself.

"Yeah, and last night, he was out there in pouring rain. Quite a rainstorm we had."

I agreed.

"I don't know if all of this is connected, but I thought you should know," Eli said. "I'd say it's all coincidence if I believed in coincidence, which I don't."

"I don't believe in coincidence, either," I said.

THIRTY-FOUR

I HEARD RATTLING at my door and opened it to find Luigi with a ladder. His string of Italian was clearly an apology. Either he hadn't known I was in the room or he was sorry he'd made so much noise or sorry he hadn't knocked. Pointing, explaining, he got the message across that he wanted to clean the glass over my door, the transom, as he'd done up and down the hall. I said, "No problem," making gestures to indicate he should go ahead, and his big smile indicated that he understood. The language barrier had not proven to be an impossible obstacle in this case.

I closed the door so Luigi could position the ladder. A moment later I saw his face above the door. He was smiling at me, using a squirt bottle and cloth, wiping the glass. I sat on the side of my bed, thinking about the transom, open at about a forty-five-degree angle. The space was too small—too awkward—for anyone to crawl through it. But if someone had a ladder, he might climb up and toss something onto the bed. A heavy barbell-like object with a key attached.

Another thought rocketed through my mind: Cat burglar. A cat burglar would need some kind of equipment. A rope? Something at the end of it to secure it to the wood frame of the transom? I didn't know how these things worked, but I could imagine possibilities. Luigi had already cleaned the transom above Sophie's door, so there would be no fingerprints on the glass, but a cat burglar would wear gloves anyway, wouldn't he?

Luigi's face disappeared after a few minutes' work, and I hurried to my door. I managed to make him understand that I wanted him to move the ladder to room twelve. I think he tried to tell me he was finished with that window, but we set up the ladder and I began to climb. I don't know what else Luigi was saying, but the anxiety in his voice made sense. If a guest fell off his ladder, he'd be in trouble. I was careful as I examined the glass and the area all around the transom. No marks on the wood that made me suspect someone had been rappelling. It would be easy to get the perfect trajectory from here and toss the key on the bed. That much, I confirmed.

But why would a cat burglar murder Sophie? Who would have access to a ladder, anyway? Or time to set it up after pushing Sophie out the window? None of my theories made any sense.

I thanked Luigi and said goodbye. No doubt he was glad to get away from me, with my crazy ideas. I had learned nothing. Maybe I would learn something from Bianca or Marisa.

I FOUND THE bed and breakfast, *Residenza Eduardo*, but Bianca was not there. Eduardo—I assumed the handsome man who greeted me was the owner—spoke good English and maybe because I was so sorry that I'd missed Bianca, he was more forthcoming than I might have expected. Yes, Signora Moretti had been there, but she had left this morning. He and his wife were very fond of Signora Moretti. She came to Florence often and always stayed with them.

Then a woman wearing rhinestone-rimmed glasses, apparently his wife, joined us. "How do you know Bianca?" she asked, and I could see she would need a little more convincing.

"I know all the Morettis," I said. "I was at the villa twice last week—and I was hoping to see Bianca again before I go home. I had some questions about the museum in Siena." I don't know where that came from— just the sudden memory that Bianca had mentioned going to a board meeting at the museum in Siena. "You don't know if she's still in Florence, do you?"

The woman adjusted her glasses and narrowed her eyes, studying me. "Perhaps you can reach her by telephone," she said. No way I'd know how to reach Bianca by telephone, and this smart woman knew it. I thanked the couple and went on my way.

I HAD BETTER LUCK at *Vivere la Toscana!* Marisa was there, and Cristiano was not. I had managed to come at a slow, quiet time.

Marisa greeted me from behind the counter. "Jordan! I was hoping I would see you again." She spoke to the other young woman in a green tee shirt and picked up something before she came out from behind the counter. "You did not get the recipes from the cooking class." Her expression was sympathetic, as if to say, *I wish the cooking class had been a more pleasant experience for you.* She handed me a small spiral-bound booklet.

I thanked her and told her I looked forward to trying out some of these wonderful recipes at home. "Do you have time to talk?" I asked. She directed me to the green plastic chairs next to the rack of brochures that advertised their diverse Tuscan experiences. I asked,

"Did you hear about the girl named Sophie? She was on the Vespa tour Friday."

"Cristiano told me what happened," she said. "Such a sad thing. Yes, I remember her. She came here one day and said she had gone to our website and had reserved a place on the Vespa tour. She asked some questions, and then she stayed for quite some time, hanging about, as you say."

I didn't correct her. She had the right idea—*hanging out* or *hanging around*. "She told me she had wanted to stay in a villa in Tuscany but did not have enough money," Marisa said. "She had a room in a convent. When Cristiano told me what happened to her at *Convento di Santa Francesca Firenze*, I realized that was where you and your uncle were staying, also. You must have known her."

"Yes. I was fond of Sophie, and I'm trying to understand what happened," I said.

"Cristiano said she took her own life," Marisa said.

"The police seem to think so. I'm no expert, but she didn't seem suicidal to me." I shifted in the uncomfortable plastic chair, considering how I might draw information from Marisa without misleading her or revealing too much of what I knew about her family. "You said she had questions. Did you mean questions about the tour?"

Marisa's brows pulled together.

"I gave her a brochure about the Vespa tour, but as we stood here, she took one of these." Marisa reached for a brochure with a photo of herself in a chef's hat on the front. "And then she had so many questions about *me*. Where did I train to be a chef? Where was my home? I was a little uncomfortable, but I found myself saying, 'I grew up at the Moretti Villa, where you will be on Friday on the Vespa tour.' And she said, 'Will I see your *Mamma*?' It seemed a very strange thing to ask. And then Cristiano called for me, and I was glad. The girl—Sophie—was still here when I left on a walking tour."

"Where is Cristiano today?" I asked.

She gave an exaggerated shrug. "He has not been here. No one knows where he is, but sometimes"—she gave a little wave that I interpreted: *He has a hangover* or *he's with a woman.*

"Sophie told me she'd been out partying with Cristiano Friday night," I said.

Marisa gave a little laugh. "I am not surprised."

I left without much new information, but what Marisa had told me aligned with what I knew of Sophie's plan to find Bianca Moretti. The clever girl had done her research on the Morettis, but she may have believed Bianca was Marisa's mother.

Starting down the creaky stairs, I saw Cristiano on the street. "You!" he cried from a distance, looking up at me with a wild expression. I hurried down the steps, not wanting to encounter him midway and risk a push from him. At the foot of the stairs, he faced me, impossibly close. I could smell his breath, the hint that he had tried to mask the smell of alcohol with peppermint.

"What do you want from me? You have caused trouble enough!" he said.

"Marisa gave me recipes from the cooking class," I said. I started to reach into my tote bag, where I'd dropped the little booklet, but he grabbed my wrist.

"You should not be here," he said, each word sharp as a blade.

"You should take your hand off me," I said, my words just as sharp.

He did, but he continued to glare at me.

I took a step back, put my palm out in protest, and said, "I have no business with you, Cristiano. I'm leaving now."

"The *polizia* came for me this morning!" he said.

I had started to go around him, but I stopped. "You were arrested?"

"Not arrested. I had done nothing! But I spent the morning at the *questura*. I was treated like a criminal. Put in a room to wait. Questioned by a stupid detective. Questioned about everything I had ever done. They took my phone."

I thought of Eli's words: *Don't get yourself arrested in Italy.*

"Was this about Sophie's calls and texts?" I asked, feeling a rush of sympathy for the man, though I couldn't make myself like him.

"Of course! It is your fault! You told them about me—I know! But no matter how they tried, they could not find anything to charge me," he said with a sneer.

"I didn't mean to cause trouble for you. But the texts and calls between you and Sophie worked in your favor, didn't they?" I said. "And they proved Sophie had plans for that night."

He snorted. "You have no idea what it is like when the *polizia* come!"

"Did you get your phone back?" I asked.

He pulled his phone from his pants pocket, as his answer.

"Go away," he said. "Do not come back." And he began taking the stairs two at a time.

"Cristiano—I'm sorry," I called. "Sorry you had to go through that."

He paused but did not look back.

THIRTY-FIVE

HEADING BACK TO the convent, I felt the heavy weight of failure on my shoulders.

I was no closer to proving that Sophie had *not* taken her own life. And I was having my own doubts. For a teenage girl who was already upset by the thought that her father was cheating on her mother, the truth—so much worse than she'd suspected—must have been devastating. I could only imagine the shock of discovering that other family. Seeing her father's happy face prominent among the Moretti family photographs. She'd wanted to spill it all to someone—Cristiano, Sister Assunta, maybe even me—but she couldn't say the words. Maybe she had felt so powerless that she just didn't want to live.

But in the depths of my heart, I couldn't believe it.

What else could I do? I had asked a lot of questions and had few useful answers. The only person I hadn't spoken to was Bianca. She could have contacted Sophie. Sophie could have let her into the convent. And she could have left the convent in the frantic moments just after Sophie's body plunged to the ground. The police that were in the *piazza* for crowd control would have rushed to the body, made calls, focused on securing the area from the pulsing crowd—but would they immediately have guarded the door of the convent, so that no one could have left? Still, even if that scenario *could* have happened, there was that locked door.

I stopped at a *gelateria* and ordered a cone of some exotic flavor, chocolate-based. Walking on with my cone, I thought about Sophie's exchange with Varinia Santoro the morning before her death. I kept trying to find meaning in Sophie's words as they played and played again in my mind: *Something I saw when I was going to my bathroom.* Something about Varinia, surely, because she had practically frozen when Varinia spoke to her. *You seemed very confused,* Varinia had said. Sophie was drunk, and Varinia had wanted her to believe that whatever she'd seen was imagined, rather than real. But what was it that Sophie had seen?

I finished my *gelato* and walked a little faster. My phone rang as I crossed the *piazza*, heading toward the convent. "Alex!" I said. "I'm glad it's you. I should've called you earlier."

Though he tried for initial pleasantries, I detected something ominous in his voice.

"Are you all right?" I asked, thinking first, as I always did, about his health.

"Nothing wrong with me," he said, "but I'm afraid there's something very wrong here. Bianca came back, and—Jordan, this is all so terribly confusing."

"Bianca's back? Isn't that a good thing?" I said before it hit me. Bianca would have come back for one reason, only. She had returned to tell the Moretti family everything.

And that was exactly what she'd done.

"I can't even begin to tell you how it all happened, but Angelica is beside herself. The very idea that Raffaele has a family in another part of Italy, that he's deceived everyone for many years, and Sophie was his daughter"—Alex's heightened emotion was not like him, but he had witnessed Angelica's reaction to this shocking news. How upsetting it must have been to him—to everyone at the villa.

"I'm so sorry, Alex. It's hard to believe," I said.

He waited a beat. "Jordan, you didn't know about this, did you?"

I hesitated, but I had to be truthful. "Not until yesterday," I said. "I couldn't tell you, not on the phone. I saw Raff at the police station. That's how I found out."

He didn't reply immediately, but then he said, "I'm going to stay here a while longer. For Angelica. Rob and Ambra have asked me to stay."

"Of course you should," I said.

Before we ended the call, I asked if Bianca was still at the villa. Alex said she was clearing out all of her things. He had no idea where she was going.

I was sure I'd never have the chance to ask her any questions about Sophie.

"So cruel," Alex said. "So very cruel." I suspected he was talking about Bianca, the cruelty she'd shown in revealing Raff's treachery to Angelica. Like hitting Angelica with a brick.

But Alex could have meant Raff, who had left so much heartbreak in his path.

PAUL HAD TEXTED ONCE, earlier in the day. Apparently, he'd spent the afternoon making and receiving calls to and from Paris and the States. He would come by for me at six-thirty, he said. "I want to show you a sight you should not miss. Please be sure you will be warm."

I checked the time as I approached the convent, glad I'd have a chance to unwind—more than two hours—but also feeling the electric anticipation of being with

Paul again, something new and thrilling and confusing, too, because in a couple of days we'd leave Florence, and what then? Could I be satisfied with calling it an exciting, lovely fling and letting it go at that?

Just outside the entrance, Ivonna passed by on her Vespa and waved. She pulled her motorscooter around to the side of the convent, and, since I'd followed her on Sunday, I knew she'd be coming through the garden and entering the building near the breakfast room. I retrieved my room key from the office and went to meet her.

She used the stepping stones that led around the fountain but did not continue into the maze of hedges—or past that into the property I'd discovered on Sunday. Outside the French doors, where I waited, Ivonna stopped to clean off her boots. "So much mud!" she said. "What a rainstorm last night! Were you awake when the storm came?"

"I wasn't here last night," I said.

Ivonna winked, surprising me, for she was typically so formal. "He is very handsome, *Signora*."

What could I say? I gave a little laugh. "He's quite charming." I told her I wasn't expecting to be at the convent tonight, either. My uncle was in Tuscany, I said. He wouldn't be back until tomorrow, at the earliest.

When she finished wiping her boots on the grass, also using a tissue she'd pulled from her backpack, we went inside. I stopped at the vending machine for a bottle of water and bought one for Ivonna, also.

"How much longer will you be in Florence?" she asked.

"We're scheduled to leave on Friday," I said, and I felt a stitch in my chest, knowing then that what I'd been thinking had just become more real.

She thanked me for the water. "You are kind. I will miss you," she said.

"I'll miss you, too," I said. "I'll miss Florence—everything about it."

A minute later—maybe more than a minute because the elevator took a while—I was on my floor. A couple of turns, and I came to the hall with all the guest rooms, mine at the other end. Luigi had opened an access panel and was shining a flashlight into the mechanical shaft. I hadn't seen behind the access panel next to my room, but one would expect the mechanical shafts to be similar in their contents. I noted that this one was located next to number 11, the room that belonged to Varinia and Carlo Santoro.

I greeted Luigi. He smiled and nodded, always a pleasant man, but I could see he was distracted. I wished I knew how to tell him that I was an architect and the pipes and ductwork and wiring, especially in historic buildings, were all interesting to me. He didn't seem to be bothered by my curiosity, so I moved closer. He focused the beam of his flashlight on the narrow section of floor just inside the large rectangular opening. A long moment—both of us studying what we were seeing—and Luigi looked back at me. His expression told me what I had no trouble understanding: *These muddy footprints are not mine. Who has been here?*

THIRTY-SIX

"Do you know if there are any plans—blueprints, architectural plans—of the convent?" I asked Ivonna, trying to curb my impatience. I had waited so long for the elevator that I finally ran down the hall and took the stairs. Then I'd had to wait for Ivonna to finish a phone call.

From her seat behind the computer, she frowned. I tried to clarify. "Drawings of the building. Construction drawings."

"The building is very old," Ivonna said.

I didn't expect to find plans from the fifteenth century, but I'd hoped there might be as-built drawings, done when renovations had taken place. Clearly there had been a few renovations over the period of five centuries.

Her expression changed suddenly, her eyes widening. "There is a book in the library that might have pictures."

I sighed, and I'm sure I sounded disappointed. "Where is the library?"

She must have read my mind because she said, "I do not mean the big *biblioteca* for the city. No, I am thinking of our library on *il primo piano*." She gave a little laugh. "We call it our library though it is really a very small reading room, with only a few books. But I know of a book that one of our own Sisters wrote about how *Convento di Santa Francesca Firenze* survived the flood of 1966. Do you know of that terrible flood?"

"I've heard stories." Mostly, stories about the important art that was lost—thousands of paintings, frescoes, and sculptures, destroyed by water or mud. From all over the world, volunteers—"mud angels" they were called—flocked to the city to help in the rescue effort.

"There was so much damage to the convent, but many donations came in, and we were able to repair." Again, a smile. "I do not mean that *I* was alive when it happened. I was not, of course. My *mamma* was very young, herself, but my *nonna* has told stories, and Sister Assunta, also. She showed me the book, and I remember many pictures."

Pictures weren't the same as floor plans, but they might be useful. I asked Ivonna if she could show me to the reading room. She wasn't able to leave the office, but she told me how to locate it and said, "The room is never locked, and you will have no trouble finding the book." She gave approximate measurements with her hands—an oversized book.

The small reading room, on Alex's floor, was furnished as one might expect to find in an elderly grandmother's house, complete with a profusion of doilies that I imagined the nuns crocheted. I sniffed the musty air, though the room looked clean—no visible cobwebs or dust. The smell became stronger when I reached the two shelves of books. Most of them looked old enough to have survived the 1966 flood, which might have accounted for the odor. Only one book was eleven by fourteen. I pulled it out, felt a surge of satisfaction that this had been so easy, so far, and sat down at a round table that was covered with a crocheted tablecloth.

It didn't help that I couldn't read Italian, but the photographs were instructive—many photos of the flooded grounds and building. Others showed the construction work in progress, and not just in the basement, which must have contained at least four feet of water, judging from the "before and after" pictures. It seemed the flood—and the subsequent donations that Ivonna mentioned—had offered an unprecedented opportunity. The large central skylight was installed, perhaps an after-the-fact of a roof damaged beyond repair. But the pages of the book that intrigued me most were the parts about the installation of new mechanical, electrical, and plumbing systems, contained in two mechanical shafts that ran vertically through all the floors.

And yes, there were a few drawings. Three pages of drawings.

I took the book to Ivonna and asked if I could get copies of pages, making the drawings larger. She was happy to oblige. Moments later she returned to the counter with my book and spread out the copies for me to approve. As I examined them and concluded that they were as sharp as we could get, Varinia Santoro came into the office, carrying her drawstring bag that apparently held clean laundry. Ivonna produced her room key. Staring at the drawings I'd had Ivonna copy, Varinia said nothing. Nothing to me, not even *grazie* when Ivonna handed her the key. She blinked several times in rapid succession as she regarded the elevations, a section showing the vertical shaft, and a couple of detail drawings that showed how the components fit together. I had the distinct impression that she knew exactly what they were.

Ivonna's smile was amused, as she watched the hasty retreat of the tall, big-boned Varinia, decked out in a flowing caftan that seemed highly inappropriate for a trip to the laundromat. "A very unusual woman, and her husband, also," Ivonna said. *Peculiar* was the word that came to my mind. Before I could add a comment, Ivonna leaned on the counter and said, *sotto voce*, "She has only once allowed the housekeeper to clean their room."

"Did the housekeeper say there was anything odd about what they had in the room? What was so secretive?" I asked, also in a stage whisper.

"Signora Santoro wanted only the sheets changed and the floor swept. She would not let the housekeeper clean the bathroom."

I asked how much longer Varinia and Carlo were staying, and Ivonna said they were scheduled to check out on Friday. Friday, the same day Alex and I planned to leave.

I thanked Ivonna for the copies. A thought struck me at the door, and I turned back. "Did anyone else ask to see this book? Recently, I mean."

Ivonna thought about it.

"It was some time ago, many months. I have worked at the convent two years, and I had not been here long. Some members of a historical society met with Sister Assunta, and they took this book for a while. I think they wanted to make it available for people to buy online—because it was fifty years since the flood."

In the reading room, before I replaced the book on the shelf, I checked the Amazon site on my phone and keyed the title into the search box. There it was. This book had come out last year as an e-book.

Another trip downstairs and outside, to the garden. I was surprised that no one else was there. Luck seemed to be with me. I had seen the old grilles along the wall at the foundation level, vents for the basement, but only at a distance. I studied one of the drawings I'd brought with me, the elevation that helped me judge which vent might be closest to the mechanical shaft that Luigi had been inspecting. Even with the aid of my phone's flashlight I probably wouldn't get a clear view of the basement area—or was it just a crawl space?—but the wheels of my mind kept turning, spinning out possibilities. Perhaps I could see enough to confirm that if someone managed to enter the basement through the vent, it might be possible to gain entry into the mechanical shaft.

I squatted in front of the old, rusty, decorative grille. The ground was muddy, and I wasn't the first to be at that spot since the heavy rain. The footprints were not clearly defined, but I tried not to disturb them. Examining the grille, I drew in a sharp breath. The grille wasn't attached. Screws should have secured it within the opening, but they were gone.

I removed the grille, set it against the building, and used the flashlight to illuminate the unfinished area. My heart began to thrum. I knew what I needed to do. I had to get in there. My experiences in tight, dark places came flooding back, and even if I could make myself go in, would I be able to squeeze through the rectangular space? I looked behind and around me again. No one else was in the courtyard, and maybe that was a sign. I took a long, deep breath and climbed through the opening.

The drop to the ground was about two feet. Once inside, I tried to think of historic buildings in Savannah with their old basements or cellars—nothing new to me, though I wouldn't be checking out this kind of space alone, and we'd bring plenty of light with us. The smell was what I'd expected—musty. This was much more roomy than a crawl space. I could move around.

Though my light wasn't bright, I was able to make out a metal enclosure, a little room with a door. I knew from the drawings that it enclosed the furnace, electrical panels, the ductwork and wiring that threaded through the vertical shaft, as well as water pipes affixed to the side of the shaft. All of this would be accessible only with a key—one of Luigi's keys. The keys that were stolen when he was mugged.

I had what I needed. To be sure there was nothing more I could accomplish here, I made a sweep with my flashlight before I turned it off. I hoisted myself up at the opening, and scrambled through it.

I put the grille back in place. With my phone, I snapped several photos of the ground in front of the vent. Bending to make a closer examination of the footprints, I saw that the partial impressions were distinct enough to suggest they were made by a small shoe. Smaller than mine.

Just in time, I turned toward the French doors, which opened for two women I recognized from the breakfast room. Speaking in Italian—I was pretty sure it was Italian—they were deeply involved in their topic and barely noticed me.

My heartbeat was slowing—nearly back to normal. I headed to my room. Luigi had left the hall and locked the access door. But I'd seen the muddy footprints just inside the mechanical shaft. I had figured out how someone was able to enter the garden, the basement, and the mechanical shaft, to get to this floor. And I believed I knew who that someone was.

THIRTY-SEVEN

"JORDAN, THAT IS ALL—quite extraordinary," Paul said.

We were in the back seat of the car that had brought him to the convent, now headed south, away from the Arno. All that I'd discovered and concluded since we'd last texted, I simply couldn't contain. I couldn't stop myself, even knowing, as I did, that Paul was taking me to some special place and *that*, not the identity of jewel thieves, should be my priority tonight.

Paul's slight frown indicated curiosity, though, not frustration with me, so I let it all spill out. "I've been wondering if Carlo could walk. I've seen his feet move—just enough to make me suspicious. But I couldn't imagine why anyone who could walk would want to be in a wheelchair. Now it all makes sense. No one would guess that he's the cat burglar."

Paul's response was an amused smile.

"You don't believe me," I said.

"I believe everything you have told me, Jordan. The man is small enough to climb up the vertical shaft, which would be too tight for most men, and his feet are small enough to make the footprints you saw in the mud and on the floor when the access door was open. But these things are, as they say, circumstantial."

He was right. I had nothing concrete, just as I had nothing concrete to prove that Sophie had been murdered. Maybe I was looking a little downcast because he took my hand and gave a gentle squeeze. "And yet," he said, "circumstantial evidence can be quite powerful."

I thought of all the strange, suspicious behaviors the couple had exhibited, and I began to recap for Paul. The housekeeper could only enter the Santoros' room when they were present and she was never allowed to clean the bathroom. What were they hiding? Varinia's trip to the laundry hadn't sent off bells of alarm until I realized that the person who entered the convent through the basement could not have missed getting mud on him—not just on his shoes, but on his clothing, as well. "Whoever climbed up the vertical shaft came out onto the hall through the access door, which is adjacent to the Santoros' room," I said. "Varinia was probably waiting, watching, and she may have wiped up mud that was left in the hall, but Carlo had locked the access door behind him, overlooking the mud that Luigi later discovered."

A thought zipped through my mind, so reasonable that I couldn't imagine why I was just now thinking it. I said, "Sophie saw something on Friday night, the night the police thwarted another burglary. What if she saw Carlo coming from the access door? It would be just five or six steps to his room, and maybe Varinia had their door open, but if Sophie had even a glimpse—no wonder Varinia tried to make her believe she was so drunk she couldn't trust what she saw."

"Are you saying there was *another* attempted burglary?" Paul asked.

"*Two.* Eli said there was one Friday night and one last night, and the jewel thief is likely a cat burglar."

"I did not realize you and Eli were conspirators in his investigation." Again Paul smiled. It was a warmer smile this time. "Now it is not only the young woman's death that you feel you must explain, but the burglaries in Oltrarno, as well. You have a heart for making things right that are wrong. I love that about you, Jordan."

The word *love* jolted me, brought me back to the moment—being here with Paul, so close to him, so little time left with him, this night that he'd planned for us. I gave a long, deep sigh, exasperated at myself, and then I said, "Your patience with me is more than I deserve. I love that about you, Paul."

With our fingers entwined, we rode along in silence for another few minutes, until a huge bronze statue of *David* came into view, atop a hill that our car was ascending. Paul announced that we were arriving at *Piazzale Michelangelo*.

THE PANORAMIC VIEW of Florence from *Piazzale Michelangelo* was even more stunning than the view from the Westin's rooftop bar because tonight we were in time to watch a spectacular sunset. Unlike the pricey rooftop bar, here was an experience that ordinary people were enjoying. Children licking cones of *gelato*, couples pushing baby carriages, lovers wrapped in each other's arms. Like Paul and me, perched on stone steps, watching the purple and orange sky turn to pink. A romantic setting without the distraction of servers or menus or wine selections.

Not that I'd ever forget the Westin. Not a chance.

This was the iconic view on so many postcards and promotional materials—the old city walls, the tower of the *Palazzo Vecchio*, and the red dome of the *Duomo*. Now I had seen the city laid out before me from south of the Arno, as well as north of the Arno, the view from the Westin that featured the spires and towers of Oltrarno.

Sunset faded into twilight. Paul said, "We have just enough time to go inside *San Miniato*." The church's green-and-white marble façade, classic Romanesque, had already caught my eye. As we walked uphill to the church, Paul related the legend of St. Minias. A victim of persecution, the story went, he was beheaded in A.D. 250. He picked up his head and walked from the banks of the Arno to the site where the church would be built in the eleventh century to honor him. Fascinating story, and, for this architect, an even more fascinating architectural gem.

At eight o'clock, a docent politely announced to the visitors—about a dozen of us—that it was time to close the doors.

"You planned everything perfectly," I told Paul. "The thirty-minute drive, the sunset, even time for a substantial little tour of the church. Perfect timing."

"And now we will walk to a little *ristorante*, just past the city walls, where we have a reservation. It's all downhill, and you have your sweater. It should be a nice walk," he said.

"A lovely plan," I said.

And the evening went exactly as he had planned. Fine Tuscan cuisine in a setting that managed to be warm, inviting, and elegant, all at once. Taxi back to his hotel, to his room.

And all of it was lovely.

ELI'S CALL CAME the next morning while Paul and I were having room service in his sitting area. Touristy breakfast of blueberry muffins, orange juice and coffee. Paul, fresh from the shower, wore the bathrobe the hotel provided. He had let me sleep until the knock on the door announced room service. I'd managed to slip into a little silk kimono that took up scarcely any room in the bottom of my practical tote bag.

Hearing the jingle of my phone on the bedside table, I said, "It's probably Alex." I hadn't turned my phone off because I wanted Alex to always be able to reach me.

But it wasn't Alex. I looked at the caller's I.D. "Eli. Why is Eli calling me?" I said.

"Shouldn't you ask him?" Paul said.

Eli apologized for calling so early, though it was nine o'clock, which was not early by my calculations. He'd called to say he was going back to Pisa tomorrow to check out some new developments related to his story on the Camorra, and he didn't expect to be back before I left for home on Friday. He wanted to meet Paul and me for lunch today. "I wasn't able to reach Paul, but I left a message. I figured you could reach him." He chuckled.

"He's right here, actually," I said.

"Ah—I figured as much," Eli said. But I wasn't sure he had.

I told him that whatever they decided about lunch was fine with me, and then I handed the phone to Paul and finished the last of my muffin during the length of their good-humored conversation.

"Eli is renting a Vespa for the day," Paul said, with a laugh. "He's a funny fellow, but one for whom I have deep respect."

"Maybe he just wants us to see him riding a motorscooter," I said, smiling at the picture in my mind.

Paul had suggested a café just around the corner from the convent. Lunch at one o'clock—yes, I would be hungry four hours from now—would let us visit with Eli and we could still leave for Fiosole in time to look around the little town before the birthday party. As my clothes from last night wouldn't do for the occasion, I would need some time at the convent to get ready. Paul—the wheels of his mind always turning—said, "I will go to the convent with you, if you agree. Perhaps the good Sisters will not mind if I enjoy the lovely garden while I wait for you to make yourself even more beautiful."

He deserved a kiss for that. One kiss led to another, and one thing led to another, and as the silky kimono slipped to the floor, it seemed so right, being with Paul like this, that I could almost make myself believe it would last forever.

THIRTY-EIGHT

PAUL WAITED IN the garden, as he'd planned. He'd picked up a newspaper, the French *La Monde*, on our walk from the Westin. He'd also attracted the attention of two elderly French-speaking women. As I entered the garden, I saw the three of them in conversation and knew he was charming them. I took the opportunity to walk over to the vent I had examined the previous evening. The footprints I'd seen in the area had been wiped away.

Paul tore himself away from the women, or at least that was how it appeared to me. We went inside to the office where I turned in my key. The office worker who had never spoken three words to me was most gracious. She actually had a nice smile—I'd never seen it before—when she gazed at Paul. I shook my head and gave a little laugh after we left the office. Paul pretended not to know what I found amusing.

He'd brought the gift for his friend Salvatore, the book wrapped in brown paper. I said, "Let me take that. I'll carry it in my trusty tote bag."

He handed it to me and pushed open the heavy wooden doors. Before us, Varinia Santoro stood at the curb beside Carlo's wheelchair. The heavy-looking rucksack strapped to Varinia's back seemed strangely at odds with the fancy caftan over loose-fitting pants. Apparently she owned two such outfits, which she alternated. As we came closer, I saw that Carlo was almost hidden by a large duffle on his lap, like something from the military.

They were leaving.

I met the couple with a cheery *"Buon giorno,"* and Varinia returned a less enthusiastic greeting. I started to make introductions, but before Paul could work his charm, before he could even speak, Varinia's attention shifted to the taxi that came to a stop at the curb. The driver of the Fiat barely managed to emerge from the car before Varinia was crowding him, launching a verbal attack, with wild gestures, as she towered over him. It was an incredible thing to watch, the large woman's aggression, the way she intimidated the driver, who was not a small man, certainly not as small as Carlo. As quickly as he could, the driver managed to get back into the taxi and the car sped away, burning rubber, so to speak. I had to wonder if Varinia ever browbeat her husband like that.

I had figured out what the problem was, from her gestures, even before she said, "Fools! I asked for a taxi with a *lift*! How could they send such a car for a person in a chair?"

"Will the driver call for another taxi, one with a lift?" I asked. Not that anyone could expect the driver to be helpful, given the way she'd treated him.

Carlo muttered something. Varinia bent down, and they spoke for a minute. I glanced at Paul, but his expression— the attentive observer—gave nothing away. And the couple's exchange was scarcely more than a whisper. Perhaps they suspected that Paul understood Italian, and, indeed, he did.

Varinia straightened to her full height and adjusted the straps of her rucksack that dug into her shoulders.

She had to be carrying fifty pounds. "Carlo is afraid we will miss our train," she said. "I have pushed the chair all over Florence. *Santa Maria Novella* is not far. I can get us to *la stazione*."

With that load? I wondered, but I was more curious about why they were leaving today. I asked, "Weren't you planning to stay until Friday?"

She frowned, and I had the feeling she was trying to remember when she'd given me that information. She hadn't, of course. Ivonna had told me.

"We changed our minds," she said, and in that moment as we stared at each other, there was no doubt in my mind that she knew what I knew, and she knew that I knew there wasn't a thing I could do about it. With her lips curling in smugness, she said, "So we will say *Ciao*." She gave the chair a push, and it began to bump on the uneven surface of the *piazza*. Carlo tightened his grip on the duffle, pulling it even closer to him, and it occurred to me that the duffle *must* contain the stolen jewels. Either the duffle or the rucksack. My stomach sank at the possibility—the very real possibility—that these two were getting away with burglary and with murder, the murder of the poor man who'd happened to be in the wrong place when the burglary occurred.

"Varinia—why don't you let us call another taxi?" I called to her. It was a desperate attempt on my part to delay—but for what purpose, I couldn't have said. Nothing was going to change in the time it would take a taxi to arrive, yet I knew if they crossed the *piazza* and disappeared into the crowded street beyond, I'd never see them again.

"Please wait, *Madame*," Paul said, producing his phone from inside his jacket. "I will make the call."

Paul's voice triggered a peculiar reaction in Varinia. She stopped her furious pushing and jerked her head around to see Paul as if she'd suddenly realized that this impressive man who'd called her *Madame* might be someone with authority, someone she should fear. Not Italian. Not American. If she and Carlo were connected to the Camorra, she was sure to know of INTERPOL, headquartered in Lyon—but was I giving her too much credit? Those thoughts careened through my mind, as Paul's intense gaze held hers. And then she turned back to her task, without a response, and began to push the wheelchair with astonishing energy.

At the same time, I heard the sound of a motorscooter approaching and saw Eli coming toward us on his Vespa rental. He did not look like a biker. He raised his hand to wave at us, and the scooter wobbled. He leaned into a turn and stopped too close to us, grinning, having great fun—until I pointed and said in a hushed voice, "They're the jewel thieves! Do something! They're getting away!"

His expression transformed in an instant to all business. "You gotta be kidding!" he said, and he looked at Paul for confirmation.

"I think she is right," Paul said.

"Can you stop them? Maybe you can ask them some questions?" Again, I was grasping at anything to delay.

Eli didn't hesitate. He revved up the scooter, got his balance, and headed toward them. For a moment I thought he was going to run them down! Varinia had apparently heard him behind her. She looked around again, then turned back, pushing harder. I thought Carlo would spring out of the wheelchair, as it bounced along the irregular surface of old stones.

Eli pulled up beside them, passed them, turned the Vespa toward them, and leaned in. I saw what he was trying to do, a maneuver like so many cop shows where the squad car makes a swift turn and blocks another vehicle. But Varinia and the chair were flying. Eli didn't run into them. They ran into Eli. At the last moment, Varinia made an adjustment, but it was too little too late. She lost control, and the collision propelled Carlo and the duffle from the wheelchair. The Vespa turned over; Eli was thrown free. Varinia wavered for just one moment, and then she sprinted across the *piazza* without a backward glance.

Before Paul and I could reach him, Eli yelled, "Call the police!" But Paul was already on his phone. Though Eli's voice was thick with pain, maybe nothing was broken. He was scrambling to his feet. So was Carlo—scrambling. Nothing wrong with his feet or legs as he crawled to the wheelchair, which was damaged beyond repair.

And he was crying. Weeping. Wailing. Moaning something in Italian. Trying to scoop up something from the pavement.

It was a lot to take in, all in a matter of seconds. The little mustache barely hanging on. The high-pitched voice. The delicate facial bones. The eyes, more distinct now that his spectacles lay near the bent wheel of the chair. No wonder Carlo never let anyone get close, never looked anyone straight-on. Carlo was a woman.

That, I had not guessed. Nor had I ever imagined that the wheelchair had a particular purpose. The twisted chair lay on its side. The metal tubing had broken away from the arm rest, and out of it spilled brilliant rainbow colors, a cascade of jewels, shimmering in the sunlight.

THIRTY-NINE

THE WOMAN we knew only as Carlo made no attempt to escape. She sat on the hard stones of the *piazza* and wept until the *polizia* arrived. With each moment, each gesture, each sob, Carlo became more and more a woman. The way she wiped her eyes. The way she hugged herself. Even the way she rose to her feet. Watching as the police officer handcuffed her and put her in the back of a squad car, I had to marvel that she'd pulled off the masquerade as a man for so long. The wheelchair was a clever touch, indeed, for more reasons than one.

Eli had serious abrasions on his arm that I thought should be treated, and he was limping, but even though I expressed my opinion, as did Paul, and even though one of the officers suggested that he needed medical attention, Eli wouldn't hear of it. He was interested only in the news story. And what a scoop he had! Squad cars kept arriving, even after Carlo was taken away—cars of the *carabinieri* as well as the *polizia municipale*. Eli had explained, the night of Sophie's death, that both branches of Italian law enforcement often showed up at a crime scene and clashed over which one would take charge. That night the *carabinieri* had backed off. Just a suicide, they had concluded, nothing that demanded their skills. Today the men in *carabinieri* jackets held their ground. I didn't need to speak their language to get the gist of the heated conversations. Everyone in law enforcement seemed to be making and receiving calls.

Meanwhile, the *polizia municipale* put up crime scene tape around the wheelchair and the Vespa and around the jewels. No one dared to disturb the tiny precious rocks that had spilled out on the *piazza*, though the sparkling gems found their way into dozens of cellphone photos. Eventually someone came to take official crime scene photographs.

Eli was in the middle of all the commotion. When I saw him getting into the back of a squad car, I felt a surge of panic, fearing he was under arrest. Eli's own words—*Don't get yourself arrested in Italy*—echoed in my mind. But just before the policeman closed the car door, Eli gave us a wave and a wink, and I was sure he was telling us that this was what he wanted, a ride to the *questura*. He would give a statement, yes, but he'd be in a position to obtain much information for his own use.

Paul and I had kept our distance. We'd expressed wonder at the revelation that Carlo was a woman, and we'd speculated about where Varinia might have gone, but mostly we'd remained silent. Silent and watchful. I kept thinking I should tell someone what I knew about Carlo and Varinia. After a while, a uniformed officer approached us—approached Paul, actually—and said something in Italian. Paul showed his passport. A gesture from the policeman told me he wanted me to produce mine, as well, and I did. He took a few minutes to examine the passports, not just a cursory glance. I was getting a little nervous by the time he handed them back to us.

He asked Paul a question. I could tell by his inflection. He scribbled on a little notebook, apparently noting Paul's answer. He must have asked where we were staying because Paul said something about the Westin and *convento*. Another question. Paul said, "Carlo," and then turned to me. "Can you give the *gendarme* their names?"

"Carlo and Varinia Santoro are the names they used," I said.

A few more questions and answers. The policeman touched his cap, nodded, and left us.

"He wanted to know if we were witnesses to the accident." Paul smiled. "That was his word—*accident*—and of course neither Eli nor Varinia intended to crash. I told him what we saw, as innocent bystanders."

"Innocent bystanders?" I gave a little laugh and a shrug. "I guess you could say so."

"We were not involved." Paul was quite serious as he said it. "I told the *gendarme* that Eli was coming to meet us for lunch. I told him that you were staying in the convent, as were Carlo and Varinia Santoro."

"I need to tell someone how Carlo gained access to the building and used the mechanical shaft to climb up to the third floor," I said. "The muddy footprints are evidence. I took photos outside, which is a good thing, because those prints have been wiped away. But maybe Luigi didn't get rid of the footprints inside the access door on my floor, next to Carlo and Varinia's room." I sounded a little breathless. A little manic. No wonder Paul had raised his eyebrows. I couldn't quite read him, but he wasn't reacting the way I expected. I wanted him to agree that what I had discovered was a critical piece of evidence, and the police should be informed.

But he didn't. "The jewels have been recovered," he said. "Carlo has been arrested. I think he—*she*—will quickly confess, judging from the tears. And Eli will fill in the blanks, as they say. I think it is all over, and you don't have to be involved."

"Eli doesn't know about the footprints," I said. "I never got a chance to tell him."

Paul's sigh seemed a bit longsuffering. "Ah, Jordan," he said.

And then a black SUV screeched to a halt, not more than twenty feet from us. Chief Inspector Eleanora de Rosa emerged from the vehicle, along with three men, all four of them looking very officious. She made the rounds, speaking to the men—not a female in the bunch—then bending down to get a closer look at the jewels, without crossing the yellow tape.

Apparently, the jewels had made this a high-profile crime, worthy of the Chief Inspector's attention.

"I'll tell *her*," I said. I didn't wait to find out whether Paul approved or not. I took several steps toward Chief Inspector de Rosa, but I didn't get too close. A uniformed officer gave me the evil eye. I put on my best smile for him and waited until the Chief Inspector stood up straight. She turned around and met my gaze.

I felt Paul's arm brush against mine. He had come up beside me, and it occurred to me that *he* was probably the reason Chief Inspector Eleanora de Rosa was walking toward us.

"Signora Mayfair," she said. At least she'd remembered my name. I tried not to make too much of her tone. She may as well have said, "*And here you are again.*"

But her gaze did not linger on me.

I made introductions. "Chief Inspector," Paul said, with a deferential nod.

"Signor Broussard, are you part of the *Signora*'s investigation into the young woman's suicide?" she said. I appreciated that she was speaking English. Maybe she didn't know Paul spoke Italian and she may not have been fluent in French.

"I must confess that I have provided very little assistance, but Jordan has proven herself quite capable without my help," Paul said, with the smile that was, as always, charming.

"You should not waste your time on that case," the Chief Inspector said, "either of you," and she cut her eyes at me, scolding, or maybe warning.

"I do not doubt the case is in good hands," Paul said, his manner still amiable, almost teasing. I didn't consider it flirtatious. Maybe it was a European thing, this little banter. "But you may be surprised to know what Jordan can tell you about this one," he said, indicating the crime scene.

Chief Inspector de Rosa's large dark eyes betrayed her. A flicker of curiosity appeared—and then it was gone. But I had my cue, and I took it. I told her about the mechanical shaft. I showed her the photo on my phone of the muddy footprints outside the decorative vent in the courtyard. I told her about the footprints Luigi had discovered inside the access door that was just a few steps from Carlo and Varinia Santoro's room. I explained that Luigi's keys had been stolen during a mugging, and one key would have given Carlo access to the mechanical shaft, while another would have opened the gate to the courtyard. "Though Carlo could have scaled the wall," I said. "I expect the duffle bag has all the equipment a cat burglar needs." I remembered I wasn't supposed to know that a cat burglar had committed the Oltrarno burglaries, so I added. "Carlo would have to be a cat burglar, don't you think, to climb up the mechanical shaft?"

She gave me a long, hard look. She studied me for what seemed like a full minute, and then she took action, barking orders, all around. "You will make a statement at the *questura*, yes?" she said to me, but I don't think I had a choice. Without waiting for me to agree, she ordered someone to bring a squad car around for Paul and me.

Paul glanced at his watch, and I knew he was thinking about the birthday party for the old artist, but there wasn't anything we could do about it now.

The Chief Inspector, flanked by an entourage of law enforcement officials, headed toward the big wooden door of the convent. Paul and I, in the back seat of squad car, headed to the *questura*.

IT TOOK A WHILE. Though I was not charged with a crime, was not even a suspect in a crime, I couldn't help feeling that this was a genuine interrogation. A detective, who spoke excellent English, took my statement and followed with questions of his own. My heart was fluttering through it all, as I tried to explain clearly what I knew and how I had come to know it. After more than an hour, he let me go with a pleasant smile and even thanked me for my assistance.

Paul had spent less time with another detective in another cubicle—"twenty minutes, perhaps," he said, when I asked. "I had little to offer, as an innocent by-stander." True, Paul didn't have as much to tell as I did, but I suspected his air of authority was an advantage I didn't have. He'd given his statement, and that was that. I'd had to prove myself. In the end, though, I believed the detective considered me a credible witness, not a crazy, wannabe sleuth.

Paul summoned the car he had hired on other occasions, and we headed for Fiesole. Given that we hadn't taken time for lunch, we weren't too much behind schedule. We'd have a little while to fritter away in Fiesole. Paul, who often seemed to be reading my mind, said, "If you like, we can get something to eat in the town."

"I'm sure there will be food at the party," I said. "Cake, at least."

"Cake and plenty of wine," Paul said. "You still have the gift, I hope."

I patted my tote bag and felt the rectangle that was the art book.

The narrow walled road began winding up, up, up, past stands of straight, skinny cypress trees. Paul took on the role of tour guide, such a natural role for him. He pointed out an ancient Dominican monastary and recited the history of a famous quarry, where stones were excavated for the buildings in the ancient town. The driver stopped a couple of times to give us panoramic views of Florence. He let us out in the main square. He would wait in the vicinity until we needed him to meet us, after the party.

Fiesole was a pleasant little town, with a *duomo* prominent in the *piazza*. A tour bus pulled in behind a hop-on, hop-off bus, and while Paul and I were deciding where we might go before time for the party, twenty or more tourists filed out of the bus. They were chattering, and I recognized English, the way Americans speak English. On another day I might have been interested in knowing where they were from.

Paul had mentioned the Roman theatre, an amphi-

theater that had been restored in the archaeological area
that included other ruins. It sounded like something an
architect should see, but when I heard the tour guide say
that the archaeological area was not a long walk, Paul
and I exchanged a look that said we'd rather stay clear
of tours this afternoon. I was glad he felt the same way.

"The Villa Medici has wonderful gardens, spectacular views," he said. I hesitated, and he said, "If you
like, we can have a glass of wine or a coffee at one of
the little cafés."

"Do you mind?" I asked.

"Of course not. I enjoy showing you the historical and architectural sites, but I have seen them all.
Whatever you like," he said. "It's not long now until we
should make our appearance at Salvatore's birthday."
He smiled, and I believed him. The party was what he
cared about. As for me, I was still trying to process
what I'd learned about Carlo and Varinia.

We found a small table just outside a café. We had
just started in on our wine, glasses filled to about two
fingers, of course, when Paul's phone chirped. He answered, said, "Eli! Where are you? We didn't see you
at the *questura*," and turned on the speaker function
so I could hear.

"I didn't stay there long," Eli said. "Gave my statement about the crash. Just the facts. I didn't get into *everything* I knew." Paul gave a wry smile. That was what
he had done, of course.

"I've been at my hotel, pounding the keys," Eli went
on. "My source at the *questura* won't talk in person. He
likes to call from the men's room, I think. So here's
the thing. *Breaking news!*" he said, mocking a news-
caster's voice.

Carlo had confessed, had been fingerprinted, and had given up Varinia. The two had been pulling off burglaries in Italy for months, and, as Eli had suspected, the burglaries were connected to the Cammora. "Carlo is Carlotta Raimondi, and she *is* married to Varinia." Eli paused for effect. "Varinia is Vicente Raimondi."

FORTY

IT SHOULDN'T HAVE been such a shock, given that we already knew Carlo was a woman. But I hadn't seen it coming. Varinia—Vicente—had played his part just as effectively as Carlotta had played hers. Both had criminal records for petty crimes. Eli said that in each new town, they came up with a different disguise. Once Carlotta had been Vicente's daughter. Another time they had pretended to be female cousins. The only consistent element was the wheelchair. As I listened to Eli, I could only shake my head.

"Once it all came out that they were looking for Vicente Raimondi," Eli said, "the police had no trouble finding him at the train station. He'd ditched the wig and the dress and cleaned off the make-up. Looked like a regular guy, I guess, but they had his mug shot. My source said he was standing at the tracks, about to board a southbound train, looking like he didn't have a care."

"Or trying to," I said, finally finding my voice. "Playing a part."

"The two should have been in show business," Paul said, with a half-smile.

I hadn't been amused by any of it, but Eli's hearty laugh came from the speaker and Paul's smile broadened, and I realized that there was, indeed, something comical about the charade the pair had pulled off. The part that wasn't funny, of course, was the death of an innocent man who had been sleeping in the shop that Carlotta robbed.

And then I thought of Sophie. Did these two push her out of her window because she knew—or they thought she knew—what they were doing? There was still the locked room. Unless they simply confessed to her murder, and that wasn't likely, we would never know.

Some distance from us, a motorscooter passed through the *piazza*, not going very fast. I thought of Florence, the streets full of scooters and bikes. Not so, here in Fiesole. I remembered the crash, just a few hours ago though it seemed much longer, the frightening moment Eli was thrown from the Vespa. I asked him, "Are you going to the doctor?"

"Me? Nah. Somebody cleaned and wrapped my arm at the *questura*. I have some pain pills I'll take when I can sleep. Miles to go, yet. I was lucky. I'll say that." Eli chuckled. "Small price to pay for the story I got."

Paul and I left the café a few minutes later. It was a nice walk through quiet, narrow streets to our destination, a fifteen-minute stroll. Salvatore's unpretentious house was in a row of other similar ones, two-story stucco with red tile roofs. A cluster of balloons, all different colors, was tied to the wrought-iron fence at the gate.

At the nearby cross street, another motorscooter appeared—or was it the same one we'd seen in the *piazza*? Practically creeping at first, the Vespa accelerated noisily when the driver, clad in bikers' black boots, pants, jacket, and full-face helmet, saw that I was looking. A chill traveled down my spine. But Paul gave no indication that he'd noticed the scooter. He opened the wrought-iron gate, and we made our way along the cobblestone path. "May I have the gift?" he said.

I took the brown package from my tote bag and handed it to him. The front door flew open and two small boys came running into the yard. Strains of harp music drifted from inside.

Nothing amiss here. It was a party! I could just hear Alex saying, "I hope you're not going to start imagining some sort of intrigue, Jordan, as you have been known to do."

IF SALVATORE CORSINI was not absolutely delighted with the first edition art book that featured his early mosaic, his ability as an actor surely rivaled his talents as an artist. A big tear rolled down each cheek into his neatly-trimmed white beard. He made no effort to wipe them away. His wife, Nicola, was one of those Italian beauties who looked to be the age of his granddaughters—mid-forties was my guess. She tried to dab at his tears with a tissue, but he pushed her hand away. He sat the entire time, a plump little man who wouldn't have measured five-foot-two, standing. Someone pulled a chair beside him for Paul and one for me, and someone else brought us exquisitely-painted goblets of excellent wine, and not just two fingers' worth. After a few minutes of being polite, I left the men to talk, Salvatore holding Paul's hand in both of his wizened old hands.

Paul had said "small party" but in my imagination, an Italian ninetieth birthday celebration would be a big, lively party. There were platters of *antipasti* and *bruschetta* and plenty of wine. The music was splendid. But it was low-key. As I wandered around, meeting the guests, I decided that everyone except Paul and me was family. Salvatore's seven children by three wives—none by Nicola—were present, along with their children and grandchildren. One young woman, married to Salvatore's great-grandson, was nursing a baby, so there was at least one great-great-grandchild. Even the harpist was a granddaughter, a teacher at the Fiesole School of Music. I learned much of the family history from a stylish woman who reminded me of Angelica Moretti. I was admiring a large mosaic that extended most of the length of the hall when the woman came out of the bathroom and struck up a conversation with me.

"What do you think of it?" she asked.

"Extraordinary," I said. It was a wedding scene, people, birds, flowers, and butterflies, created with what had to be a million tiny tiles. Having seen the photo of that other mosaic in the art book, I had the impression that this was from the same period, and the woman confirmed.

"It was a wedding gift to me, but when we divorced, I told Salvatore I did not want it. I'm sorry for that now." She introduced herself as "the second wife, Serafina, the mother of four of his children. I have the record for the longest marriage to Salvatore, eighteen years." I managed to say my name before she told me that Paul Broussard had been a frequent visitor to their house when she was married to Salvatore, and she always hoped he would marry their daughter, but the daughter was happily married to a plastic surgeon who kept her beautiful, so all had ended well.

Serafina was a wellspring of information that I did not need, but she was entertaining. My impression, from her gossip, was that Salvatore's family were all congenial with each other, and the more delicious the scandal that might erupt about one of them, the more they all enjoyed it.

Back in the midst of the party, Serafina stuck with me. Nicola joined us for a minute and told me, "It is the best birthday for Salvatore because his friend Paul is here." Her English was hesitant, which may have been the reason she seemed shy. Or it could have been that Serafina's personality simply overshadowed hers.

"Would you like to see Salvatore's studio?" Serafina said, and without waiting for my answer, she said, "Nicola, please bring the key."

And that was how I got a private tour of Salvatore Corsini's studio. A separate building behind the house, opposite a small, elegant courtyard, the studio contained what must have been a hundred pieces of art, all sizes. Spectacular mosaics that represented the life's work of the old artist. Something about the deeply personal nature of Salvatore's art made me wish Paul was my tour guide, not Serafina.

Paul and I said our goodbyes soon after the cake was served. Family members were leaving, too. There would be no big Italian meal, even for family. Paul closed the wrought-iron gate behind us and we began to walk back the way we had come. It was still light, a pleasant walk, but cooler than before. The party had lasted only about an hour and a half.

"Is everything all right?" I asked Paul, who seemed unusually quiet.

He said, "I do not think my friend has long to live. He didn't speak of an illness, but he no longer goes to his studio. He said, 'I am very tired.'"

"He's ninety years old," I said. "He has earned the right to be tired."

"I always imagined him dancing, laughing, drinking wine, working furiously! Defying old age until one day he was just—gone." Paul smiled. "I didn't imagine what old age would look like on Salvatore."

Our conversation made me think of Alex, the person who, in my mind, would always defy old age, and I felt a stab of guilt that I hadn't been in touch with him all day. He was supposed to come back to the convent today—wasn't he? With all that had happened since we'd spoken yesterday, I couldn't remember exactly how we left things. I dug my phone out of the depths of my tote bag and checked for a message or a missed call, but there was no sign that he'd tried to reach me.

"I need to call Alex," I said.

"I will call our driver," Paul said.

We moved apart a few steps while we each made our calls.

Alex answered and sounded perfectly chipper. He was back at the convent, and I had told him I was going to a party with Paul this afternoon, so he hadn't been expecting me to call. "Is the party over already?" he said. "I thought Italian parties lasted all night and into the morning."

"I'll tell you all about it," I said. "I wish you could have seen this man's studio."

The noise came upon us so fast that I barely had time to turn and see the motorscooter speeding toward us. Toward me. I heard, as much as I felt, the bump. I was aware that my feet had left the ground and my phone had flown into the sky.

FORTY-ONE

THROUGH IT ALL, I was conscious, but there was a gauzy quality to reality.

I was aware of Paul's voice, mostly reassuring, but when he spoke in Italian—on the phone, calling for an ambulance, and then to the paramedics when they arrived—he sounded anxious, even apprehensive. I couldn't tell how seriously I was hurt. Something hurt. One whole side of me hurt. Eli had walked away from his accident, but when I tried to move, Paul touched my shoulders and I knew he wanted me to lie still. Funny— I think he was speaking to me in French. In my next coherent thought, emergency personnel were lifting me onto a gurney. I gathered from the agitated voices that they didn't want Paul to ride with us, but he did.

And then an oxygen mask went over my nose and mouth, for the duration of the trip. I needed to speak, but I couldn't seem to shape thoughts into words anyway, so I closed my eyes and tried to will all the spinning in my brain to settle down. It wasn't long to a medical facility that must have been just outside of Fiesole. "I'll be close by," Paul said, as we made our way down a corridor, and a moment later a couple of nurses and a doctor were taking care of me. My clothes, torn and splotched with blood, were ruined. I thought I must be near-dead, to get so much attention, but it was soon apparent that they just weren't busy at the little medical center.

Eventually I realized I was not near-dead. I got my wits back enough to talk with the doctor. He asked where I lived, and I was able to tell him. He knew of Savannah, having trained at Emory University Hospital in Atlanta. Maybe he was trying to distract me, telling me how he'd owned a motorbike during his time in Atlanta and he'd been in a similar accident, but he hadn't caused it. He was struck by a Range Rover as he maneuvered his motorbike in traffic.

No broken bones, the x-rays confirmed. "You have some nasty bruises and abrasions," the doctor said, "but you will be all right. You were fortunate."

My left hip and thigh ached, but the stinging pain was worse—my left arm, all the way down to my hand where the skin had peeled away when my body skidded along the ground. A couple of pain pills later, I began to drift off. I asked for Paul. The pretty young nurse said, "Rest for a little while, and the *signore* can take you home."

PAUL WAS SITTING in a chair beside my bed, reading a newspaper, when I awoke some time later. I couldn't say how much later. When I moved, I groaned, and he looked up. Standing over me then, he reached for my hand—my right hand, the one not bandaged—and bent to kiss it.

"I was very worried," he said, still holding my hand. I nodded.

"They tell me you will be fine." He brought my hand to his cheek and held it there for a minute.

"Alex?" I said. "I was on the phone with Alex."

"We have been texting all along, and we have spoken, also," Paul said. "Incredibly, your phone still works."

"Alex must be worried."

"Naturally. He wanted to be here, but I convinced him to wait until I knew more. And then I told him that you will not need to stay." Paul smiled, as if remembering their conversation. "You can call him in the car. I think relief will come to him only when he hears your voice."

I shivered. The exam room was cool—typical— and my hospital gown was thin. Paul covered my arms and pulled the sheet up to my chin, but it offered little warmth. He rang for a nurse, and she brought a blanket. She also left a bottle of water and a cup. "After the doctor sees you again, if you are feeling well enough, he will let you go," she said, on her way out.

"Is that better?" Paul asked, adjusting the blanket, very attentive.

I nodded, closed my eyes, and tried to shut out the scene that kept replaying in my mind. A minute passed, or more. Time was fuzzy. When I opened my eyes, Paul was still standing over me, and he seemed to pick up where we'd left off. "I sent the driver to buy something for you to wear. Your clothes"—he made a face that would have said everything, but I already knew about my clothes. "It is late, but he was resourceful. He went to one of the hotels and found this in the gift shop."

Paul picked up a bag from beside his chair, pulled out a white velour robe, and laid it across the blanket. I pulled my hand—my good one—out from under the covers and touched the soft material. Very plush. Paul showed me a pair of ballet house slippers to go with the robe, though he assured me that my strappy sandals were not ruined.

"You've taken very good care of me," I said.

He smoothed out a wrinkle on the robe, a surprisingly domestic kind of gesture for Paul Broussard. "I only wish I could have prevented this terrible thing. I still can't believe it happened—or understand why."

"Have you talked to the police?"

"Of course. I will not rest until they find the person who did this."

I asked him to raise the head of my bed and put the pillows behind me to prop me up. He poured some water for me. I was sure that anything Paul could do for me, he would do—which made it that much harder for me to say what I had to say.

"Paul, it was Bella."

He drew in a sharp breath. "Bella?"

"It was Bella on the Vespa." My throat was trying to close, but I couldn't stop now. "I think she was trying to kill me."

"Impossible, Jordan! You are mistaken!"

"Paul, I saw the sapphire bracelet."

The color drained from his face. His shock was genuine, no doubt about that. The bracelet he had given Bella was distinctive. A minute passed, frozen silence. And then there was that moment when something changed between us. His resolve took over. I saw it in the set of his jaw and heard it in his voice. "Bella is in Cortona," he said. "I spoke with her last night when I was in the car, before I reached the convent. She was regretful that today would be her last day in Cortona. She plans to return to Florence tomorrow. You and Bella have not had the friendship I had hoped, but you must know she would not do such a thing."

I hadn't imagined she'd go so far as to try to kill me, but now I believed that she would, indeed, do such a thing. And I could see how she managed it. Paul would

have told her that we would be in Fiesole at the birthday
party. She took a train to Florence—maybe a late one
last night—rented the Vespa this morning, and came to
Fiesole to wait for us. All the puzzle pieces came into
place in my mind, but I couldn't shape the words. All
I could say was, "The bracelet. That moment just before she hit me—she might have wanted me to see it."
It was an image burned in my mind. I felt the grimace
on my face, as I remembered.

Paul hesitated, as if he had to let my words sink in. But
then he gave one of those quintessential shrugs. "You are
imagining these things. I understand, Jordan, that you
have been through a terrible ordeal, and the pain medi-
cine may have made you dream this—this scenario."

True, I was a little woozy, but I was dead-sure that
it was Bella on the Vespa.

Even if Bella hadn't seen us in the main square, she
would have waited near Salvatore's home. How hard
could it be to find the studio of the famous Salvatore
Corsini? Anyone in Fiesole would be able to give her
directions. I wanted Paul to understand, but while I was
still trying to say the words, the door opened, and the
doctor entered, with the pretty nurse behind him. He
gave us a cheery greeting and asked how I was feeling.

"Ready to go home," I said. Home to Savannah was
what I really meant.

The doctor checked my chart, listened to my heart,
pronounced me fit to leave, and said goodbye. Paul went
to summon the driver. The nurse helped me dress, gave
me some written instructions and a little bottle of magic
pills that I was sure I would be glad to have. Another
nurse came with a wheelchair, much like the one that
had been used to transport jewels.

In the car, I called Alex first thing.

"I can't take you anywhere," he said, after I had convinced him that I was all right.

"Seems that way," I said.

He had questions that Paul had not answered to his satisfaction. I said, "I'll tell you all about it at breakfast. Don't worry about me. I'll see you in a few minutes. We're on our way to the convent now."

Paul's slight frown told me he hadn't planned to take me to the convent. An awkward moment passed after I had ended my call to Alex, before Paul said, just above a whisper, because we had no privacy from the driver, "Jordan, won't you come to the Westin? I want to be sure you have what you need. If you will be more comfortable in your own room, I will arrange it. At least I will be nearby if you will go to the hotel."

I was tempted. And I wouldn't have wanted my own room. I would want to lie next to Paul, sleep and wake with him beside me. But I couldn't pretend nothing had changed with us.

"I'm a mess," I said. "I need my own clothes. Maybe with some time alone, I can figure things out that seem so confusing."

He didn't ask what things. He didn't make any further case for the Westin, and I would have been astonished if Paul Broussard had done anything but what he did.

He told the driver to go to *Convento di Santa Francesca Firenze.*

FORTY-TWO

ALL I WANTED was sleep.

Alex had met me downstairs and insisted on seeing me to my room. It was probably a good idea. I was wobbling a bit. I give him credit; he didn't ask a single question about how this had happened, who was responsible, or why—nothing. He accepted my promise that I would tell him everything at breakfast.

Paul had left me with only a request that I call him in the morning—or if I needed him for anything before then—and a light kiss on the cheek.

I dug my scarred but functional phone out of my tote bag and put it next to my bed, within easy reach. The display of the time showed 11:42 p.m. The written instructions from the nurse indicated I could have two more pain pills at midnight. Close enough. I washed my face, brushed my teeth, took the pills, managed to change into pajamas, and crawled into bed.

Maybe I thought the meds would knock me out and I would wake in the morning feeling, if not brand new, pretty good. I'd never had much experience with painkillers. It was a strange night. At times I felt I was sinking into a deep, black hole, and at other times bizarre scenes played in my mind that could have been actual or imagined. Once I thought I heard voices and I went to my door, opening it to see Varinia in the hall. I called to her, and she ran, and then I woke to the knowledge that I'd been in my bed the whole time. But it seemed so real!

All night, I kept being pulled in and out of that eerie dream world. The numbers on the face of my phone told me I was awake almost every hour, but it took several attempts for me to stay awake long enough to get myself up and across the hall to the bathroom, something I should have done before going to bed. And then, somehow, I found myself on the other end of the hall, in front of Sophie's door. I don't know how long I stood there before I realized that something else had invaded my dreams. I knew what had happened to Sophie. I had the solution to the locked door murder.

Stumbling like a drunk, I made my way back to my room, to my bed. A moment later I was sinking again into a troubled sleep, but, in what seemed like no time at all, my phone was jingling. I managed a hoarse answer. It was Alex, making sure I was all right, wondering if I was able to come down to breakfast. It was eight-thirty.

I told him I could be there a few minutes before nine, before the unsmiling woman would close the doors of the breakfast room. Dragging myself out of bed, I realized that recovery was going to take a while longer than I'd thought and tried to remember where I'd put my pain pills.

And then I had a flashback of something during the night, a dream, fully realized as I'd stood in the hall in front of Sophie's room. There had been a moment when I knew how the murder was accomplished, had the solution right there in my grasp, but for the life of me, I couldn't remember what I'd figured out.

THE PICKINGS WERE SLIM in the breakfast room, but I wasn't all that hungry. I had toast and jam. Alex had the cereal that looked like a version of Rice Krispies, the only cereal option left. The fruit was gone. We both had coffee, and plenty of it. The *Caffe Lungo* had run out but Alex brought me something else that did the trick. The strong brew was as black as tar, and, after all, the caffeine was what mattered. He'd filled our cups to the brim.

The staff and the few guests that remained in the breakfast room at closing time looked at me with more curiosity than sympathy. Just one woman ventured to ask what had happened to me. I was sure that was what she asked, though she spoke Italian. I said, "Vespa," and that apparently told the story. She nodded and said something else that I gathered, from her kind manner, was some expression of compassion. I said, *"Grazie,"* and it seemed to be the appropriate response.

Alex first asked about my injuries, and I assured him that although I probably looked terrible, I was mostly sore. He might have told me I *didn't* look terrible, but I wouldn't have believed him. More worrisome to me than my bruised hip and thigh was my arm, where it would take a while to get back that layer of skin. The thought of changing the bandages made me a little queasy, and I pushed back the plate with half a slice of toast on it.

"Maybe you aren't ready to be up and about yet," Alex said.

"I'll go back to bed in a little while," I said. "You've been patient. I have a lot to tell."

And I told him. I spared nothing, not even Paul's reaction when I'd identified Bella as the Vespa rider. Alex adjusted his glasses a couple of times, trying to be a good listener, but his brow furrowed, and I sensed he experienced, vicariously, the pain and fear I'd felt. I was reminded that my uncle was my advocate, always. My deep, noisy sigh signaled the end of my recitation, and even then, Alex didn't speak, but he reached across the table with his palm up, inviting me to put my hand in his. I did, and he squeezed. It was like a shot of energy.

"I would never have accused Bella if I hadn't been sure, absolutely, one-hundred percent certain. You know that, Alex. Didn't Paul know that? No one else who owns a sapphire bracelet would have any reason to run me down!" I said, my voice wavering. I blinked and blinked again. I was not going to cry! "It's just as well this way," I declared. "I'm going home tomorrow."

"Paul wouldn't want to think his daughter was capable of such violence, but I expect he'll come around," Alex said, sounding more like a professor now than an affectionate uncle.

He withdrew his hand from mine and picked up his cup.

"Am I being ridiculous?" I asked. "I've tried to get past the stunts Bella pulled at the Moretti Villa, accusing me of making her fall on the construction site and then accusing me of stealing her precious bracelet. But this—this was an attempt on my life. I can't just let it go."

Alex, still holding his cup in both hands, gave a firm answer. "No, you are not being ridiculous."

"But should I go to the police? I'd have to go to Fiesole today."

Alex waited a moment before he said, "I would hope Paul will follow through."

"I don't think he will," I said. I reached for my half-eaten toast and took another hearty bite. I wasn't queasy anymore. My anger had restored my appetite.

We were silent for a moment, and Alex went back to refill our cups. Most everything but the coffee had been taken away. "These Vespas! Two incidents with motorscooters in one day," Alex said, when he was back at the table. In one of their calls while I was getting medical attention in Fiesole, Paul had informed Alex about Eli's collision with the wheelchair, about the jewels that spilled out, solving that crime, and about the revelation that Carlo and Varinia were Carlotta and Vicente. As we lingered over our coffee, we talked about the Moretti family, too. It seemed like a kind of "debriefing," a way of winding up our time in Florence, trying to make sense of it all. But we still didn't know how to make sense of Sophie's death.

Alex and I were the last to leave the breakfast room. I was heading straight to my bed. Alex said he'd be working in his room, and I promised to call if I needed anything.

I was supposed to call Paul, too. I would, but I wanted my head to be clear when we spoke. I was feeling the effects of the meds I'd taken a little more than an hour ago. The caffeine I'd consumed had not served its purpose.

I fell into the same kind of drugged sleep as before. Varinia and Carlo took over my crazy dreams. I hadn't yet incorporated the personae of Carlotta and Vicente into my consciousness. Carlo did wheelies with the wheelchair, and jewels spilled out, making a glittering river in our hallway. Varinia undressed, down to a sleeveless leotard and tights. Carlo jumped out of the chair and began to dance. Musicians paraded through the hall. Someone carried a paper lantern on a pole. A string of motorscooters frightened me, and I called for Paul, but he was nowhere to be found. And then I saw Varinia at Sophie's door, standing with feet planted wide apart, arms braced against the door jamb, palms flat, shoulder muscles rippling. Carlo scampered like a monkey up Varinia's back and tossed something through the open transom.

I bolted up in bed, let out a groan and grabbed my bandaged arm, which I'd swung about too freely. When the pain had subsided, I reached for my phone and called Paul.

"I'M GLAD TO hear your voice, Jordan," Paul said. Nice words but without the warmth I'd come to expect in his voice.

"Paul, I need your help. I know how Sophie was murdered," I said.

"*Mon Dieu!* Tell me!" That was the Paul I knew, and I felt a rush of shame, knowing that even as I considered reporting his daughter to the Fiesole police, I had to call on him now, in this other matter. It was the only way, the only chance that I could get justice for Sophie.

"I need you to ask Chief Inspector de Rosa to come back to the convent," I said.

The sound Paul made was something like *Ha!* "Do you think I can persuade her, in a decision about one of her cases? You give me too much credit, Jordan."

"I *know* you can persuade her," I said. "I would go to her, myself, and plead with her, but it wouldn't work. She thinks I involve myself too much in things that aren't my business."

And maybe I do, I could have added, but no one else is trying to solve Sophie's murder.

"You told her about the mechanical shaft," Paul said. "You provided evidence."

"Maybe she simply didn't get a chance to say thank you," I said.

I wasn't sure Paul appreciated my sarcasm. He said, "I spoke with her just one time, yesterday. My statement, at the *questura*, was that of a tourist who saw the Vespa and wheelchair collide, and nothing more. Why would the Chief Inspector believe I can provide valuable information about activities in the convent, where I am not staying?"

"I know women, and I have a good sense of that particular woman," I said. "She'll listen to you."

A moment's hesitation, and then, "I want to help. I do, Jordan. You have a big heart, and you believe with your whole heart that Sophie was murdered. But what you are asking me to do—I will need to offer more than simply a pleasant request."

"More than just charm. I know." I was smiling now. "You can tell the Chief Inspector that I can show her forensics people where to check for fingerprints. I know how the key got into the locked room."

"Are you sure?"

I couldn't say I was positively sure. I couldn't say that a dream had led me to the solution. This wasn't the same as my absolute certainty that Bella was riding the Vespa and that she deliberately ran me down. I said, "Can't you just trust me, Paul?"

"That is not the point," he said, and then, with an air of formality, "I will do what I can."

"Paul—thank you. This is for Sophie," I said, but I think he was already gone.

FORTY-THREE

THEY CAME. A couple of *polizia*, and the detective in sharp-toed boots that I remembered from the morning he had removed Sophie's personal effects. I heard their voices in the hall.

It was after one o'clock. I'd been trying to clean up, hard to do with my bandaged arm that I couldn't get wet. I couldn't take a proper shower, but I'd managed a sponge bath. Even washed my hair in the sink, one-handed. Fresh clothes, make-up, I was as good as I would get today. No more pain pills, if I could get by without them. I went into the hall and saw Ivonna.

She rushed toward me. "I heard what happened to you!" She clasped her hands and seemed to search for words, but gave a little cry instead. What was there to say, after all?

"I'm all right," I said. "I need to tell them where to look for fingerprints."

Ivonna's eyes widened. I suppose I did sound too self-important. "You called for them? They didn't say anything except to tell me I should unlock the door to room 12."

I would have explained, but there wasn't time to fill her in. "This may prove that Sophie was murdered," I said, at the door of what had been her room. I saw the techies at the window, preparing to dust around it, I presumed. That wasn't going to get them what they needed.

The detective heard us and came to the door. "You have a room on the hall," he said, studying my bandaged arm, as if deciding whether to ask. He remembered me from that first encounter but if he knew I'd had any part in getting them to come back, he gave no clue.

"The door was locked from the outside, but the key was found inside, on Sophie's bed," I said. "I know how it was done."

He gave me a hard look. I wondered what his instructions had been.

And then I heard the voice of Chief Inspector Eleanora de Rosa, coming from the direction of the elevator. Something I couldn't make out, and a husky laugh. Beside her, Paul. He'd apparently come with her from the *questura*, having done exactly what I asked. Even so, I couldn't ignore the fact that the two made a handsome couple.

"Ah, *Signora*, I was sorry to hear about your misfortune," she said, with more irony than sympathy as she glanced at my bandaged arm. Someone like myself who meddled in criminal matters was bound to get hurt, her tone seemed to indicate.

"How are you feeling, Jordan?" Paul came closer to me and regarded me with—pity? Was that what I saw? I hoped not. Maybe just kindness. I wasn't sure what I wanted from him.

"Much better," I said. I thanked both of them for making this happen—and so quickly.

"Monsieur Broussard puts much faith in your theory, *Signora*. He is very persuasive." Eleanora de Rosa paused for a significant beat. "I agree you were helpful in showing how the jewel thief disappeared into the convent after each burglary. You leave Florence tomorrow, yes? So if you can prove to us that this suicide is actually a murder, it must be today, yes?"

Patronizing as she was, she was giving me a chance. Paul's charms were exceptional, but I couldn't believe the Chief Inspector would have engaged the *polizia*'s resources today if Paul's appeal hadn't ignited something that was already there. Maybe she'd had her own misgivings about the way the investigation was handled. Maybe she'd had to admit that it was suspicious for Sophie to make plans to meet Cristiano and then decide to kill herself.

"The locked door has always pointed to a suicide," I said, "but the murderers could have come out into the hall, locked the door, and then they were able to get the key back inside, through the transom." I pointed up, to where the glass was angled open.

The Chief Inspector looked up. "They?" she asked.

"We knew them as Carlo and Varinia."

"The jewel thieves? But what reason did they have to harm the girl? Do you believe she was part of their criminal activities?" I took note that de Rosa's question sounded genuine.

"No, nothing like that. I think Sophie saw too much." I explained the exchange between Varinia and Sophie that made me believe, in hindsight, that Sophie had seen Carlo coming from the access door. "Though she knew nothing about the jewels, if Sophie knew Carlo was not wheelchair-bound, Carlo and Varinia couldn't have that."

"That is speculation. The girl is dead. She cannot tell us. You have not explained about the fingerprints that you offer as proof." The Chief Inspector was growing a little impatient.

"I think you'll find Varinia's—Vicente's—fingerprints on the door frame." I moved into the doorway and showed how Vicente would have set his feet against the door jamb. I raised my right arm and spread my fingers, holding my hand a few inches away from the frame, not to leave my prints. I couldn't raise my left arm.

"Let me," Paul said.

I moved back and Paul took my place. He was about the same height as Vicente, his shoulders broad and strong, like Vicente's. As he stood in that position, though his outstretched hands weren't touching the wood, he provided a powerful image that indicated where Vicente's prints might be. "Carlotta was small and agile. It was nothing for her to climb upon Vicente's back, onto his shoulders, and toss the key through the open transom," I said, suppressing a smile as I thought of my dream. "I climbed up on the caretaker's ladder myself and checked the angle. I saw how the key could land on Sophie's bed."

Chief Inspector de Rosa appeared stunned. I wasn't sure whether she was astonished that I'd climbed on Luigi's ladder or that I'd actually figured out what had happened.

Our silence must have told Paul that he could end his demonstration. He moved from the door frame. He came to stand beside me and gave me one of his trade-mark smiles.

The detective had listened to all that was said, but he waited until de Rosa spoke to him, and then he called to the other *polizia*—all in Italian, but I could follow. They came to the door jamb and began to work with their kits. We moved further into the hall. The Chief Inspector mused, "I do not think we will find the cat burglar's fingerprints. She would have known to wear gloves, not to leave her prints on the metal of the key ring. But if the man's fingerprints prints are where you say, it will be interesting to hear his explanation."

That was my thought, but I didn't see the need to add my comments.

She said something else to her detective, and then turned to Paul. "I will go now. Are you coming with me? We can take you to your hotel, if you wish."

Paul thanked her but said no, he would walk when he finished here.

"I hope the fingerprints match," I put in.

The Chief Inspector looked at my arm and said, "An unfortunate accident on the streets of Fiesole, yes?"

I felt Paul's gaze on me, and I wondered what version of the incident he had given her. I wondered how Eleanora de Rosa would respond if I asked for her help with the Fiesole police. Could I reveal to her—or to the authorities in Fiesole—that my attacker was Paul's daughter? Bella was dangerous. No telling what else she might do. Maybe I could ask the Chief Inspector to check with the Fiesole police, to see if they had any suspects.

But all I said was, "Unfortunate, yes."

"Fiesole is supposed to be a quiet town." She gave a dismissive wave. "With all the tourists that come to Italy now, these little towns are no safer than Florence."

"No place is always safe," I said, "not even a convent."

I heard my name and saw Alex. "What's this?" he asked, regarding the activities at the door of Sophie's room. "I've been calling you, and you didn't answer."

"I'm sorry, Alex. I left my phone in my room," I said.

Paul said hello and Alex returned the greeting. Neither seemed as easy with each other as they had been before—before Fiesole. Or maybe that was my imagination. As we talked, Chief Inspector Eleanora de Rosa made a quiet departure without a word of farewell to either Paul or me.

"I suppose she didn't get a chance to thank you for your observations," Paul whispered.

"What observations?" Alex asked.

"I'll tell you everything, later," I said.

"You're always saying that," Alex said. He looked from me to Paul and back again. "I was wondering if you feel like getting some lunch, but you may have other plans."

Paul spoke up, saying he needed to go to his hotel, and I wondered if Bella was arriving from Cortona, if he was planning a heart-to-heart with her. He could have had a ride with the Chief Inspector, I noted.

Alex suggested the café just around the corner, an easy walk. I could do that. "Let's meet downstairs," he said. "Ten minutes? Is that enough time?"

I said ten minutes would be fine.

"Sorry you missed your ride," I told Paul, when Alex was gone.

"I wanted a moment with you, Jordan," he said, touching my arm, directing me farther from the doorway where the *polizia* worked. My back next to the wall, his face close to mine. "Can we see each other tonight? It is our last night in Florence."

"I know. I can't believe it," I said.

"A quiet dinner?"

"Yes. Alex and I have to be at the airport early, and I won't be one hundred percent." I was already wishing

I hadn't told Alex I'd go out for lunch, but maybe I just needed to work through the pain. "But I wouldn't want to leave without a little more time with you."

"We will make it early. Let me call for reservations, and I will let you know." He took my hand and pressed my fingers to his lips. For a long moment we looked at each other without words. I wondered what we'd say tonight, how we'd find the right words. Or if we could.

When he'd turned toward the elevator, I started to my room. Ivonna came up beside me.

I'd forgotten all about Ivonna. She'd made herself as inconspicuous as the proverbial fly on the wall.

"It is hard to take in that Varinia and Carlo were not what they seemed, and they were criminals. Jewel thieves and murderers," she said, "and they were guests of our convent, doing terrible things. If they were responsible for Sophie's death, I hope they will pay dearly."

"So do I," I said.

She walked me to my room. She might have wanted to talk more, but I said, "I have to get my phone and meet Alex. We're going to lunch."

"I'm glad you are feeling better, *Signora*," she said, and then, with a mischievous smile, she added, "Signor Broussard, he is, as you said, very charming."

I gave a dreamy sigh that made her laugh and said, "Yes, he is."

ALEX AND I shared a pizza and a large bottle of sparkling water. Back in my room, I took another nap. It helped, after going out for lunch. I didn't want that feeling of cobwebs in my brain that came with the pain pills, but I could have used one. I was sore all over my body now, not just where I had bruises and scrapes. I dreaded the flight home. Tomorrow, at this time, we'd be in the air.

Paul called, as promised, and said he'd made reservations for seven at a little *ristorante* not far from the convent. He would be by for me at about six-forty-five.

I began to pack.

FORTY-FOUR

THE *RISTORANTE* WAS somewhere in the Oltrarno district, hidden away on a narrow street. It reminded me of the restaurant near the city walls, downhill from *Piazzale Michelangelo* and the little church, *San Miniato*. That was just two nights ago, incredibly. We'd dined on the terrace, and it had been cool. Tonight was an even cooler night, and I was glad that Paul had reserved our table indoors. The décor brought to mind understated elegance. Dark reds, brocades, and rich, dark wood, white tablecloths and sparkling crystal. We were seated in a small alcove, for optimum privacy. Very intimate. Paul knew his restaurants, all right.

"Will you have wine?" he asked, looking up from the extensive wine list.

"I'll have a glass," I said. My reward for laying off the pain meds since morning.

The evening began as others had, with quiet talk, our heads bent toward each other. A slow, easy prelude to dinner, sipping wine, sampling the colorful selections from a plate of *antipasti*. We could almost pretend tonight was no different from the others.

We had just ordered when Paul touched his jacket, then took his phone from the pocket. It must have vibrated. He would not have committed the *faux pas* of letting his phone announce itself with an annoying sound, but I wondered why he hadn't turned it off. He looked at the display. "I need to take this call," he said, and he excused himself.

It wasn't a leap for me to come up with Bella's name. Who else would it be? Paul would not let a business call interrupt our dinner. I took another sip of wine and thought I might change my mind about having more than one glass before the night was over.

Paul returned to the table after a few minutes, and he was smiling.

"I do apologize, Jordan, but you will be glad to hear this," he said. "The caller was Eleanora de Rosa."

I didn't have to feign surprise.

"She also apologized for calling tonight," Paul said, "but she knows you are leaving tomorrow and you would want to know how the investigation is proceeding. Much has happened since we saw her. She assumed—correctly, I am glad to say—that you and I are together."

She might have called *me*, I thought, because I gave my cell number at the *questura*, but who could blame her for wanting to have another chat with Monsieur Broussard?

"You were correct, also, in your assumption that the fingerprints on the door frame matched those of the jewel thief, Vicente," Paul said.

The confirmation came as a relief, more than I'd expected. Maybe I hadn't been certain, just hopeful. I made a sound, part-sigh and part-laugh. "The *pubblico ministero* is the Prosecutor," Paul said. "It is customary for him to become involved early in the investigation."

Paul continued, saying that even with the fingerprint match, Vicente would not confess, so the Prosecutor determined that he should deal with Carlotta. She was the weaker one. Furthermore, she had not intended to kill the man in the shop. Though Carlotta must pay for the crime that occurred during her commission of a burglary, the Prosecutor would recommend a lighter sentence if she would implicate Vicente in what was looking like a cold-blooded murder.

"The Chief Inspector did not reveal the details of the Prosecutor's deal, but Carlotta took it," Paul said.

As he repeated Carlotta's story, the scenes played like a tragic movie in my mind.

Vicente, in the persona of Varinia, had knocked on Sophie's door and asked to look at the parade from Sophie's window. Sophie allowed it, but Vicente could tell she had misgivings. Finally, he asked what was wrong, and Sophie's impertinent response let him know she had seen too much and he could not count on her silence. I imagined what she might have said: "What are you doing, you and that little man—if he is a man—who can walk as well as I can?" Why did Sophie have to be so bold? If only she'd told *me* her suspicions, I would have followed through—somehow. She didn't have to die.

"Vicente then pushed her through the window." Paul hesitated for a moment; he also must have felt the scene was too real. "He locked Sophie's door, using the material of the caftan to protect the key from fingerprints. He hurried to their room and told Carlotta what he had done. He said if they could return the key to the room, it would look like a suicide. Carlotta slipped on gloves. Vicente had a clever plan, but he did not wear gloves. His only worry was that Sophie might have survived the fall from the window. Carlotta said they did not know for sure that she was dead until morning."

I could see how easy it was to get rid of the key. Amazing, how easy. "Everyone on the hall had gone out-

side to see the festival," I said. "There was so much con-
fusion on the street, around Sophie's body. No one came
up to the room, or even to the hall, for several minutes."

"Time for Carlotta to climb upon Vicente's shoulders and toss the key through the transom. Carlotta
told the rest of it exactly as you said." Paul picked up
his glass. "To you, Jordan, for your determination to
find the truth."

Our glasses touched with a sound like the chime of
a tiny bell. I took a sip and raised my glass again. "To
justice for Sophie," I said.

THE NEXT TIME Paul's phone alerted him, he looked at
the display, turned off the phone, and put it back into
his pocket. "I do not need to reply to this text," he said.

"Bella?" I ventured.

He nodded. "I expected her back mid-day, but she
sent a text—after I had waited for her—saying that it
would be tonight."

It took a fair amount of restraint not to say that Bella
surely knew the questions Paul was waiting to ask her,
and she was postponing that confrontation as long as
she could. At some point Paul would have told her that
I was flying out Friday morning. She knew he would
be with me tonight. Tomorrow, with me out of the way,
Bella would have a better chance convincing Paul that
she was perfectly innocent. She hadn't been in Fiesole,
riding on a Vespa, guilty of a hit-and-run.

"She's back in Florence now?"

"Not yet. She said it will be late and she will see me
at breakfast."

So I'd made another correct assumption.

I took a bite of the saffron-flavored mashed potatoes that came with the codfish. Paul had ordered duck breast. He cut off a portion, then laid down his knife and fork. His expression was earnest. "I should not have left my phone on," he said. "I hadn't heard from Bella. I suppose I was worried. But the interruption—I don't want it to ruin the evening, Jordan."

"Eventually we would've had to talk about Bella, anyway," I said.

He didn't agree or disagree. He waited, and then said, grudgingly, "I know she is difficult. I try to make— as you say—boundaries. I told her today that I will be flying to Paris tomorrow afternoon, with her or without her."

"She knows you wouldn't leave her here," I said.

Paul gave a little laugh, with no joy in it.

After a minute, I said, "You know she could have killed me. What are you going to do?"

My bluntness did not settle well with him. He picked up his wine glass and turned the stem around and around. "I do not believe it. I cannot believe it," he said, setting the glass down without taking a drink. "I know you are persuaded by a bracelet that you may have glimpsed, but it all happened so very fast. I do not believe it was possible to identify the person on the Vespa, whose face was covered by the helmet, who could have been a woman or a man. I am afraid your feelings toward Bella have intruded."

And that didn't settle well with me.

"Is that it?" I said. "I'm just wrong? Maybe you can forget about it when I leave?"

"Jordan, please," he said in a quiet voice that managed to convey a great depth of emotion.

"You don't want to know the truth, do you?" I said.

I think it was the first time I'd come to grips with that, myself. Paul hadn't seen the bracelet, but for some reason that could only be pathological, Bella had held out her wrist, the instant before impact, to make the sapphire bracelet visible to me. Paul could believe me—or believe Bella, who was supposed to be in Cortona. It struck me that her intention, all along, might not have been to kill me but to test Paul: Who would he believe?

The waiter returned and refilled Paul's glass. He gave me a splash of wine to replenish mine. I took another bite of the fish that had lost its flavor, somehow, and Paul ate some of the duck breast, finally. He'd never answered my question, but I was pretty sure I knew the answer. He was afraid of what the truth would mean, in his carefully constructed world.

And then he said, suddenly, "Please don't ask me to choose."

I considered what he was asking. "I won't," I said. He didn't see the inevitable yet. Bella would force him to choose. But I didn't say it.

If I had a few more days, I'd take matters into my own hands. I would go back to the Fiesole police. I would tell them the Vespa rider was wearing a sapphire bracelet. I would tell them that I'd seen only one bracelet like it, ever.

But I was going home, putting it behind me, and maybe that was how it should be.

We finished eating and drinking and did not order dessert or coffee. Paul called for our driver but may have told him not to hurry. As we waited outside on the dark, quiet street, Paul wrapped me in his arms, and we kissed for a long luscious moment. It was not the kind of kiss that should have meant goodbye.

"Ah, Jordan," he said. "Do you know why you have captured my heart?"

The sweet, quaint expression was one Alex had used, speaking of the girl he'd met in Italy, fifty years ago, and had never forgotten.

I answered, truthfully. "No."

"I wish I could tell you," he said. "I wish I knew."

What do you do with a man like that?

FORTY-FIVE

"SOMETIMES I THINK I need to get off of all these damned boards," Alex said, sinking into the big comfy leather chair in my sunroom, against the late afternoon shadows that fell across the back yard. It was October, one of the most pleasant months in Savannah. Days were still hot, but the evenings were lovely.

I handed Alex a drink. Alex wasn't much of a drinker, except that he loved good wine, but he'd requested a gin and tonic, and he looked like he needed a lift this evening after a full day in a board meeting.

"Maybe it's just too soon," I said, sitting across from him, in the rocking chair that I used to rock my babies. "We've just been home three weeks. Maybe you aren't sufficiently rested."

"I must say, I feel tired. Weary."

Again, that was unexpected. I felt a sudden shiver, remembering Paul's worry about Salvatore Corsini, who had said, "I am very tired." But Salvatore was ninety years old. I shook the thought out of my mind.

"You know, I should fix something for us to eat here," I said. "We don't need to go out."

"No, no"—Alex waved away the suggestion. "Just give me a few minutes. They're expecting us at Noble Fare."

"I doubt they'd have to close their doors if we had to cancel," I said. "Let me stir up something. How about a western omelet and a nice salad? I have some fresh fruit I can cut up."

Alex made an exaggerated frown. "*Please*, Jordan. When I can have the catch of the day, and Chef Patrick's cheesecake?"

My desk phone rang. I was close enough to reach it. It was Julie, just leaving the bike shop, where she'd been working for months. Sometimes I thought about her expensive Cornell education and wondered if she found it useful in her present employment. The upside was that she didn't seem unhappy. Quite the contrary. And sometimes I thought about Sophie, how her mother would surely give anything to have her daughter with her. I reminded myself to count blessings.

Julie asked if I needed her to pick up anything for dinner on her way home.

"Remember—Alex is in town. We're going to Noble Fare," I said.

"Oh—that's right." She didn't say she'd forgotten. When had Julie *ever* called to ask if she could pick something up for our dinner?

I whispered "*Julie*" to Alex, and, as I expected, he said, "Ask her to join us!"

I didn't have to beg.

"In case you're worrying about how I'm dressed," she said, "I have a change of clothes here, so I won't have to wear my biking shorts. Noble Fare! I'll even put on mascara."

"See you at seven," I said. I hung up and thanked Alex for including his great niece.

"Nothing livens up an evening like a young person," Alex said.

"You mean *I'm* not cheery enough for you?" I said.

"Let's face it, Jordan. Neither of us has been *cheery* since we returned from Italy." He lifted his glass and clinked the ice, looking thoughtful. "I had an e-mail from Angelica last week. Very sad, all that she's gone through. Victor's death, then the awful disclosure that her son was leading a double life, and then the grand-daughter she never knew, murdered."

He took a drink and then another. I remained silent, waiting for him to continue, in his own time. After a minute, he said, "Raff has removed himself from the business—or—I expect Angelica gave him the boot, though she didn't say so. Bianca has moved her things to Florence and Raff has gone back to Sophie's mother, to whatever the place was that they live."

I supplied, "Casa Vittoni."

"That's it." Alex touched his temple and shook his head, as if he should have remembered. "I wonder if Raff plans to live his life as Leo Costa from now on."

"I wonder how long it will last with him and So-phie's mother."

"It has already lasted twenty years," Alex said.

"Yes, but they had something that held them together. They had Sophie," I said. "Now they have to live with how everything turned out—all the lives ruined."

Alex gave me an indulgent smile, and I realized I was still consumed with everything that had happened in Florence. I stood up. "I'll get my things and then we probably should head to the restaurant."

Alex emptied his glass and stood up, too. "On a happy note, Angelica said Marisa and Jake have gone to the Moretti Villa to live and work."

"They've left Cristiano? Good for them."

"And now they're his competitors. They will be a

perfect addition to the *agriturismo*," Alex said, adding, with a scowl, "I never liked that Cristiano fellow."

A minute later I locked the front door and we began to walk down Abercorn. Noble Fare was not far. Driving would be more trouble than it was worth, but I said, anyway, just in case Alex wasn't feeling up to walking, "I assumed you wouldn't want us to bother with the car."

"For goodness sakes, no." Alex's step seemed to be lighter, suddenly.

We waved to my neighbor, Mr. Duff, who was working in his flowers, in the cool of the evening. We turned on East Gaston Street and stopped to chat a minute with Miss Emma, who was closing up her little shop, Antiques and Rare Books. "I haven't forgotten about that book," she said, in her squeaky voice. "I'm still trying to get it for you."

"No hurry," I said.

I told Alex, as we walked on, about the art book Paul had bought to give his artist-friend for his birthday. His had been a first edition, but I was sure there must be a copy somewhere I could buy at a reasonable price. I just wanted to be able to look at that stunning mosaic by Salvatore Corsini, the one inspired by his grandparents, and think of him.

"You can probably find it yourself. You can find anything on the Internet," Alex said, as if he were teaching me something I didn't know.

"It's not on Amazon, but Miss Emma has her ways of finding old books, and I'm glad to give her the business," I said.

Alex waited a moment and then said, "You haven't said anything about Paul."

"No, I haven't." I waited to see if he'd come back with

something clever. When, instead, he hiked his chin, I said, "He called a few days ago. We had a nice long chat. Did you notice the pink roses in my dining room?"

"I wondered about those. Two dozen?"

"I didn't count, but I think it has to be three. You know how Paul goes overboard," I said.

A little farther on, Alex said, "Maybe I shouldn't ask, but I've fought my curiosity as long as I can. What about Bella?"

"Bella is in Switzerland. I gather it's a kind of psychiatric clinic, but the amenities sounded like a resort," I said. "Paul did his own investigation, and he discovered that Bella had done what I said—she'd taken the train, rented the Vespa, waited for us, all of it. I think she tried to convince Paul that she was just trying to scare me."

Alex gave me a look. Sure she was.

I'd like to believe it.

"So Paul came around to the truth. I thought he would." Alex sounded a little smug.

"This place in Switzerland—sounds like Bella might be there a long time," I said.

We left it unspoken that Paul had apparently *not* shared his findings with the police.

"I hope Paul made amends for not taking you seriously enough," Alex said, and as an afterthought, "Ah, yes, the roses." Then, with a sideways glance, "Is that enough?"

It was a good question I couldn't answer yet. "He might come to Savannah in early spring," I said. "I suggested February."

If Alex was surprised, he managed not to show it. "February. Mild weather like this," he said, "but by then, things are beginning to bloom. February is really the best month in Savannah."

"Everything feels new in February," I said.

At Chatham Square, just a block from Noble Fare, SCAD students, presumably, were making a video. I had to get over this thing, thinking of Sophie each time I saw a vivacious young woman, thinking of what Sophie might have done with her life.

Alex said, "Angelica invited us back in a few months, to stay at the Villa. It would be delightful, with Marisa and Jake managing the activities, the new rooms"—his voice trailed off.

I picked up the thread. "But you didn't make any promises."

"I wasn't sure my traveling companion would be ready to go back soon," he said.

"Not soon. Not anywhere." I amended the serious tone. "Oh, Italy was wonderful. All of our trips have been wonderful. But do you realize that we always get ourselves into trouble?"

"You do," he said, and then, with a deep sigh, "I have to say, Jordan, this one took a lot out of me." Then his voice lilted. "There is something to that line, *Il dolce far niente.*"

"A sweetness for doing nothing," I translated, to Alex's surprise. "I don't see you doing nothing for long. But I get it. This one took a lot out of me, too."

Passing a magnolia tree, I thought I saw a butterfly flitting around it, lighting, finally, on one of the broad leaves. But maybe I imagined it.

* * * * *

ABOUT THE AUTHOR

PHYLLIS GOBBELL'S LATEST MANUSCRIPT, *Treachery in Tuscany*, is third in the Jordan Mayfair Mystery Series that began with *Pursuit in Provence* (2015) and continued with *Secrets and Shamrocks* (2016). She also co-authored two true-crime books based on high-profile murders in Nashville: *An Unfinished Canvas* with Mike Glasgow (Berkley, 2007) and *A Season of Darkness* with Doug Jones (Berkley, 2010). She was interviewed on Discovery ID's "Deadly Sins," discussing the murder case in *An Unfinished Canvas*. Her narrative, "Lost Innocence," was published in the anthology, *Masters of True Crime* (Prometheus, 2012) and is now available as an audiobook. She has received awards in both fiction and nonfiction, including Tennessee's Individual Artist Literary Award. An associate professor of English at Nashville State Community College, she teaches writing and literature.